CATCH THE RISING SUN

Book #3

CATCH THE RISING SUN

From the Secret Diary of Eddie Ocean

E. O. TEST

ISBN-10: 0985305037
ISBN-13: 9780985305031

AUTHORS NOTE

Disclaimer: This is a work of fiction. The characters named in this story are fictional and their actions should not be assumed to be true depictions of anyone's character or behavior. Any incidents herein are fictitious.

Dedicated to my soul mate, Margaret Ann.

Chapter 1

ISLA DE PINOS

02:05, MONDAY, APRIL 22ND, 1974. NEAR THE SOUTHERN COAST OF ISLA DE PINOS, CUBA

Our destination was *Isla de Pinos*, a large island located south of the Cuban mainland. Two hundred yards off the coast, I slowed the boat and steered toward a desolate area of low swampland that was believed to be uninhabited. We were searching for the entrance to a narrow creek, a tributary of the Jacaro River, and a passage that would allow us to bypass the mouth of the river, where the Cubans had stationed gunboats. The creek would allow us undetected entry farther upstream and close to our team's rendezvous point near a prison complex.

"Cut the engines," Carlos ordered, his voice hushed.

Our clandestine mission to rescue Katarina Romero from the Russian butcher Nikko Nikonov was finally underway.

A gentle breeze pushed our drifting boat toward the island's southern shoreline. The long, sleek boat began a slow rotation as she turned portside to the wind. We passed between a pair of mangrove-covered limestone upcroppings that formed two peaks rising about 20 feet above the surface of the Caribbean Sea. Hundreds of chattering seabirds perched among the mangrove branches became silent and craned their necks as they nervously observed us: intruders moving slowly between their rookeries.

"*Bueno*. These islets will provide us with cover," Carlos said as he held night vision binoculars to his eyes and began scanning the swampy shoreline.

"Looks good, *chico*. No activity. Let's go ashore," Carlos whispered. I restarted the engines.

The powerful motors of the 30-foot cigarette boat were surprisingly quiet. The CIA had modified this vessel to run fast and stealthily. Intelligence reports stated that Katarina Romero was being held captive in the *Presidio Modelo* prison complex on the *Isla de Pinos*. It was an old prison complex that had been built under the dictatorship of Gerardo Machado between the years of 1926 and 1928. Five large circular buildings had been constructed with layers of prison cells tiered six stories high. The prison cells encircled a central observation guard post.

After the revolution in the 1950s, when Rafael Cato seized power, he began using *Presidio Modelo* to imprison Cuban political dissidents, counter-revolutionaries, homosexuals, Jehovah's witnesses, and anyone else deemed unfit for the new norms and dictates of the Socialist Cuban state and its new dictator. The prison complex was designed to house no more than 2,500 prisoners in humane conditions but, at one point, Cato inhumanely packed over 6,000 prisoners into the obsolete prison, where they suffered greatly in deplorable conditions. The island prison had supposedly been shut down and put out of commission in 1967, but Cato secretly continued to use one of the five prison silos to hold unfortunate people who had dared to personally offend or cross the vindictive Communist dictator.

"Carlos, can you see the prison? Are we in the right location?" I asked.

"I can't see shit through these mangrove branches! We need to find the creek and enter the river to move farther inland," Carlos said.

"Look! Over there—an opening in the mangroves," I said. We had found the tributary.

"I'll drive, Eddie. You go to the bow and guide me forward."

At the bow I used hand signals to direct Carlos as we entered the mouth of a deep, meandering creek. The narrow waterway cut a path through the dense mangrove swamp, but many branches extended out over the water, obstructing the channel. Shrill screeching sounds of mangrove branches scraping along the hull and cabin of the boat were not conducive to our covert operation.

"Ahh shit! Slow the boat," I muttered after a thin mangrove branch that had snagged on the bow rail broke free and whacked me across the face like a bullwhip.

"That's gonna leave a mark," Carlos said and then slowed the boat as I dodged more oncoming mangrove branches and vines. Now the loud, high-pitched scraping sounds were replaced by low thuds and the snap of cracking branches as we pushed onward through the thicket of clawing tree limbs. Soon the narrow waterway opened into a wider body of water, and we could now see over the canopy of mangroves.

Carlos seemed relieved and exhaled heavily. "We have entered the Jacaro River." A moment later he made a pointing motion and whispered, "Look. There it is." On the high ground in the distance, the daunting, tan-colored walls of the *Presidio Modelo* prison were silhouetted against the black night sky. We counted five circular structures rising six stories tall above the foliage.

Carlos momentarily examined the area with his binoculars and then set them aside in order to better steer the boat. "That's where they have her—Katarina is in there!"

"But which one?" I asked.

"No clue, *chico*. I just hope the CIA knows."

Our boat was hugging the shoreline and moving slowly upriver. I directed Carlos toward a break in the mangrove-lined riverbank, where two boulders stood like bookends, framing a small sandy-white beach. As the bow of the boat gently touched land, I jumped off and tied a line to a sturdy mangrove root. Then Carlos cut the engines.

"What do we do now?" I asked him.

"Now we wait for the plane."

Our plan called for three heavily armed Special Forces operators from Brigade 2506 to parachute onto the roof of the secret prison camp where the Russian Nikko Nikonov, a/k/a "Nicky the Knife", was holding Katarina captive. The commandos would invade the prison camp, avoid or kill any hostiles, and then bring Katarina down to the boat. Our exit strategy was to run the Cuban Navy gauntlet at the mouth of the Jacaro River at full speed and escape into the Caribbean.

"I hear a plane!" I whispered.

"From which direction?" Carlos asked. Since having his ears cut off by Nicky the Knife, Carlos had had his hearing become impaired, especially when it came to identifying the direction from which sounds were emanating.

"Over there—from the northwest."

"Good! The plane must be ours!"

A small plane devoid of any aviation lights was coming in fast, skimming the surface of the water to avoid radar detection. Suddenly the pilot pulled her up, and the plane began to climb at a very steep angle until it looked like a small black fly hovering above the prison. The aircraft slowed and then circled once around the prison complex before accelerating, losing altitude, and flying back in the same direction from which it had come.

"Did you see anyone jump?" I asked.

"No, it's too dark. But they must have jumped; the plane is leaving."

"So now what?" I asked.

"We wait for them to come down. Bring the flashlights up from below deck."

Ten minutes passed before the popping sound of distant gunfire came echoing down from the high ground.

"Those are M3s—grease guns. I would know that sound anywhere, *chico*! Our boys are up there, all right." Then several loud booms echoed off the tall walls of the cavernous buildings.

"Those are M79s—grenade launchers. They must be blowing the hell out of that place!" Carlos had a big smile on his face as the popping sounds increased in intensity.

"Now the Commie bastards are returning fire. That's the sound of an AK47." Although I could not tell the difference between the distant popping sounds of gunfire, Carlos could as he interpreted variations in the reports of the furious gun battle.

We saw a small flash of light high on a rooftop before we heard a thundering blast. *KABOOM!*

"That was C4! They must have blown the top off that damn prison! Damn—I wish I were up there!" Carlos was still smiling—an expression I had not often seen on the man's face.

"How are only a few men going to take over that fortress?" I wondered aloud.

Carlos chuckled. "By element of surprise, *chico*! Careful planning and a few men who fight together as a machine can sometimes accomplish the seemingly impossible. Plus the reports say that the prison is lightly guarded. Only a few VIPs are being held captive here."

"Why aren't you worried?"

"Worried? Why worry? Would that help?" Carlos asked, still smiling, and then he added, "I bet they have no more than half a dozen guards up there. That prison was closed down several years ago. Today Cato uses it only for special guests—his VIPs—dissidents for whom he holds a personal grudge."

"Then why Kat?"

"Are you kidding, *chico*? She tried to poison the bastard!"

"Oh—so Cato must have discovered the poison cigar that Kat gave him, right?"

"Isn't that obvious, Sherlock? Cato was clearly enthralled with Katarina but then suddenly kidnapped her and tossed her into that dungeon. The fact that he handed her over to the Russian butcher Nicky the Knife means that he has sentenced her to a slow, painful death for her betrayal." Another large explosion reverberated off the concrete walls.

"Our men will be on their way down that hill before those commie bastards even get their pants on!" Now Carlos was laughing, probably imagining the panicking guards running around half-dressed trying to find their weapons.

How can he be so confident? How does he know our guys aren't the ones getting shot all to hell?"

The gunfire ceased, and five minutes of silence passed, "It's all over Eddie. Soon we will know who won that little skirmish."

Little skirmish? If that was a little skirmish, I sure would hate to get into a full-out battle with el Muerte's *boys!*

Carlos stood on his tiptoes, peering into his night vision binoculars. "Hey! I saw a light! Look! A light coming downhill—they are halfway down."

"Where?" I squinted to focus my eyes.

"At ten o'clock high. Someone with a flashlight—coming downhill fast! Follow me!" Carlos jumped off the boat and ran over a small sand dune and onto a trail leading uphill through the mangrove thicket. He paused at a fork in the path. One side branched off to run parallel to the beach; the other bifurcation continued to run uphill toward the prison.

"These are deer runs. Our brothers are coming downhill on this deer trail," Carlos said and pointed his flashlight toward where he had seen the light moving. He flashed his light off and on three times but then gasped, "*¡Ay, coño!*"

"What's wrong?"

"Are you blind, *Gringo*? Don't you see all those lights coming down the hill now? More of them than I thought. Must be a dozen guards chasing them now! Quick, take this gun and follow me!" Carlos pulled a pistol from his side waistband and then another from behind his back. He shoved the second gun at me as we ran uphill on the deer path.

SUNDAY, APRIL 7TH, 1974. TWO WEEKS EARLIER, AND BEFORE THE RESCUE MISSION. UNDER THE OVERPASS IN MIAMI.

I was lying on the ground outside my cardboard shack, suffering from food poisoning caused by tainted *paella*, when Carlos woke me. "Snap out of it. Drink more water. The Cubans have captured Katarina. I need you to help me take a fast boat to Cuba. We must go there to find her. We will take two of our best special force operators. We will rescue Katarina from the Russian butcher. We must go now! My car is down below." The look of fear and panic on Carlos's face was unsettling. I had never before seen him show fear. I grabbed my backpack and stumbled down the slope.

With tires squealing, Carlos took off toward the city. "First we must stop off at Katarina's apartment to collect a few weapons and her passport and IDs. From Cuba we will take her to our safe house in the Cayman Islands. If she has been harmed, we'll return to Cuba to kill more of the Communist bastards," Carlos said as he drove the car at breakneck speed. We arrived at Kat's apartment within several minutes.

"Let's go!" Carlos shouted as the car screeched to a halt. He ran up a flight of steps to the second floor with me following close on his heels. Carlos used a key to open Katarina's apartment, and we went inside.

"Where's the bathroom?" Feeling like I might vomit again, I went into the bathroom and stood hunched over the toilet but only suffered from a series of dry heaves. After splashing my face with water and taking a drink, I looked at my reflection in the mirror.

What's this? Someone had written on the mirror when it was fogged by steam. *Maybe it's a message left for us by Katarina!* After leaning close to the glass, I breathed heavily out from my mouth to re-fog the mirror, and more letters become visible as well as a drawing. In the middle of a large heart-shaped drawing, I saw the letters **KAT + E.O.** *Katarina must have drawn this after getting out of a hot shower.* I closed my eyes and imagined her standing in front of the mirror with her thick hair standing tall atop her head, wrapped up tight in a bath towel. *This is the same childish doodle that I drew in the sand on Smathers Beach in Key West! Is it possible? Does Kat secretly love me? Has she been hiding her feelings for me all this time?* When I came out of the bathroom, Carlos was digging through Katarina's bedroom closet.

"I'm in here, Eddie. Check those dresser drawers over there," he demanded.

When I entered the bedroom, I froze in my tracks. I could not believe my eyes. Katarina's bedroom was decorated like that of a young girl. *This is not what I expected. That cold, sterile safe house that she pretended was her home was a better fit for her aloof personality. This stuff can't belong to Kat!* Many sweet and sentimental knickknacks and memorabilia were placed all about her room.

On her long dresser were two framed photographs, one at each end. I picked up the nearest picture. *That's us!* It was a photo of Katarina dancing with me at the Tropicana in Cuba. She was wearing that sexy Latin Rhythm dress. *She is so beautiful.* I put it down and went to see the other picture. It was a shot of us standing near the seawall outside our hotel in Cuba. *What's this red smudge?* I picked up the picture to get a closer look and recognized Katarina's lip prints in red lipstick on the glass picture frame planted just above my sunglasses. *She kissed the left side of my chest. She kissed my heart! Does Katarina secretly love me?*

"Come on, Eddie. I got her passport—let's go!" Carlos rushed toward the door, and I began to follow him out but then stopped short.

"Wait, Carlos!" I went back and grabbed the picture and shoved it into my backpack.

You really had me fooled, Ms. Katarina Romero! Beneath that gorgeous, cold exoskeleton…underneath that hard, tough, icy façade, you hide your tender heart! Katarina, now I know that you are *capable of heartfelt love!*

"We have no time to waste, Ocean!"

"Okay, Carlos, let's go! Let's go find Katarina!"

Carlos drove south on Biscayne Blvd. Again he was racing through the streets of Miami like a madman toward a safe house located in Key Largo. Docked there was a customized cigarette boat that could get us to Cuba in a matter of hours.

"Carlos, your driving is gonna get us killed! What good will we be to Katarina dead?" I exclaimed as I clung white-knuckled to the dashboard.

"Shut up! Just hang on, *gringo!*" He pushed the gas pedal to the floor, and the 1962 Chevy Impala SS veered into the passing lane and blew past an eighteen-wheeler as the telephone poles along the roadway flickered by like rungs on a picket fence.

"Shit!" I felt the nausea returning again from my bout of food poisoning, and Mr. Toad's Wild Ride courtesy of *el Muerte* did not help my situation. I stuck my head out of the open window, but the wind blast was painful. Thankfully, I did not vomit. Half a dozen times I thought we were going to have a head-on collision as we raced south on the Overseas Highway. The Impala suddenly turned off US Highway #1 and roared down a dirt road before slowing and then sliding sideways to a halt on a crushed limestone driveway near the front porch of a small fishing cottage. Somehow we had made it to Key Largo in one piece. Through a cloud of white limestone dust, Carlos ran toward the cottage while I opened my door and fell out face-first onto the ground, clutching my backpack to my side.

"Thank God!" I said as I stood up on shaky legs and stumbled toward the cottage. By the time I entered, Carlos was inside the shack, arguing with two men.

"*No!* We must go *now!*" Carlos shouted as he pounded his massive fist down onto the kitchen table.

"Negative, Carlos. We must have a solid plan in place...and this full moon is in a bad phase for a covert operation," a tall, thin man said as he wiped the thick lenses of wire-rimmed glasses with the tail of his bright tropical shirt.

"If we wait there will be nothing left of Katarina to bring home, damn it! Nicky the Knife has her! Look at my head!" Carlos leaned down and pulled back his thick black hair, exposing the holes on the sides of his head where the Russian had carefully, surgically removed his ears.

The other guy, a short, stocky fellow, was leaning backward, balancing on the back two legs of a wooden chair and smoking a cigarette. He said, "We know about your ears, Romero. But you will only get more people butchered or killed by acting rashly. Be patient, *el Muerte!*"

Carlos's face was turning red. "Give me the keys to the boat—we're leaving now, Fatso!" he yelled, and then used his foot to kick the guy's chair, sending the stout fellow toppling over backward so that his head crashed hard onto the wooden floor.

"Shit!" The enraged man scrambled to his feet to confront Carlos, but before the two behemoths could come to blows, the tall guy wearing the wire-rimmed glasses moved behind Carlos with cat-like quickness and plunged a hypodermic needle into the side of his neck. Carlos groaned and staggered forward, falling face-down onto the kitchen table, unconscious.

"Why did you do that? Who are you guys?" I asked, raising my fists to a defensive position.

"Don't worry, Ocean, that was just a sedative…it was for his own good. He was about to get you both killed, kid," said the tall, thin guy.

"How do you know my name? Who are you guys?"

They looked at each other.

"Go ahead, Buzz. We can tell him. He's been working with 2506. I think Katarina Romero is this kid's girlfriend," said the tall guy as he carefully unscrewed the needle from the glass syringe.

The stocky guy righted his chair. "We are with the CIA, Ocean. We are here to help you and your dissident friends plan a mission to rescue your Cuban girlfriend. You can call me 'Buzz,' and my partner here goes by 'Willard.'"

"Buzz, she's not my girlfriend. I wish she were—but she's not."

"Well, none of that really matters right now, Ocean. Let's face it: The odds of us getting her out of Cuba alive are slim to none," said Buzz.

"What? Then Carlos is right! We have to go now!" They must have seen panic overcoming me.

"Keep your cool, kid. With our help, you just might have a shot at saving Katarina. But we gotta keep her hot-headed Uncle Carlos under wraps until it's go time." Willard caught Carlos just as his limp body slithered off the table. He lowered him gently to the floor. "Get his legs, Buzz," he said and grabbed Carlos under the armpits.

The pair of spooks ordered me to stay at the fishing shack until I was contacted, and then they took Carlos outside and put him into the back of a black SUV.

"How long? How long are you going to leave me here?"

"We'll be in touch, kid. Just stay put and keep your head down!"

After watching the SUV drive off, I looked over my accommodations. The small, rustic cottage was well stocked with dry goods and bottled water. *How long do they expect me to stay here? Take that boat, dude. Uh—take it where?* Quickly I began to go stir-crazy and was overcome with worry for Katarina's safety. I decided to take the boat for a joy ride to break the monotony, but when it wouldn't start, I discovered that the agents had disabled the boat by removing some ignition parts.

Two weeks passed. Then suddenly, unannounced, the CIA guys showed up on the porch of the fishing shack. They had Carlos in handcuffs, and he was not a happy camper. He had that dark, sinister, penetrating look that only the eyes of *el Muerte*, the zombie, could convey.

They pushed him inside the shack, and the stocky guy, named Buzz, asked him, "Carlos, if we turn you loose, you are not going to do anything stupid, right?"

"Not if you give me the keys to the boat, Fatso!"

"Don't go off half cocked, *el Muerte*. Sit still so we can tell you the plan." Carlos sat down. "Okay, let him loose, Buzz," said the tall guy.

Buzz unlocked the cuffs from Carlos's massive wrists. Carlos started to stand, hesitated for a moment, and then sat back down. The men joined him at the kitchen table and proceeded to tell us the details of their rescue plan.

The tall guy looked at his watch, "Carlos, you will leave in two hours. It's the new moon—the darkest night of the month. When you arrive in Cuba it will be after midnight, and you will have the support of three of the brigade's best commandos. They will drop in by air—the best way to get to the top of the prison undetected. You must be at the designated place on the Jacaro River before 0200."

Carlos was visibly angry, "But it's been two weeks! What are the chances that Katarina is still alive?" His voice was a mix of anger and despair.

"What chance? Well a much better chance than if you had gone off under a full moon without a plan and only the kid to help you, Carlos. They would be feeding pieces of both of you to the caimans right now...that's for damn sure!"

Chapter 2

THE JACARO RIVER

"**H**ijo de la gran puta!" Carlos pressed the side of his pistol up to his right temple and swatted with his left hand at the mosquitoes that were pestering him. I knew from my time living with the Whatchacallit Tribe in the Big Cypress that swatting only drew more of the little bastards, so I endured their bites in silence. The gunfire and explosions had ceased, and now we listened to the nighttime sounds of the swampland, thousands of croaking frogs and chattering crickets serenaded us as we stood near the bifurcation in the deer path.

"Let's move up." Bent at the waist, Carlos started lumbering forward. Unlike the larger North American Whitetail, most Cuban deer are only the size of large dogs, thus the deer path leading up the steep hill toward *Presidio Modelo* was narrow, and the dense foliage bordering each side of the trail arched over the passageway, forming a shoulder-high tunnel. The footing on the trail consisted of loosely packed sand, which provided very poor traction and further slowed our ascent.

Suddenly Carlos stopped moving and crouched down beneath a bush at the side of the deer run. I followed his lead. The sound of distant voices calling out commands in Spanish became audible. We crouched down, listening. Suddenly the sounds of heavy breathing and grunting filled the air as two men with guns slung over their shoulders and carrying a makeshift stretcher came crashing through the overhanging branches and burst into view from a bend in the path less than 10 yards away. Carlos stood up to greet the commandos and, with his pistol, motioned for them to take the path leading downhill toward the boat.

As the men rushed by in the darkness, I could see a woman with a white bandage wrapped around her head lying supine on the stretcher. *That must be Katarina! Thank God they got her!* Following the stretcher-bearers was a third man, who stopped beside Carlos, and they spoke briefly in Spanish. Then the stranger ran past me down the trail. Carlos said, "Eddie, go with them! Get them home safe! I still have unfinished business." Carlos turned from me and ran uphill.

"Where the hell are you going, Carlos? We gotta get out of here, dude!" It was no use; Carlos disappeared into the darkness. Confused, I hesitated but then followed the commandos down to the boat. The three men were loading Katarina onto the boat as I untied the line from the mangrove root and climbed aboard. The two stretcher-bearers went below deck with Katarina, and the third guy stood at the bow, his machine gun aimed toward the deer path.

"Carlos, we've got to go, man!" I shouted out toward the shore.

"Shut up. Keep your voice down!" The guy who seemed to be in command glared at me, his black eyes glistened in the dark; his face was painted green.

"But we can't leave Carlos!" I insisted.

"It was his decision to stay...*el Muerte's* choice. So get this tub moving before someone puts a bullet through your head!" The guy used the barrel of the machine gun to motion for me to take the boat downriver. When I continued to hesitate, searching the land with my eyes, he turned to face me and trained his sights right at my forehead. Reluctantly I backed the powerful boat out into the river and turned her downstream just as the other two commandos came up from below deck and took defensive positions near the bow.

"Go! Go! Go!" the commander said and redirected the gun from my head toward the shoreline. I took one last glance at the white, sandy beach, hoping to see Carlos before slamming the throttles forward. The boat shot up onto plane, and we raced down the river, throwing off a huge wake that crashed upon the mangrove-covered shoreline of the otherwise calm river.

We were rapidly nearing the mouth of the Jacaro River and the open sea beyond, when suddenly the dark night exploded in a bright, blinding light. Off our starboard beam a powerful spotlight illuminated us, and the rumble of a Cuban gunboat's engines could be heard as the craft began to accelerate and move off from the shoreline toward the main river channel. *They're gonna cut us off at the river's mouth.*

"Get your head down, kid!" someone called out as all three commandos began unloading their guns at the spotlight. I squatted down a bit, but with the boat up on plane, I could not see forward over the bow. We were running at full open throttle, and I needed to navigate the channel, so I was forced to stand back upright on my tiptoes to see the channel markers as incoming bullets whistled overhead and a burst of machine gun fire stitched a row of holes down the side of the cuddy cabin.

Suddenly there was a thundering boom as the water a few yards off our port bow exploded as if an underwater depth charge had gone off. The huge geyser of water showered down upon us as we raced past the point of impact.

Damn! That was close! I tried to push the throttles farther forward, but they were already wide open.

"Bésame el culo, cabrón!" someone called out as the other guys began cheering. We had won the race to the mouth of the Jacaro River, and the gunboat's spotlight was fading into the night. But just when we thought we were out of danger, more bullets began

whining overhead. I noticed small flashes from the muzzles of gunners firing at us from a rock jetty off the starboard beam. All three commandos ran to the starboard gunwale and began peppering the rock jetty with gunfire as red-hot brass cartridges bounced around my ankles and littered the deck with hundreds of spent shells. Then the gunfire from the jetty ceased, as we got out of range, and we entered the open water of the Caribbean Sea.

We were now racing southeast toward the Cayman Islands. The spotlight of the Cuban gunboat was just a speck in the distance.

"Good job, *Gringo!*" a green-faced commando said as the other two reloaded their weapons.

"Look—the starboard motor is smoking!" I said as we all turned our attention to the plume of blue-black smoke lying close to the surface of the water behind the boat. I shut down the failing engine and continued running at half throttle on the port engine. From the cockpit I could see splintered fiberglass and dozens of bullet holes dotting the starboard side gunwale of our boat. I turned my attention to the cuddy cabin, where a large bullet hole had been blown through the hatch right next to the door's latch. *Kat!*

"Someone check on Katarina," I said, and I nodded my head toward the cuddy cabin.

The commander went below and then popped right back out. "She's okay—as good as can be expected."

"Take over, sir. I want to see her." I said.

"No, kid. She's in no mood for visitors, I assure you. She told me she does not want you or Carlos to see her."

"Why?" *Why would Kat not want to see me?*

"Just get us to Grand Cayman, pronto! The girl needs a medic," the commander said to me and then stood guard, holding his machine gun in front of his chest, blocking the cabin door.

"Speaking of Carlos, who's gonna go get him? Why did he stay behind? What did you say to him back on that island?" My head was full of questions. Nothing made sense.

"After Carlos knew Katarina was safe, he asked me two things. First he wanted to know her condition—what they had done to her— and then he asked me if the Russian butcher, Nikko, was among the guards chasing us," said the commander.

"They call him Nicky the Knife. Well, was he there?"

"Yeah."

"Carlos has vowed to kill that man for cutting off his ears."

"That's why Carlos chose to stay—he said he was going to kill the Russian bastard."

"That's crazy! That's a suicide mission," I said as I brought the boat up to three-quarters throttle.

"Yes—a suicide mission. Even in the darkness I could see the rage and the hatred in *el Muerte's* black eyes. He was *loco*."

Chapter 3

THE BIKER BABES

06:21, MONDAY, APRIL 22ND, 1974

Rhythmically, gently, the bow of the boat rose and fell as we ran on only one engine at half throttle through a series of small swells rolling in from the southwest Caribbean Sea. I tried to calculate the remaining distance to our destination, Grand Cayman. *Let's see, we ran the gauntlet at the mouth of the Jacaro River at approximately 3:15 am…so we have been averaging about 18 knots for nearly three hours. We should have covered about 60 nautical miles…that means we've got at least 125 miles left before Cayman. We should arrive just after lunchtime, dude.*

Looking up from my chart, I watched the eastern sky begin to brighten and the ocean turn deep purple as a blood-red sun broke over the horizon directly ahead of my bobbing bowsprit. The sky above the rising fireball turned brilliant, the colors red and orange against the blue sky providing the first blush of day. I glanced down at the compass and adjusted my heading two degrees to port, the bearing that would lead us to George Town Harbor on Grand Cayman Island. The reflection of my face in the windshield was aglow from Mother Nature's lovely early morning light show. *With that sun rising directly over George Town, you don't even need a damn compass, Sunchaser Eddie Ocean; just follow that sun.*

Rising and falling with the rolling sea, the two commandos sleeping at the bow were being gently rocked to sleep like babies in a cradle, but their commander was busy in the stern sitting in a deckchair and studying a nautical chart. When I turned my head toward the stern, I heard an unusual rattling sound coming from the remaining engine. *Better hope that port motor didn't take a slug too, dude!*

The commander began speaking into a handheld radio that he held close to his face. Momentarily there came a response. The sound of crackling static prevented me from understanding the squeaky voice coming over the receiver as the commander turned his head and listened intently. Then he bent down and made some marks on his navigation chart before saying, "Ten-four. Over and out!" The tall, wiry soldier stood up, clipped the radio onto his utility belt, and then walked toward me at the helm.

"Ocean, we got a change of plans. We need to go to the airstrip on the south end of Cayman Brac, not George Town Harbor."

"Why? That will add at least forty minutes to our trip, and you said Kat needs medical attention."

"Just do it, Ocean. Cayman Brac isn't as busy—the small airstrip has fewer prying eyes, and the CIA has a charter flight waiting there to take us and Katarina to Miami."

"What about this boat?"

"'*Us*' means me and my men—not you, Ocean. You need to get the boat repaired and then bring her back to the fishing shack in Key Largo."

The look on his face made me resist protesting his plan. "Aye-aye, Captain," I said as the commander handed me his chart. I adjusted our course for Cayman Brac. Now the sun was no longer my guiding light as it rose a few degrees off the starboard quarter.

"Okay, our new course is set, sir. Can I see Katarina now?" I asked.

"Do you understand English, kid? I told you she doesn't want to see you. She was adamant—said she would kill me if I let you come down. Can't you get more speed out of this tub?"

"I'll try, sir." I pushed the remaining engine a bit harder, praying that it would hold up until we made landfall.

When we docked on the south end of Cayman Brac it was 02:15 pm. While I was busy securing the stern dock line, the commandos hustled Katarina off the boat. Once again they carried her on the litter, and I got only a glimpse of her as they trotted up the dock toward a waiting Jeep. Kat's entire head seemed to be wrapped with gauze. I could only identify her by her long, slender build and the black, silky hair sticking out from the bottom of the head bandage.

"Hey, wait for me!" I called out as I secured the dock line to a cleat. The commander stopped, turned, and called back to me, "Ocean, you stay put. Monitor channel 66. We'll tell you where to take the boat for repairs. I'll see you back in Florida, kid."

"Shit!" I threw the bitter end off the line down to the dock and watched the soldiers drive away toward the airstrip with Kat lying in the back of the Jeep.

FRIDAY, MAY 3RD, 1974. GEORGE TOWN, GRAND CAYMAN ISLAND

After a wait of over two weeks for engine parts and repairs, the port-side engine was finally repaired, and I received the boat shortly after 3:00 pm on Friday. With both tanks full, and extra fuel stowed in a 55-gallon drum strapped in the stern, I departed for Key West. I planned on shortening the long haul around the west end of Cuba by passing through Cuban waters very close to the island. If the weather remained favorable and the Cuban navy didn't catch me, I hoped to make Key West after sunrise on Saturday.

EARLY SATURDAY MORNING, 04:00

After rounding the western tip of Cuba, I estimated that I was in Cuban waters somewhere northwest of Mariel Harbor. Now I was driving away from Cuba on a northeastern tangent toward Key

West. In the distance to my southeast, the lights of Havana became visible, and behind me, rising high like the back of a giant dinosaur, the black peaks of the *Sierra de los Organos* mountain ridge were outlined against the early morning sky.

The peaceful mountains were quite beautiful, but as I was looking up at the highest peak, the lights of a boat became visible as it traveled near the Cuban shoreline. Obviously my running lights were turned off, so I knew that the other crew could not see me at such a great distance. Still, to be sure, I altered my course slightly to see if the boat would follow suit. *Is she just passing through or are they tracking me?* Within a minute the other boat also changed course, a sure sign that she was tracking me.

Damn! They must have me on radar. In order to conserve fuel, I had not been running at full speed, but now I gunned the engines and put her wide open before taking a look back just in time to see the running lights of the pursuing boat go out. *She knows I spotted her.* Now the horizon was black again, and I couldn't tell if the other boat was gaining on me. *I'll be out of Cuban waters soon. Hope I have enough speed!* Apparently the other vessel was no match for the spooks' supercharged cigarette boat. Like a bottle-nosed dolphin, I was flying up and out of the water in great leaps and bounds through the three-foot chop toward Key West. Once I was sure that I was out of reach of the Cuban navy and in safe waters, I stopped the boat and topped off the nearly empty fuel tanks from the 55-gallon drum. Then I was back underway.

Thoroughly exhausted, I was in Key West Bight just after sunrise, refueling the boat. My plan was to, after eating a hearty breakfast, take a two-hour nap and then be on my way to Key Largo, but my alarm failed to go off and it was after 6:00 pm when I awoke. I double-checked my watch, "Damn, you slept all day, dude!" I muttered and sat up on the edge of my bed rubbing my eyes. *Might as well get some dinner before heading out.* I walked over to the Half Shell Raw Bar and had a combination seafood platter that I washed down with ice-cold beer.

As I finished my meal, the rumbling sound of motorcycles caught my attention. I paid my tab and went outside to see what was going on. A long parade of motorcycles was traveling down Caroline Street. As I stood there admiring the passing choppers, a female biker pulled over to the curb in front of me.

"Get in," she said and nodded to the sidecar attached to her bike.

"Where you going?" I asked.

"Just down to Captain Tony's," she said.

"Cool, I dig that dive bar." I climbed in and off we went.

The curbs were lined with motorcycles parked tightly in long rows. She pulled in beside a Road King with massive saddlebags, and when the biker chick got off her motorcycle I was surprised to see that she was well over six feet tall. "You coming in, dude?" she asked as I climbed out of the sidecar.

"In a minute. Go on ahead."

The bikers began gathering at the bar, and the fact that they all seemed to be women really piqued my interest. I was hesitant to go in because there were hardly any other guys inside. The parade of tattooed babes dressed in black leather outfits, leather jackets, and harness motorcycle boots just kept on coming. They filled the cramped space as the tourists hurriedly guzzled their drinks and fled the scene.

Some of the babes started reaching up under their shirts and removing their bras, then twirling the undergarments in the air before tossing them up onto the rafters to join the impressive collection of undergarments hanging from the ceiling. I was standing out front looking in and thoroughly enjoying the freak show when suddenly I felt a sharp set fingernails take a bite out of my right ass cheek. "Hey!" I turned around and found a pair of identical twins laughing at me.

"What's the big deal?" I said.

In harmony the girls pointed at one another and said, "She did it!" The pair of biker chicks wore identical black leather outfits, had short blonde hair, blue eyes, and stood about 5'4" tall. They appeared to be a bit older than me, maybe in their late twenties, and had a hard sensuality about them.

"You're kinda cute, dude. Want to join our party?" the one on the left asked me.

"Who are you people?" I asked. In unison, the pair turned with the precision of synchronized swimmers. On the back of their jackets was an embroidered, circular logo with the image of a howling wolf; the words SHE-WOLVES encircled the toothy carnivore.

"Huh, so you're the 'She-Wolves,' eh? Is that some kind of gang?"

With a bright, pearly smile and a twinkle in her light blue eyes, the chick on the right said, "Yeah, we're here for the full moon howling. Tonight begins the full moon celebration. So are you gonna join us or not? I guarantee you will have a ball!"

The offer was very enticing, but when I glanced over at the bar scene and saw that the biker babes were getting really animated, loud, and rowdy, I had second thoughts. The volume of the music had been cranked way up, and a topless, heavily tattooed chick was trying to climb the hanging tree that grows right in the middle of the place. Near the pool table a pair of 200-pound chicks were going nose-to-nose in a shouting and shoving match. *Dude, you don't want to be the only piece of meat among that pack of crazed she-wolves!*

"Come on, we'll buy you a drink handsome."

"No thanks, ladies, I'm a sailor, and I gotta get my ass up to Key Largo tonight."

"Why not leave in the morning, sailor boy? I'm sure that your ass can wait a few hours." They both closed in on me like a pair of hungry *Canis Lupi*, and I backed away right into a chopped Harley.

"Shit!" I yelled as the bike hit the asphalt.

"Holly crap!" The twins echoed in harmony. "That's Massive Mary's chopper!"

Wide eyed, I glanced over at the gang of bikers in the bar. The tall chick who had been trying to separate the arguing giants saw the bike go down and started tugging on the sleeve of one of the two behemoths. The pair stopped shoving one another and stared at me with wide eyes and flared nostrils.

Holy crap is right! I was about to make a dash for it when the hot little identical twin seductresses latched on to my arms like a pair of pit bulls.

"Hold on, sailor boy. Massive Mary's gonna want a word with you!" One said. I was almost free of the twins' grasp when a gorilla-sized female grabbed me from behind and put me in a full nelson. She held me there with thick hairy arms as Massive Mary's seething, red face appeared an inch from mine.

"You'll pay for this, dude!" she said, spraying me with spittle that reeked of Wild Turkey before backing off to upright her fallen Harley. "Shit! Look at that scratch!" She squatted down, then got up, then down again beside the motorcycle like a sumo wrestler doing warm-up squats before a bout.

"I'm sure we can buff that right out, ma'am," I said sheepishly.

"You see that dent, moron? And that's a custom paint job!" She slowly rose to her feet, pounding a fist into her palm as the tattoo of a hula girl shimmied atop the flexing muscles in her forearm. "Oh boy! You're gonna pay for this, all right," she repeated, pounding that fist.

"Hey, give me an estimate. I'll gladly pay the damage." Fifty hardnosed She-Wolves were now outside Tony's, surrounding us and thoroughly enjoying the confrontation and anticipating the beat-down.

The two giants looked at one another. "What do you think, Big Betty?" Mary asked her partner.

"I say 500."

"Five hundred...$500?" I asked.

"Yeah, dude. Five hundred or two extra-large cans of whoop-ass: your choice!"

"I'll pay the money! I choose the money-option, ladies. But I don't have that much on me right now." I felt the sweat forming on my brow.

"Then you'll have to earn the money, dude! Take him inside!" Massive Mary ordered Big Betty. With Big Betty's inescapable full nelson applied to my neck, she lifted me off the ground and started carrying me inside. When I tried to run, my legs flailed the air helplessly like a ragdoll being carried away by a big, hairy Saint Bernard. When I stopped running, my legs just dangled, swaying from side to side like a pendulum with each stride of the hairy mammoth. The lyrics of "Gimme Shelter" by the Rolling Stones greeted me as she carried me inside. The deafening music was blasting out from the jukebox.

"War, children, it's just a shot away."

"Get his shirt and pants off!" Mary demanded. Mick's lyrics were not comforting me.

"It's just a shot away!

"Rape, murder!

"It's just a shot away.

"It's just a shot away!"

"Hey, wait!" I tried to resist, but a dozen hands yanked off my clothes.

"Okay, put him on the bar!" The wolf pack cheered and howled as Big Betty released her wrestling hold and hoisted me up by my waist and onto the bar, clad only in my dingy tighty-whitey underpants. I stood there, hunched over, trying to protect my vital parts as someone turned the volume on the jukebox even louder so the music could be heard over the howling crowd of crazy women. "Wild Thing," by the Troggs, came blasting out over the speakers.

"Dance, or you'll get the whoop-ass option." Massive Mary's booming voice was barely audible above the ruckus.

"Dance?" I whispered in dismay and remained standing hunched over. Then I saw the hula girl tattoo start dancing again, each time Mary pounded her meaty fist into her palm. *You better dance, dude!*

"Yeah, yeah, yeah!" Mary hollered as I gyrated my hips to the music.

"Wild Thing...I think I love you...*but I wanta know for sure!* Come on and hold me tight...I love you."

Biker chicks were pushing toward the bar, and the gals up front began sticking dollar bills into the elastic waistband of my underpants.

"Wild Thing, you make my heart sing.

"You make everything....groovy! Dah...Dah...Dah,Dah Dah... Dah,Dah!

"You move me!"

There were too many dollar bills for my 32" waistband to hold, so the chicks started stuffing them down my shorts. Mary began collecting the money and counting the bills. She made me dance to three more songs, and then she let me come down from my impromptu stage.

"Okay, Wild Thing, you paid off the debt. Now I'm gonna buy you a drink." She slammed her fist down on the bar, and then two shots of Jose Cuervo appeared. "Drink!"

"No, that's okay...I gotta get going. But thanks."

Big Betty and Massive Mary pinned me up against the bar. Their combined girths threw an eclipse over me. "Drink!"

"I guess one won't hurt." I threw back the shot and gasped, "Whoo momma!" Betty pounded her fist on the bar again and two more shots appeared. "Again!" she said.

I woke up the next morning in the bed on the cigarette boat. The twins were sprawled out next to me, one on each side. Their leather biker garb was strewn all around the cabin. I sat up and realized that something was around my head like a headband. I pulled it off.

"What the hell?" I said as I held a black leather thong at arm's length.

I took the biker twins, Missy and Sissy, to breakfast that morning at a nearby little Cuban restaurant and was shocked to learn that one was an attorney and the other a CPA living in downtown Miami.

They gave me business cards, and then I walked them to their room at the Eden House Hotel on Fleming Street.

"Are you gals heading home today?"

"Hell no! The Full Moon Celebration starts tonight. All the She-Wolves will be howling at the sky by midnight! Tonight's the big party, dude!"

"Big party? What the hell was that last night—just a little shindig? You She-Wolves almost partied me to death!"

"Look us up in Miami, and we'll teach you how to party, sailor." That's what the twins insisted on calling me: "Sailor." With a pounding throb in my head but a smile on my face, I returned to the boat and then set a course for Key Largo.

MONDAY, MAY 6TH, 1974, 01:00

My eyes were burning with weariness as I navigated the shallows off the coast of Key Largo. With only the light cast from a sliver of crescent moon high overhead, I located the narrow channel that led to the dock at the Key Largo safe house. No lights were on in the deserted little shack, so after tying up the boat I located the hidden key from a rafter above the back door and went inside, where I collapsed on the bed and fell into a deep sleep.

In the morning, the sounds of chirping birds greeted me as I rolled my aching body out of bed and made coffee. *I gotta get up to Miami to see how Kat's doing. How you gonna do that dude? You have no money and no wheels. Guess I'll have to hitchhike.* The conversation taking place inside my head was interrupted when I noticed an envelope on the kitchen table. "Ocean" was scribbled on the outside. *What's this?* I looked inside and found ten $100 bills. *A thousand bucks! Huh, the spooks left a grand lying right out in the open…this must be my pay!*

With the newfound money, I bought a bus ticket to Miami and arrived there late in the afternoon. *I'm starving! Hey, look, dude—an orange rooftop up ahead—that's a HoJo's—yum!* After eating a dinner of fried haddock and clams at the Howard Johnson's Restaurant and Motel, I got a room for the night. *In the morning I'll deposit this cash into my bank account and then go find Katarina.*

The next morning, after having a big breakfast at the HoJo's, I walked to my bank, where my favorite teller, Ms. Julie, was on duty. I went over to her window.

"Hi, Julie."

"Hello, Mr. Ocean, we haven't seen you for a while. Making a withdrawal today?"

"No, ma'am, I only have about a buck left in my account, but I want to deposit $700 cash." Julie gave me an odd look. *She's probably wondering how I blew over a hundred grand...the money that I paid the hospital for Brownie's surgery and the rest to save Lucas's farmhouse.*

Julie was paging through her ledger with a furrowed brow. "Huh, you say you have only a dollar left?"

"Actually I should have $1.06, Julie."

"You must have bought yourself that new boat, Captain Eddie," she said as she continued looking up my account information.

"No, Julie, I wish I *had* bought a boat. Just had to take care of some friends instead. It was an emergency," I said as I slid the envelope containing seven $100 bills across the counter and beneath the teller's window.

"Hey, Eddie! Your balance isn't $1.06. It's $120,001.06!"

"What? No way, dudettee. Where did that 120 grand come from?"

"Yep. You have over $120,000 here!" she said with a smile.

"Hey, Julie, do you think Brownie found out that *I* paid for his surgery and paid me back? The guy has a high-paying job in L.A. now. He's an architect."

"Don't know. Let me see where these funds came from. No Eddie, not from L.A.—this money was transferred from an account in Minnesota. Came from the account of a Mr. and Mrs. Fry."

"Fry? Who in heck are the Frys?"

"Says here that there is a letter for you. I'll get it from the mail-room. Excuse me." Julie left and returned with an envelope. "Here you go." She slid the letter across the counter, and I opened it.

"Oh yeah, I do know them! Marty and Gabby Fry—the inventors that I chartered down to Key West. This note says that Marty perfected the sample of the glue formula that I gave to him. They patented his sticky glue formula and then sold the rights to the Triple M Company of Minnesota. Wow! Sold that damn formula for close to a million bucks! They say the agglutinate is revolutionary and that the 120 grand is my finder's fee for the sticky note idea…a 10 percent cut!"

"Wow, a million dollars just for glue? Hey, what's that?" Julie pointed to a small yellow pad that was sticking out of the envelope.

"Don't know…let's see." I picked up the little pad. "Julie, it says that these things are called Stick-It Notes." I pulled the top sheet off and stuck it on the window between us.

"What are you supposed to do with them?" Julie asked.

"Leave notes for people, I guess. I used labels like this to identify all the rigging on the sailboat on that Key West trip…did it to teach the Frys the equipment and how to sail the boat. Boy did that pay off!"

"Huh—yeah. These little notes might be useful around here. How do I order some for the bank?"

"Forget about the stupid sticky notes, Julie. Let's see my bank statement, babe!" I could not believe my eyes! Julie was right. I had over 120 grand in my account. "Yee-ha! I see a boat in my future, Ms. Julie!"

Chapter 4

A LOST KAT

The jubilation caused by my newfound fortune quickly faded when I opened my backpack to stow away my bank statement. Whitest, with his black bead eyes and sober teddy bear expression, gazed up at me from the open backpack as if to ask, *Really dude, you're happy? What about Katarina?* Under the white teddy bear was the photo of Kat and me standing arm in arm by the seawall in Cuba. The red smudge of her lip prints visible above my heart brought me back to reality and reminded me of my priority, *Kat needs you. You need to find her, dude!*

Julie interrupted my thought. "You should be able to buy a fine boat with that much cash, Eddie."

I zipped shut the backpack to escape Whitest's accusatory stare. "Thanks, Julie. I plan to. But first I need to check on another friend," I said and slung the pack over my right shoulder.

"Take care, and good luck," Julie said as the next guy in line stepped up to her window.

As I walked to the bus stop, I wondered where to start my search. *In the Cayman Islands, the commandos told me that Katarina was badly in need of medical care. Guess I'll look for her at Jackson Memorial Hospital.* At Jackson I found nurse Patty Whacker working on the fifth floor and asked her for help. "Patty, could you find out if Katarina Romero is a patient here at Jackson?" I asked her.

"Sure, Eddie. I'm about to go on break. I'll go down to Admitting to see if she is our patient. Won't take long. Why don't you wait for me in the cafeteria."

"Thanks, Patty."

Patty found me in the cafeteria ten minutes later and delivered bad news: "Katarina is not registered here. Sorry, Eddie."

"But Patty, they probably have her registered under a false name. Some bad dudes are after her." I persisted and took the photograph from my bag. "Here—this is what she looks like. She must be here."

"Wow, she's gorgeous," Patty said with a frown. "Let me make a copy of the picture." Patty went behind the nurse's station and then came back around the counter and returned the picture to me. "Eddie, Jackson is a big place. We have over 1,500 beds."

"I know, but I'll check everyone of them—one by one if I have to."

"They won't let you wander around in here all day. And some of the units are isolation units, Eddie. Tell you what: I'll get my friends to have a look around for you. That's all we can do. Go home and come back in the morning."

"Thanks, Patty. I'm going down to Phlebotomy. I'll get Uranus to help look, too."

Patty, Uranus Johnson, and some of their co-workers searched every nook and cranny of Jackson Hospital's vast complex that day, but they couldn't find Katarina Romero. The following morning I returned and received the bad news.

"Eddie, I'm sorry. We've checked every room and unit. I'm sure your girlfriend is not here at Jackson." Patty seemed perturbed.

"Well, thanks for trying, Patty. You're a good friend." I tried to give her a kiss on the cheek, but she turned her back to me and said, "Maybe Uranus had some luck."

But Uranus concurred with the nurses: Kat was not at Jackson. "Try Cedars of Lebanon Hospital. It's just across the street, dude," he suggested.

"Okay, thanks, Vampire. I just gotta find Kat." But Kat was not registered at Cedars Hospital either. *Maybe she was treated, discharged, and sent home. Should have checked her apartment first, dummy!*

After riding the bus back across town, I found Katarina's Brickell Avenue apartment empty. *Looks like she moved out.* I stood outside looking through the front window, wondering where she might have gone. *Maybe she's at the safe house.* But the safe house in Coconut Grove was also vacant. *Where are the spooks hiding her?* I wondered as I took a slip of paper from my wallet. The scrap of paper had two phone numbers scribbled on it—my CIA contacts. *I'll find a phone and give them a call.* I dialed the first number from a phone booth outside a nearby convenience store. *"The number you have dialed is no longer in service.* Both phone numbers that the CIA had provided to me were now disconnected. *Great! Now what?* I decided to go to the Little Havana section of Miami in search of leads.

The bus dropped me off downtown at Southwest Eighth Street, and I began to walk west, away from the city and into Little Havana. Soon all the signs were printed in Spanish. On my left I passed the Cuban Memorial Plaza and stopped to look at a string of small monuments commemorating the 1961 Bay of Pigs invasion. The pain of the Cuban exiles was palpable in that plaza, and it made me wonder about what might have happened to Carlos Romero.

A wave of shame and guilt for leaving Carlos in Cuba came over me as I walked along the landscaped median. I came upon seven monuments and stopped in front of the one of the Virgin Mary to say a brief prayer for the safety of Carlos and for luck in finding Katarina. Then I noticed a huge raised map of Cuba and read the weathered inscription authored by the Cuban patriot and poet José Martí.

"La patria es agonia y deber." Huh, Spanish. *I wonder what that means.*

I decided to ask a middle-aged woman standing nearby, "Señora, what do those words mean?" I asked and pointed at the map.

"No speak English. You speak Spanish to me!" she said.

"But this is America. I don't speak much Spanish, ma'am."

"No es America! Es Miami!" she insisted and then walked away in a huff.

"It says, 'The homeland is agony and duty.'" A young woman wearing a colorful flower-patterned dress stepped up beside me. I turned to see the attractive young woman standing next to me as she gazed intently at the inscription. Her thick, shoulder-length auburn hair glistened with hues of red as the gentle breeze ruffled it. She turned to look at me, and as our eyes met, the pupils of her sky blue eyes visibly dilated. *She is so pretty, dude. So sweet and fresh. Don't I know her? She seems familiar.*

"Are you a tourist?" she asked me.

"No, I've been living here in Miami—under a bridge near Overtown."

She looked me up and down; my outfit was casual but clean and well tailored these days. "Under a bridge? Ha, so you're a joker. What's your name, joker?"

"Sunchaser. What's yours?" I don't know why, but I gave her my Indian name.

"Sure, 'Sunchaser'—pretty common name. I should have guessed. My name is Maggie."

"Hello, Maggie, pleased to meet you." We shook hands, and then I asked, "Is there a place to get coffee nearby?"

She did a double take to see if I was serious and then started laughing. "You *are* a joker, a real wise guy, aren't you. Follow me, Joker." As we walked west I realized what had made Maggie laugh. Although I hadn't noticed before, on nearly every corner there was a Cuban coffee counter and a small takeout window. Coffee counters lined both sides of the street—dozens of them. Half a block farther west she turned left and went into an open-air coffee shop. "This is

Los Pinarenos Frutería, my favorite place for coffee. Enjoy!" Maggie said and turned to leave.

"Hey wait, Maggie—want to join me?"

"Okay, Joker, I've got a few minutes." She stepped up to the window to order.

"*Buenos días, Margarita. ¡Que linda, señorita!*" The guy obviously knew her well, and they conversed in Spanish while he made two *cafés con leche*. Then over coffee I told her about my search for Katarina after being separated from her in the Cayman Islands. Of course I left out the part about the commandos and our covert rescue mission in Cuba.

"Katarina seems to have fallen off the face of the earth," I whined.

"Sounds like your girlfriend dumped you, Joker. Maybe you should give her some time…give her some space."

"Wow, that stings. You cut right to the chase, don't you, Maggie! You think Kat dumped me?"

"Sorry, Eddie, but it seems pretty obvious to me."

"Look." I took out the picture of Kat and me. "That's her kiss on my chest." I pointed at the lip imprint. "I think we might be in love."

"Huh, she's Cuban, isn't she? She's hot. You must have done something to piss her off, Joker."

"Maggie, I think Kat is in trouble, not just pissed off."

"Well, good luck finding your girlfriend. But I've got to get to work." Maggie stood up to leave.

"Hey, where do you work?"

"Jackson Hospital. Over on 12th Street."

"You got to be kidding!"

"No, Joker. I'm not joking. I work in SICU—the intensive care unit."

"My friend Brownie was a patient in SICU, and I never saw you there."

"I received a promotion and started working in the unit just two weeks ago."

"Maybe I'll stop by and say hi sometime, Maggie."

"Don't bother unless that girl Katarina really did dump you." Maggie started walking away but then stopped and said, "Oh yeah, Joker, also don't invite me over to your place until you move out from under that bridge that you live under." She laughed and walked away. Her flowery dress seemed to glow in the reflection of the morning sunshine. I watched her get swallowed up in the crowd walking along SW 8th Street.

After wandering the streets of Little Havana for half an hour I came upon a dive bar called *El Gato Negro*. The bar was open-air to the sidewalk, and I stopped and looked into the darkness. Two middle-aged men, friends of Carlos Romero who I knew were members of Brigade 2506, were playing pool and drinking beer in the dingy, dimly lit bar.

"*Hola*! Do you fellows remember me? I'm Carlos Romero's friend, Eddie Ocean." I entered and began asking them questions.

"I'm looking for Katarina Romero. Do you guys know where she is?" They pretended to not understand me even though I knew they spoke English. Then a third, younger man, who had been playing pinball, came over to join us. He stood nearby, listening.

"Come on, dudes! You know me. I met you through Carlos Romero. I need to find his niece Katarina."

The pinball wizard responded, "We know who you are, Ocean, and we appreciate your help in the past, but now it's time for you to go back to being a sea captain. If Katarina wants to see you, *she* will find *you*." I sensed that the Cubans were hiding something from me. They were obviously giving me the brush-off. The last time I had seen them they had been friendly and treated me like a member of the gang, but for some reason I had become *persona non grata* to the Cuban dissidents. *Do they blame me for leaving Carlos Romero behind in Cuba?*

The younger guy walked me to the exit and then took me aside and said, "Try placing an ad—a cryptic message to her in the personals of the Miami *Post* might do the trick. That's how the brothers keep connected covertly."

I met with my friend Rosalina at the *Post*, and she helped me place a personal ad in the newspaper and agreed to let me use her phone number in the advertisement to locate Katarina. The ad read: ***Lost Kat. Black with green-grey eyes. Need her back desperately. Contact E.O. at 305-221-0227.***

For the next two weeks I looked for Katarina in every South Florida hospital, but to no avail. It became apparent that Katarina did not want to be found; it was clear now, she *was* hiding from me. *Maggie is right. Kat dumped you, dude.*

With Carlos Romero stranded in Cuba and the dissidents in Miami as well as the CIA spooks stonewalling me, I had no one to turn to. I was at a dead end. *Like everyone has been telling you, you're gonna hafta wait for* her *to come to* you, *dude. Might as well get a boat and get back to work.*

So with a broken heart I went to the Miami Marina to see what the sleazy yacht broker had up for sale. His inventory didn't interest me, and the boats he had were overpriced anyway. After leaving his office I noticed Fanny Licker behind the bar at the Tiki Hut.

"Hello, Fanny!"

"Hey Eddie, welcome home."

"Good to be back," I lied. *Everything I see here in Miami reminds me of Kat!*

"You want brunch, Eddie?"

"Yes please, the usual."

"Coming right up." Patty made a Bloody Mary extra spicy with extra veggies and a long Slim Jim. Even though I had money for a more substantial meal, the odd pirate's breakfast made me reminisce about happier times.

"Here you go, Captain Ocean."

I took a sip and then looked across the waterway and saw the silhouette of Dr. Jill Hamm's Brillo pad-shaped head inside the office of the Sun 'N' Fun Charters building. She started waving her stubby little arms around in the air, and then Frenchy Couture came storming out of the office and slammed the door behind him before trudging down the docks toward the sailboats. *Poor Frenchy—he should quit that witch.* Suddenly the sadness of being rejected by Katarina came over me like a storm cloud. *You're on the highway to nowhere once again, dude!*

Fanny took a long look at my face and asked, "What's wrong, Eddie? Looks like you lost your best friend."

"I guess so. Fanny, it's time for me to say goodbye to Miami. This town holds too many memories—haunting memories. Think I'll head on down the road...maybe to the Keys."

Fannie saw me gazing across the waterway. "Eddie, you're not gonna let Jill Hamm run you out of town, are you?"

"No, it's not Hamm, although it *will* be nice to put some miles between me and that little troll. I just need a change of scenery; this place reminds me of my lost love."

"The Cuban chick?"

"Yeah. Things will get better when I get a boat and get back on the ocean."

"Did you see the yacht broker?" Fannie nodded her head toward the broker across the marina.

"Yeah. He had nothing too interesting. Nothing like that awesome Beneteau that Hamm snatched right out from under my nose."

"I heard talk that the Moorings up in Dania Beach, near Lauderdale has some nice boats for sale," Fanny said as she took away my empty glass and wiped the counter.

"Really? Well I guess I'm headed up to Lauderdale to see what they have available. Thank you so much, Miss Fanny Licker."

"I'll miss you, Captain Eddie." Fanny leaned across the bar and planted a wet one on my cheek.

"I'm sure I'll be sailing through here often, babe." I stood up and pulled out my wallet. "You take care, Fanny." I paid her and left for the Greyhound station.

After riding a slow bus up to Ft. Lauderdale, I found myself walking south on U.S. Highway #1 toward Dania Beach, looking for the

Moorings Yacht Brokerage. Ahead of me to the left I spotted a familiar building. *Hey, that's the Sea School, where I got my Merchant Marine
captain's license.* Three men and a woman came out of the building as
I stood looking up at the Sea School logo.

"Is that Eddie Ocean?" a middle-aged man called out.

"Hey! Captain Huber!" I recognized my Sea School instructor
immediately.

"You coming to upgrade your six-pack license to a hundred-ton
ticket, kid?" Huber asked as the others walked toward a parked car.

"No, sir. Just passing by, heading to the Moorings in Dania
Beach—looking for a sailboat."

"That's quite a hike. Want a lift?"

"Sure, Captain Huber."

"Why don't you join us for lunch, and then we'll drop you off
afterward, kid."

"Great! I've only had a light brunch today. Where you guys
headed?"

"Southport Raw Bar off 17th Street."

"I love that place. I can already taste a dozen raw oysters with
spicy horseradish being washed down by a frosty mug of cold beer."

After lunch Captain Huber and his students dropped me off at
the Dania Beach Marina. "Ask for Big Jim Bush and tell him I sent
you, kid. Big Jim will give you a fair deal."

"Okay, will do."

"Hey kid, you are aware of that storm tearing up the Lesser
Antilles, right?" asked Captain Huber.

"Ah, no. Haven't been up on the news lately, Captain."

"The computer models have it skirting along the Bahamas,
which means rain, some heavy seas, and big swells are headed our
way for sure."

"No problem. I'll be onshore, shopping for a boat."

"Good luck and take care," Huber said as the car pulled away. He
waved goodbye, and I saluted him.

Chapter 5

EYE OF THE TIGER CRUISE

The Dania Beach Marina was full of powerboats and sailboats of every size and style. From 12-foot Boston Whalers to 150-foot-plus mega-yachts, whatever boat you were looking for could be found here. I wandered along the docks, searching for the Moorings office and checking out the sailboats that I passed. *That catamaran is a real beauty. Yeah but those Cats are probably way out of your price range, dude. Check out those nice mono-hulls instead.* My window-shopping was interrupted by a guy standing on the deck of the remnants of a fifty-year-old, 70-foot rust bucket of a trawler.

"Ahoy, mate!" I looked up at a guy wearing a dark-brown leather hat. The front brim of the pirate-style headpiece was tacked to the crown, pinned securely by the quills of three gray feathers that fluttered excitedly in the breeze. Long black braids of hair cascaded down to his chest; the twists of hair were held tight by colorful, hollow wooden beads, and the braids hung well below the puffy collar of his dingy, white, 1700s-era pirate's shirt. His dark, penetrating eyes stared down at me from a heavily weathered and deeply wrinkled face, and a black handlebar mustache extended six inches beyond each cheek before curling skyward and ending in sharp, upturned points. His triangular, foot-long goatee was braided just like his hair, the tip fastened with two silver beads.

"Ahoy," I answered suppressing a laugh. *Is this dude for real?*

"Me name be Reef Kichards," the old pirate stated.

"I'm Eddie Ocean," I said, unable to suppress the smirk across my face. *Reef Kichards? This dude is surreal! That made-up name must be a play on Keith Richards's name, and this guy is the spitting image "pirate version" of the Rolling Stones guitarist.*

"You be looking for some work, Matey? I need a hand ta take this old tub over ta the islands." Just then, two barefooted young women in cut-off denim shorts and blouses tied up like halter tops came out from the wheelhouse. They stood behind the old pirate, squirming with hands behind their backs like shy teenage girls as the breeze sensually ruffled their long black hair. The hungry, lusty look in their eyes made me realize they were probably not as innocent as they appeared to be.

"I'm always looking for work, sir, but today I'm here shopping for a sailboat."

"So you be a sailor, Mate—knew it right from the start. This job be a lucrative job if you got the balls." One of the women coughed to get the man's attention. He turned to face them, "Oh, these young lassies be my daughters, Brandy on the left and Chardonnay on the right. Girls, this here be...ahh, what was that name o' yours, mate?"

"He's Eddie Ocean," one of the girls said, and they both giggled.

"Come on board fer a cold beer, Eddie Ocean. I'll tell you about the job."

"Well, I really need to find the office...." I stopped in mid-sentence when Brandy blew me a kiss and Chardonnay winked an eye. "Well, maybe one quick drink, sir." I took a closer look at the rusty old boat. She had huge truck tires hanging off the sides as dock fenders, and streaks of rust stains were all over the hull and the wheelhouse. I had to climb up a rope ladder to board the old tub.

"Brandy, get the gentleman a beer," Reef said as I followed everyone inside the wheelhouse and Brandy ducked below deck to go to the galley.

"No offense, sir, but is this vessel seaworthy?" I asked.

"She's just like my dear departed wife, mate. She looks a little rough around the edges, but she's stout and rides like a dream."

Brandy handed me a cold bottle of Kalik Beer.

"Ah, Kalik, the beer of the Bahamas," I said and took a sip. Standing close beside me, Chardonnay started running her fingers through my hair, while Brandy closely scrutinized me with hungry eyes. Their grizzled old father didn't seem to mind his daughters' precocious behavior.

"Aren't you all gonna join me, sir?" I asked and then took a long swig of beer.

"Maybe later, mate. We've preparations to make." A translucent mist began to mask the pirate's wrinkled, elongated face as he spoke, and his words sounded like they were coming from a tape recording played at a slow speed.

I blinked to clear my vision as my body became limp. "Man, did anyone ever tell you that you look just like that Rolling Stone dude, Keith Richards?" I asked as my body began to melt. Chardonnay lowered my head down to rest on the bench seat beside her.

"You look tired, Eddie. Why not take a rest?" Brandy said as she took the half-empty beer bottle from my hand. Her voice was distant, as if drifting down to me from the ozone layer.

The next thing that I knew was that my body was being slammed violently up and down on a bunk inside a cabin below deck. I listened to a loud voice of someone in an adjacent cabin insanely screaming, "You peckerheads gone a done it! We all gonna die. Fish turds for dinner!"

As I lay on the bed listening, still in a stupor, trying to shake the cobwebs from my head, I remembered drinking beer and talking with the Kichards family in the wheelhouse but did not understand what had happened to me. *How did I get down here?* I wondered as I began climbing back up to the wheelhouse in the rolling boat. Objects were falling down and flying about the cabin, and I was being bounced off the walls as I staggered toward the steps; it felt like being inside a washing machine.

"What the hell is going on?" I said as I climbed out of the hatch and saw Reef Kichards at the helm, struggling to control the steering wheel.

"Did you enjoy your nap, mate? Welcome to the 'Eye of the Tiger' cruise!"

"Holy shit! You must be mad!" I gasped after looking out the window. It was dark now, and I saw that the lunatic was driving the boat through 30-foot seas. Our feet left the deck when the boat went over the top of a cresting wave and began to drop off the backside.

"You drugged me, you bastard! Now you are going to get me killed!"

"Don't worry, mate. We do this every chance we get! We call it 'Eye of the Tiger' cruising!" Reef was screaming to be heard above the sound of the raging storm. I could see only the glint of his eyes in the darkness as he started reciting a limerick.

"There once was a sailor from Wales.
An expert at pissing in gales.
He could piss in a jar.
From the top-gallant spar,
Without even wetting the sails!"

I looked away from the madman, and what I saw outside was beyond belief. The two girls were up at the bow, tethered to the deck with safety harnesses, and standing on top of an overturned inflatable dinghy. They held hands as the ship climbed the next huge wave and Reef throttled forward. The boat seemed to be pointing skyward at 90 degrees and sliding backward.

"Oh shit!" I screamed and grabbed a railing, but just when it felt like we were going to flip bow-over-stern and turn turtle, the old boat plowed through the breaking crest and plunged downward, sending Reef and me off the floor again and the girls flying eight feet high into the air above the bow, where they seemed to float momentarily, screaming with delight, before coming back to earth and bouncing off the dinghy and back into air as if they had landed on a trampoline. Lightning flashed, illuminating Reef's face momentarily. His eyes were as wide as the portholes, and he howled out in delight, and then a resounding, inhuman, demented laugh reverberated throughout the wheelhouse.

"You're insane, old man! We're all goners. We're dead!" A roar of thunder drowned out my scream. Then hail started pelting the ship, and the girls unclipped their tethers and scrambled for cover. Chardonnay made it inside, and I struggled to hold open the heavy steel door as Brandy approached, but a blast of seawater washed over the deck and knocked Brandy off her feet. As she came sliding along the deck toward the stern, I reached out and grabbed her arm, and then pulled her inside just before the heavy door violently snapped shut like a giant mousetrap.

"Whew! For a second I thought I was a goner," she said, her eyes wild with excitement. She laughed as she struggled to stand up in the oscillating boat. "Isn't this a blast!" She screamed to be heard as another crashing wave flooded the deck.

"We are *all* goners! Your father's an idiot! We're in a hurricane!" I yelled as another flash illuminated everyone's face. *Oh my god! They are all smiling…having a blast!*

"Don't worry, mate. Soon we will be in da eye of this tiger!"

"What, inside the eye? You mean to tell me you are driving us *into* the storm?"

"Of course, mate. It's much safer inside the hole of the storm. Not as much fun, but safer. That's where we'll meet up with our friends." *Meet friends?* Just then the largest wave yet was coming at us with a roar.

"Yee ha!" both girls squealed with delight.

"Hold on ta ya scrotum, matey. This be a big'un!" Reef again threw the throttle forward as we climbed the mounting wave.

Our Father, Who art in Heaven…. Miraculously my prayer was answered. Somehow the old rust-tub made it over the crest and slid down the other side like a big, rusty bobsled. Now calmer water was ahead of the boat. The huge rolling waves had been replaced by white, foaming spikes of water shooting up and down, making the surface of the ocean resemble the top of a lemon meringue pie.

"We be inside her now, mate. Now I just gotta find Cisco."

"Let's go!" Chardonnay chirped and unlatched the wheelhouse door.

"Come look outside, Eddie," Brandy said and pulled me out through the doorway.

I stood in wonderment, taking in a 360-degree panoramic view. A wall of water topped by dense clouds and flashing lightning encircled us now, and the boat was gently rocking.

"Look up, Eddie." We all stood looking up at a clear, tranquil, starry night sky high above us.

"Wow! This is incredible!" I gasped. "Never been in the eye of a hurricane before."

"You should try it more often. Isn't this fun?" I don't know who asked me that question; I was still staring toward the heavens.

"I think I'll consider this trip a once-in-a-lifetime experience, thank you very much," I said.

Suddenly Chardonnay called out, "Hey, here comes Cisco!" Reef turned our boat sharply to port, where a larger vessel was approaching us.

"What's going on?" I asked Brandy.

"We gotta give Cisco the stolen money. That's why Papa hired you: to help us."

"*Hired* me? I was shanghaied, not hired! Stolen money, you say? What stolen money?" Nobody was listening to me; both girls were standing by at the port side of the ship.

I noticed that the huge wall of water at our stern was coming uncomfortably close, and I signaled to Reef to have a look. He glanced back and then gave me a thumb-up signal as both boats drove forward a little faster, traveling side by side and at the same speed. Then I realized that we were pacing the hurricane, moving at about 12 knots inside the eye. Someone on the other boat tossed a heavy line down to our deck, where the girls grabbed it, and then the crews began rigging up a makeshift zipline between the two ships.

"Now come with us," Brandy ordered. I followed the girls to the stern, where they started passing duffel bags up to me from the hold of the ship.

"Is this the stolen money?"

"Duh!" I couldn't tell who said that. The girls hurriedly removed the bags from the hold. Together we dragged six large duffel bags stuffed with money over to portside.

"You're doing a splendid job, mate," Reef said with a smile as I passed by the wheelhouse.

Next, floats were attached to duffel bags, and then the bags were attached to the zipline. After that, the frantic activity came to a stop, and the girls stood looking at me.

"Well, what are you waiting for?" Chardonnay asked and held out some type of harness with a lifejacket attached.

"What do you mean? Waiting for what?"

"Didn't Papa tell you when we were weightless spacewalking outside in the storm?"

"Tell me what?"

"You have to go up with the money. Cisco will pull you up." She pointed up to a Hispanic-looking guy with an impressive handlebar mustache that was twice the size of Reef's. The Cisco Kid stood at the other end of the zipline and motioned for me to come on up!

"Why doesn't that guy just pull the bags up without me?"

"Because with the two ships rolling, that cable could break, and the money would be lost overboard. If that happens, you will be in the water to retrieve the bags, and we can pull you in."

"That's stupid! Just attach the bags securely to the rope."

"That's not the way Papa does it. Don't worry—it's easy."

"Really? Then why don't you do it, Brandy?'

"I would love to, but Papa won't let me. He says it's too dangerous."

"Too dangerous? Your papa let you...ah, what do you call that craziness...weightless space walk in the middle of a hurricane, but this zipline is too dangerous?"

"Yeah, one time the cable broke and a guy got smashed between the ships. He was flatter than a squirrel lying on I-95 for two weeks in the summertime."

"He got smashed? No way, dudettes! I ain't crazy like you people!"

"Eddie Ocean, you took the job, so you better finish it! Papa don't look none too happy." Brandy was right; Reef was standing just inside the wheelhouse, holding a shotgun, with a demented look in his eyes.

"Oh shit! Help me hook up this harness, girls."

Cisco began hoisting the bags and me up the line to his ship. Midway between the ships, the boats cantered in opposite directions, and the cable drew tighter than an extra-small G-string on a 300-pound pole dancer. *Twang.* The cable made a sound like an instrument being tuned, but it didn't break.

"*Chit! Chit! Chit!*" I looked up and saw panic in Cisco's eyes as he put some slack in the cable. Somehow I made it to the top with the money just before the cable parted with a much louder *twang*. The girls nimbly dodge the cable as it snapped back and whipped across the deck like an angry serpent.

"Hey! Now what?" I called down to the girls.

Reef answered my question. "Guess you'll have go with Cisco, mate! Don't worry—I'll send you your pay."

"But where am I going, Reef?"

"Cuba! Sayonara Eddie!" he yelled to me from between cupped hands and then re-entered the wheelhouse.

"Cuba! Hell no!" I called out in disbelief and then tossed another line down to the girls. They tied it off on a cleat, but Reef was beginning to steer away from Cisco's ship.

"Jump now!" Brandy yelled. Quickly I attached my harness to the pulley above the nylon line as it began to tighten and stretch like a rubber band. I took a deep breath and jumped. The deck of the trawler raced toward me as I went tearing down the zipline at breakneck speed.

Pop! The line broke before I reached the deck, but my momentum sent me sailing through the air like a human cannonball.

"Ahhhhggghhh!" Screaming like a madman, I was sure I was a goner when I flew two feet over Brandy's head and cleared the wheelhouse roof by mere inches as I hurtled toward the bow of the turning ship. With eyes closed, I braced myself for the deadly impact but suddenly felt my body painlessly hitting the deck and then bouncing back into the air. I landed again and bounced up, but not as high. This time on my landing, my legs found the dinghy and my head bumped the deck.

"That inflatable dinghy saved your butt, Eddie. I thought you was gonna get splattered like a love bug on the windshield of an eighteen-wheeler." Brandy was standing over me just as I passed out.

Chapter 6

SHANGHAIED

"**Y**ou was awesome, Eddie! You was like Superman! I never saw a man fly before!" Brandy was leaning over me, holding a cool, wet washcloth to my forehead. I tried to sit up but stopped and cried out in pain.

"Agghhh! What happened?" I said as I lifted my shirt to see a large, ugly blue bruise covering my right ribcage.

"You flew off Cisco's freighter! You flew through the air just like you was Superman! But you bumped your head on the landing," Brandy said.

"Flying? I wasn't flying; I was hurtling to my death! It's a miracle I survived. You crazy people almost got me killed! Where are we?"

"We out of the hurricane."

"I've been shanghaied!" I said as I gently palpated the swollen knot on my forehead.

Chardonnay spoke from just inside the cabin doorway. "Daddy said we can keep you. Isn't that great, Eddie? We gonna have lots of fun together." She was standing behind Brandy, holding the double-barreled shotgun.

"Keep me?" I sat upright. A stabbing pain shot through my right side.

"Daddy said we can share you, but only one of us can marry you. We gonna flip a coin for you after dinner."

"Marry me?"

"When you risked your life to fly home to us, we knew you was in love with us, Eddie," Brandy said and kissed the bump on my head. Then she pulled me close, burying my face into her ample bosom, her long black hair tickling the back of my neck.

"You girls are insane! Take me back to Florida, back to Dania Beach!" With my head stuck up to my ears in Brandy's cleavage, her large breasts muffled my words.

"What did he say, Brandy?" Chardonnay asked.

"He wants to go back to Dania."

"We can't go back there, Eddie. The cops are looking for us. That was where we robbed the bank," Brandy said.

"So that's why US 1 was blocked and all those cop cars were gathering. I passed the bank you robbed when I was riding the bus up from Miami."

"Yeah, so you see we can't go back there, sweetie. We're going to Nassau." Brandy released my throbbing head from her booby trap.

"Oh? Well, Nassau…that's nice," I said. My hopes of escaping this floating insane asylum were raised because I had friends living in Nassau who could help me.

"Yeah, all three of us will have a nice romantic honeymoon in Nassau, sweetie pie," Brandy said and stood up. "But for now we will have to keep you locked up until you get to know us better…then you'll forget all about Florida." The girls left the cabin and locked me inside.

Just play along until you get to land, dude. Then you can jump ship. Again a voice came from the adjacent cabin.

"There was a young maid from Madras
Who had a magnificent ass.
Not rounded and pink
As you'd probably think,
It was grey, had long ears, and ate grass!" Awwwkkk!

"Hey! Who are you? Are you being held captive? Did you get shanghaied too?" I called out, but I received no response. Eventually I fell asleep, and when I woke up it was morning. By the sounds outside and the lack of motion, I determined that the boat had been docked. My cabin door opened, and Brandy entered with a tray of food. The gun-toting Chardonnay followed her into my cabin.

"We let you sleep through the night, Eddie. You didn't want dinner, but now you must be starving, sweetie."

"I sure am, Brandy."

"Here, darling." She set the tray on my bunk and said, "Eddie I have great news! I won you with the coin toss last night!"

"Yeah, but remember you have to share him with me, Brandy!" Chardonnay said, her face twisted up in a pout.

"Eddie, as a sea captain, Daddy has the authority to marry us. So tonight after dinner we'll get hitched. Aren't you happy, Eddie?" Brandy asked.

"Ah, yeah...thrilled." *Play along for now, dude.*

"Eat up. My Superman needs to keep his strength." Brandy kissed the bump on my head, and then the girls left. I pushed the tray aside and scrambled over to the small porthole to look outside. *This looks like Nassau, all right. I'll soon be free from these loony tunes.* I returned to the food and gobbled it down like a ravenous dog.

The next thing I knew it was early evening. "What the hell? I must have slept all day," I mumbled as I peered from the porthole into the darkness outside. Again my door opened. This time Reef Kichards entered the cabin carrying the shotgun.

"Time to get hitched, Mr. Ocean. You must restore the honor of my daughters, kid."

"Restore their honor? Do you think that something happened between us? I swear I did not touch your daughters, sir."

"What do you think they were doing with you when you were drugged, kid, having a tea party?"

"Drugged? That's it...why I slept all day! You drugged me again!" Suddenly I recalled the dream that I had about rollicking with the wild, buxom sisters. *Oh crap! I thought I was only dreaming about those crazy girls.*

"Well, tonight after dinner, we will make all your moral turpitude and debauchery with my daughters honorable and legal. Looks like I'm about to be your new daddy, kid," Reef said with a wide smile that displayed a mouth full of crooked and cracked yellow teeth. He motioned with the barrel of the gun for me to get moving. "Let's go. The gals have your wedding dinner waiting." In the galley the girls were putting out food. A white wedding veil covered Brandy's face, and Chardonnay had a big red plastic flower pinned in her black hair.

"We made you all our favorites, Eddie: corndogs, pizza, and pop tarts for dessert. Would you like some wine, sweetie?" Brandy asked.

"Okay. Yum, Boone's Farm!" I said sarcastically. "It's not drugged, is it?"

"Of course not, sweetie pie, I need you wide awake tonight for the honeymoon."

"Remember, you have to share him, Brandy," Chardonnay said as she poured wine into everyone's glasses.

"Daddy, do I have to share him on my honeymoon night?" Brandy whined.

"No," Reef said and turned toward Chardonnay. "Daughter, you will have your turn. Let the newlyweds be alone their first night."

"That's not fair, Daddy. I had to share that Italian guy on my wedding night. And he only lasted a week. Then it took forever before you got me a new husband!" Chardonnay said.

"Only lasted a week? What happened to the guy?" I asked.

"He's the guy we told you about—the guy who got squashed between the boats in the eye of the last hurricane," said Brandy.

"Yeah, and he was real fun, too—much better than that pilot—but the wild cowboy was the best husband of them all!"

"Them all? How many husbands have you girls had?" I glanced over at the exit where Reef was seated at a small folding table, holding the shotgun. I was starting to get very nervous about my situation.

"I've only had three hubbies, but you are Brandy's fifth. Isn't that *so* unfair," Chardonnay said as she passed out corndogs.

"What happened to all those guys?" I asked.

"They always get kilt one way or another. Especially Brandy's beaus," Chardonnay said.

"Well at least I never had one of mine jump overboard in the middle of the night a hundred miles from land, screaming, *"God help me! Take me home, sweet Jesus!"* Brandy said.

"What made him do that?" I asked.

"Because Chardonnay would not give him even one night off!"

"Oh yeah, Brandy. Well, what about that fellow of yours who chummed the reef with pigs' blood, pretending to be shark fishing, and then jumped into the feeding frenzy screaming, *"Save me, sweet Mother Ocean!"* Brandy said as she lifted her veil and then stuffed a corndog down her throat, swallowing it whole before pulling back the bare wooden skewer and licking it with her incredibly long and pointed tongue.

"Brandy, you know that fisherman was just crazy, crazy from the git-go. I did not cause him to jump in with those sharks!" And then as if competing in some corndog eating contest, Chardonnay duplicated Brandy's corndog-swallowing feat. She made eye contact with me and slowly pulled the wooden skewer out through her pursed lips and began licking it with an equally long and pointy tongue. My appetite was rapidly fading, but I forced down a slice of cold, rubbery frozen pizza.

"Who is in the cabin next to mine?" I asked.

"That's Professor Peckerhead."

"Professor huh…of what? English Lit? He was reciting limericks to me. Why do you keep him locked up?" My mind was racing.

"So he won't fly the coop." Reef said and finished the last bite of a slice of the rubberized pizza.

"So he's shanghaied like me?"

"Okay, enough small talk. Let's get on with the ceremony," Reef said and stood up to hand the shotgun over to Chardonnay. He picked up a black book that I thought was a Bible and walked toward me, and then motioned for me to stand beside Brandy.

"Do you really want to do this?" I asked no one in particular.

"Of course, sweetie, we is in love!" *Well, just play along, dude. This can't be a legal wedding.*

"Okay, let's all have a moment of silence." Reef closed his eyes and bowed his head. I bowed my head but kept my eyes open, and I could see the title of the book. The thick black book was not a Bible. In gold letters *The Limerick* was written across the spine. Then Reef stood straight and said, "I only wish that my late beloved wife, Daphnis, could be here with us to witness the joining of our precious daughter to young Mr. Ocean; a fine and worthy lad he be. Since Mr. Ocean seems to be a fan of the limerick, a short poem to honor my dear Daphnis is in order. Without opening the book Reef began.

"Daphnis while dining with crew,
Found an elephant's wang in her stew.
Said our cook, "'Please don't shout,
And don't wave it about,
Or your daughters will want one, too.'"

"Oh, Daddy, that was so sweet!" Brandy said and then lifted the veil from her face. I could see tears forming in her eyes. Reef opened the book and told us to place our hands on its pages.

"I now pronounce you husband and wife. Eddie, you may kiss the bride." Reef said and slammed the book closed.

When I hesitated to kiss Brandy she grabbed my head with both hands and latched her mouth onto mine with the suction of a remora. The taste of corndog filled my mouth, and I felt her long tongue slithering down my throat like a serpent. It was like being kissed by an anteater.

"Gaaahhhh!" I began to gag as the tongue seemed to reach down my throat and past my larynx. I could not get air and became light-headed. At that point I must have fainted because when I came to my senses, Brandy was carrying me across the threshold of her cabin.

"Aren't *you* supposed to be carrying *me*, sweetie pie?" she said and then plunged that tongue down my throat again before tossing me onto her bed, where I bounced painfully on my bruised ribs.

Help me! My silent scream went unanswered, so I prayed that I might make it through the night to see the morning light.

I survived my wedding night, but two days passed before the girls let me leave Brandy's cabin.

"I guess we finally got you broke now, sweetie pie. Today you can come out for supper," Brandy said and helped me up to the galley. I was weak and could barely walk from the daily physical and mental demands that the sisters were putting on me. When we passed the adjacent cabin, Professor Peckerhead called out from his room, "Aaawkkk! Don't let that peckerhead fly the coop!"

That poor guy sounds demented. They've really messed him up.

Reef was in the galley. "You look like shit, kid. Are my girls too much for you to handle? You should be happy to be married to such a lively young filly as Brandy be," Reef said with a smirk. I did not respond. I just stared longingly at the exit door. Then Reef added, "My beloved Daphnis was a wonderful gal, but not so passionate in the sack. There is a lover-ly poem in the good book that reminds me of her.

"A mortician who practiced in Fife
Made love to the corpse of his wife,
How could I know, Judge
She was cold, did not budge...
Just the same as she'd acted in life."

"Ha, that's a good one, sir." I tried to laugh but could not muster one.
"You look like you could use a shot of rotgut, kid."

"No, thanks, but I sure could use some fresh air and sunshine, Captain," I said.

"Not till the girls say they got you broke. We had too many o' you young fellows run off and break my babies' hearts."

"Don't worry about me running off. This lifestyle is like dying and going straight to heaven, dude—I mean, *sir*." I lied to gain Reef's confidence.

Brandy entered the galley. "Daddy, I think we finally got Eddie broke. I left our cabin door unlocked last night, and he didn't try to run away. Professor Peckerhead was standing guard outside his door, and we didn't hear him squawk all night—not once." *Damn! The door was unlocked with only some old demented professor standing guard? You missed your chance, dude! Stay cool. Play the game.*

"Of course I didn't run. Why would I want to run off, darling?" Brandy gave me a loving smile and came across the room to me. For the hundredth time she grabbed my head hard with both hands and jammed her serpentine tongue down my throat. Over the past few days I had learned how to breathe with that damn foot-long organ obstructing my airway. I was just biding my time. Like taking baby-steps, each day I was granted a little more freedom, and the opportunities to escape were increasing. But suddenly one evening Reef announced that we were going to set sail in two days.

"We got a good blow coming up from the Caribbean. In the morning prepare the boat, and the next day we gonna set sail to find the eye of that tiger!"

"Yippee! 'Eye of the Tiger' cruising! Daddy, we can teach Eddie weightless spacewalking!"

"Yee-ha! Another hurricane! I can't wait girls!" I chimed in with false bravado. *That means tonight is your last chance. You gotta bolt tonight, dude!*

That night, just before climbing into bed and while Brandy was in the head, I tested the doorknob of our cabin door. *It's unlocked dude!* I pretended to sleep and then sometime after midnight I crept over to the door and was about to leave but hesitated. *Wait! Professor Peckerhead might be standing guard outside the door. Get something to gag him with dude.* I slipped a pillow out of its case and slowly cracked the door open and peered outside. *Cool! I don't see anyone standing guard.* But I only took three steps before I heard the Professor screaming out! He began reciting limericks!

"Aaawkkk!

"There was a young man in Peru
Who had nothing whatever to do,
So he flew to the garret
And buggered the parrot,
And sent the result to the zoo!

"Aaawkkk! Aaawkkk! Aaawkkk!"

The voice was coming from above me, and I looked up to see, to my amazement, a huge blue bird sitting on a T-shaped perch. The bird was a hyacinth macaw.

"Aaawkkk! The peckerhead bastard will fly the coop! Aaawkkk!"

"Shit!" I swatted at the huge blue-colored bird with the pillow-case, and it blinked its yellow-trimmed eyes and then ripped a hole in the pillowcase with its sizeable black beak.

"Aaawkkk! Wake up, you lazy peckerhead buggers! Aaawkkk!"

I reached up and pulled the white pillowcase down over the screaming bird in an attempt to shut the damn thing up. Cloaked in the pillowcase the bird jumped down to the floor, ran across the room and crashed into the wall. Then it began jumping up and down, rising high off the floor and into the air with it's large, black, beak protruding from the hole in the pillowcase. Now it was scream-ing even louder, "Aaawkkk! Aaawkkk! Aaawkkk!" In the dim light the bird resembled a small ghost flying about the boat. Suddenly just two feet to the right of my leg a door opened and Chardonnay reached out to grab me as I began to climb the stairs leading up to the wheelhouse but the sight of the *ghost* made her pause momentarily and she step back into her room until she realized that the *ghoul* was only Professor Peckerhead inside a pillowcase.

"Aaawkkk! The peckerhead is flying the coup! Aaawkkk!"

I made it topside but sitting there in the dark was Reef Kichards clutching the shotgun. I raised my hands to surrender, but Reef seemed groggy and slow to respond to the parrot's alarm call. Then I noticed an empty bottle of rum lying on its side at his feet. *He's drunk! Go for it, dude!* I grabbed hold of the rope ladder and glanced back to see the girls taking the gun from Reef, who had fallen off his chair attempting to stand up. When I jumped onto the dock I looked up to see the girls standing above me.

"Shit!" Chardonnay was taking aim. *You can't outrun buckshot, dude!* I dove off the dock and swam underwater until I found refuge between the twin hulls of a catamaran. The girls spent over an hour searching the water under the docks with flashlights, arguing the whole time about whose fault it was that I had gotten away. Finally they gave up and went to back their boat, allowing me to slip away to the shore. Two hours later and just before sunrise, I showed up on Conch Jimmy's stoop.

"Hi Jimmy. It's me, Eddie Ocean."

"What the wanna be, dude. You be soaking wet, mon."

"I need help, Jimmy. Can you help me get back to Florida?"

"Sure, mon! C'mon in."

Chapter 7

THE ORION

Two days after my escape from captivity in Nassau, Jimmy helped me secure a ride on a boat transporting Bahamian bread and conch meat to Ft. Lauderdale. Now I was back to where I had started my odyssey before being shanghaied by the crazy Kichard clan. Big Jim Bush was about to give me a sea trial aboard a 43-foot Beneteau Oceanis that was being offered for sale. Jim and I left the Moorings dock and motored up the Dania Cutoff Canal, heading for the Port Everglades Inlet. The sailboat was roomy, fast, and within my price range—a real beauty. I liked her even more than the 41-footer that Dr. Jill Hamm had snatched out from under my nose in Miami.

We entered the wide turning basin of the port, and Big Jim turned the boat southeast into a stiff breeze as I hoisted the main sail. Then Jim unfurled the jib. As usual I felt a surge of exhilaration when the wind grabbed the boat by her sails, heeling her to port and propelling us through the light chop with surprising speed. Once into the open ocean, Jim shut down the 54 horsepower Yanmar diesel engine. Now we could hear only the sound of the wind and the sea as the boat cut smoothly through four-foot waves.

"Sweet ride!" I called back to Jim as I stood near the bow, watching a school of flying fish gliding two feet above the white caps off our port quarter.

"Come, take the wheel. Get a feel for her. Feel her power," Jim said.

After forty-five minutes of tacking and jibbing, we ran home behind a huge blue spinnaker with the wind at our backs. I loved the Beneteau and was already sold on her, but I didn't let Big Jim know that; we had some bargaining to do. After tying up at the dock, I began to closely examine the interior and the engine compartment. *This thing is immaculate. She's probably gonna set me back 120 grand!*

"This motor has some hours on it. That's for sure," I commented with a frown as I looked at the immaculate and well-maintained single diesel engine before closing the hatch and going to the galley. "Well, this kitchen equipment is not *too* bad," I commented before walking away from the gas stove toward the chart table, where I began inspecting the boat's electronics. The boat was a creampuff, well maintained, but despite that fact I occasionally would make a negative comment about something or other.

Big Jim snickered at each of my derogatory comments and finally said to me, "Eddie, you can see that this boat is in tiptop condition. You're very lucky to find a used boat in such fine shape."

"Yeah Jim, but you know what they say: A boat is a hole in the water where you throw all your money. Can't be too careful, sir."

Big Jim was getting bored with my haggling. "Listen, kid, Captain Huber is a good friend of mine. He told me to treat you right, so when you're done kicking the tires I'll give you the bottom line price."

"Yeah, okay, I admit she's awesome, dude! What's she gonna cost me? Give me the out-the-door price."

"She's $105,000 plus taxes." Jim took a small calculator from his pocket and began punching in numbers. "That's $110,250 out the door, Eddie."

My old rule of sleeping on any big decision in order to avoid being impulsive had been torn from my rulebook when Dr. Hamm beat me to the punch on the 41-footer.

"That's a good figure, dude. You've got a deal!" Once again I would own a boat and have a roof over my head, finally! *You're back in business, dude!* The nearly 15,000 bucks left in my bank account was icing on the cake. *This might be one of the best days of my life… if only Katarina were at my side. Wish she could see my new boat. Then she would know I'm not such a loser after all.*

"Okay, kid. Let's do the paperwork! What are you going to call her?"

"The *Orion*, sir."

"Like the constellation? Nice name."

"Yeah, Orion, the hunter in the night sky. In times of trouble his presence has often brought me comfort."

"*Orion* it is," Jim said as he filled in the blocks on a registration form.

It was a done deal. Big Jim let me sleep on the boat that night, but she would not officially be mine until after my check had cleared the bank. The next afternoon I went to a marine store and bought some required safety equipment that was missing from the boat and also food for the galley. Then, after spending one more night onboard at the Moorings dock, I said farewell to Big Jim and set sail for the Florida Keys. It was a clear and sunny spring morning, and my three-day journey south was a breeze. *Pardon the pun.*

10:00, FRIDAY, MAY 24TH, 1974

The large, white roof of a boathouse loomed off my starboard beam as I neared the southern tip of Islamorada in the Florida Keys. *There she is…Bud 'N' Mary's Marina.* I fired up the diesel and then turned into the wind to drop the mainsail in preparation for entering the marina.

Bud 'N' Mary's Marina would be my home for the next few months. Captain Ocean's Sunset Cruising, became my new business and my meal ticket for the time being. A few roundtrip charters down to Key West were tossed into the mix of the nightly sunset champagne cruises that I offered. My evenings, when I did not have a sunset cruise booked, were often spent brokenheartedly reminiscing over my trip to Cuba with Katarina. But at least the work—if you can call it that—helped take my mind off her. Then one morning a surprise visitor showed up at my boat slip.

"Ahoy, Captain Ocean! Are you onboard?"

I was in the galley making scrambled eggs with green peppers and cheese when I heard the voice calling me. "Yes sir, that's me," I said as I stood on the stairs and popped my head out from the hatch to see who was calling.

"May I come aboard, Captain?" the man asked. I recognized the guy immediately.

"Sure. Come aboard, sir." It was the tall, thin guy with the wire-rimmed glasses, Willard. I had met the guy at the Key Largo fishing shack. He was one of the two CIA agents who'd helped Carlos and me plan Kat's rescue mission. As usual, the spook was wearing a tropical shirt and khaki pants, with boat shoes and no socks.

"What brings you down here, sir? I was trying to find you and your partner in Miami a few months ago, but your phone numbers have been disconnected."

"Yeah, sorry about that, kid. We didn't want to get you any deeper in the shit. The Cubans know you're not Canadian…. I'm afraid they know you're here in Florida, and they also know your name's Ocean. Do you own a gun?"

"A gun? Yeah, I got a single-shot twelve gauge—for sharks."

"Single shot? Well, that's better than nothing, I suppose." Willard nervously scanned the docks with squinting eyes and said, "Let's go below."

In the galley, smoke was rising from my burnt eggs. "Where the heck is Katarina? I've given up searching for her," I said and hustled to the stove to turn off the burner.

"Katarina has been refusing to see you, but something has come up, and it's no longer her choice. Today is your lucky day, kid," Willard said as he poured himself a cup of coffee. "Mind if I have some coffee?" He stirred in some sugar as he asked.

"Sure, help yourself. What did I do to upset Katarina? Why doesn't she want to see me?"

"You'll find out—all in due time, kid. There's a lot you don't know."

"Yeah, a hell of a lot I don't know! I have so many questions."

"I might not be at liberty to answer them, kid, but what do you want to know?"

"For starters, did you guys get Carlos out of Cuba yet?" I asked.

"Carlos is dead, kid. The Cubans caught him...tortured and killed him," the spook said without emotion."

"What? Carlos dead?" I gasped in disbelief.

"Our informant Garcia witnessed his demise. He reported that Nicky the Knife finally broke the unbreakable *El Muerte*. They tortured him for a week before he gave up the ghost in that dungeon on the Isle of Pines."

The news hit me like a two-by-four between the eyes. I was stunned. "What! Tell me that's just a sick joke, dude!" I was both shocked and angry.

"It's true, kid: *el Muerte* is dead. When Katarina found out that her uncle died after rescuing her from the prison she went crazy. She went loco—she has tried to harm herself several times."

I slumped down on the sofa adjacent to the galley, feeling sick to my stomach. *I left Carlos on that beach. I left him to a death sentence!*

"Kid, we need *you* to make Katarina understand that *she* was not responsible for her uncle's death. *El Muerte's* stubbornness and his vendetta against the Russian Butcher is what got Romero killed."

"It's true. Katarina is not responsible; *I'm* responsible. The commandos made me leave Carlos behind. They threatened to shoot me if I didn't leave the island…said that I would get Katarina killed; get them all killed if I didn't go immediately. But I should have refused to leave him."

"So you see it's true. It was Carlo's decision to stay—his decision alone. You must make Katarina understand that fact—for her own sake." Willard tasted the coffee and winced. "Shit," he mumbled.

"Hey! Now it finally makes sense. The reason Katarina hates me is for abandoning her uncle to die. She blames both me *and* herself."

"No. That's not accurate; Katarina did not want you to see her from the beginning, even before she learned of Carlos's death. She only found out about his death two weeks ago. I'm afraid she had other reasons for not wanting you to see her, kid."

"But why…so where is she now, and what is your plan?" I asked.

"Do you have someone who can watch your boat for a few days?"

"Sure, the dockmaster."

"Okay. I'll take you to Miami. Maybe you can get Katarina Romero out of her funk before she offs herself. You're probably her last chance. Nothing else we have tried has worked."

"Offs herself? Are you saying that Kat is suicidal?" I asked and sprang to my feet.

"Yeah, two weeks ago she asked us to take her to the Freedom Tower downtown. Said she wanted to go there to honor Carlos… to pray for his soul and the future of Cuba. But she was not going there only to pray. She was planning on jumping to her death. Her bodyguard grabbed her just before she took the leap. That was two days after she found out about her uncle's murder. She's made two more attempts to take her own life since then. She's on suicide watch."

"That doesn't even sound like Kat. She's tough—she's invincible! She would never give up the fight."

"No longer the case, kid. Nicky the Knife broke her spirit, too. You'll see. I've already told you too much, kid. You'll have to see for yourself...soon."

"Okay, let's go. No time to waste!" I said as I stuffed some clothes into my backpack.

Chapter 8

BLIND FAITH

We rode in silence to Miami, where Willard turned right, leaving US 1, and pulled up to the tollbooth on the Rickenbacker Causeway.

"So this is where you've been hiding her? Katarina is on Key Biscayne?" I asked.

"Yeah. We'll be there in about fifteen minutes."

From the passenger side window, I looked to the west as we crossed the bridge over Bear Cut. The setting sun burned through the distant afternoon haze, setting the horizon on fire with vibrant yellow and red hues. As we traveled through Crandon Park, the sun fell below the horizon, and the still-vibrant sky silhouetted a long row of majestic palm trees lining the beach. The spectacular "postcard image" made me long to once again share such enjoyable experiences with Katarina.

"I can't predict how Katarina is going to react to you, kid. We had a hell of a time getting her to agree to this meeting. We finally convinced her that if she was not going to see you again, you deserved an explanation—a goodbye."

"Goodbye?" My excitement and optimism at the thought of being reunited with Katarina began fading like the daylight.

"She considers this meeting to be her farewell to you. She has already delivered her swansong to the Brigade 2506 brothers; she quit the brotherhood."

"I've never seen Kat give up....give in."

"Katarina *has* given up. She's lost the will to fight. You need to give her a reason to live—a reason to fight on, kid."

"It sounds like you're describing a completely different person, not Katarina Romero, dude."

"There is something about her that I'm not at liberty to tell you, Ocean. That piece of this puzzle is up to Katarina to reveal if she chooses to," Willard said as he switched on the headlights. He drove me to a large waterfront home at the end of Key Biscayne near Cape Sable.

"Wow, nice crib!" I said.

Willard explained that a prominent anti-Castro politician owned the mansion. It was crawling with armed security guards.

"This place is a fortress," I commented.

"Yeah, ever since sponsoring the Cuban trade embargo legislation, the senator has been threatened by the KGB and the Cuban Government. After the assassination of that anti-Castro radio host over on Miami Beach last year, the senator was granted Secret Service protection. Follow me." With his long legs, Willard took the steps two at a time as I followed him up a staircase to the second floor. We went through a spacious room and out onto an open terrace. The balcony overlooked the Atlantic Ocean.

Katarina Romero was sitting in a chair behind a transparent curtain that appeared to be mosquito netting. She sat slumped over; shoulders slouched forward. Her graceful, elegant ballerina posture, which I had come to know so well, was missing. The sight of her made me pause just outside the doorway. *Is that Katarina?* I wondered why the elegant posture with which she carried herself was gone. Without speaking, Willard used a hand motion to direct me to a chair in front of the curtain. Then the spook vanished, leaving us alone.

Without greeting her, I sat down. Kat remained looking out over the ocean, which was growing dark with the dusk. She seemed to not know that I had arrived. *She's so thin and frail. She looks pale…maybe it's just this damn netting.* I squirmed in my seat and said, "Hi, Kat."

She stiffened. "What? Oh, hello, Eddie."

"Katarina, I searched all over for you…looked in every hospital in Miami and beyond for over a month."

"I know. They told me that you were such a persistent little bugger." She spoke without turning toward me.

"Well, why did you avoid me? Why hide from me? Do you hate me, Kat?"

"No—just the opposite, Eddie. I was stupid and weak like a teenaged girl, and now I've caused everyone a lot of pain…caused the death of my Uncle Carlos."

"That's not your fault. The Cubans caught up with you. They got lucky and kidnapped you, that's all. Carlos helped us rescue you. We had you safely onboard the boat, and Carlos could have escaped with us, but he wanted to stay behind to kill the Russian, Nicky the Knife. That was *his* decision and no one's fault. It must have been his fate, Kat." I leaned in closer to the netting to try to see Katarina more clearly through the white mesh. "What's with this mosquito net?"

"I agreed to see you only if they put a curtain between us."

"Why?"

"The main reason is so that we cannot touch." She turned her head toward the curtain for the first time, and I saw that she was wearing those large, dark sunglasses that she wore when she picked me up in the black Corvette. Back then, Katarina looked like a supermodel posing on the cover of a magazine. But she looked different now. Her frail body was slouched forward, and her voice was weak.

"What if I just get up and walk around this damn net?"

"*No!*" she said as she tensed up and slid to the edge of her chair. "If you do that I will call security, and our little meeting will be over."

"Okay, Kat, relax. I'll play by your rules."

"Good. Now I will tell you what happened, and soon you will know why I never want you to see me again." The feeling in my chest was as if someone had carved out my heart, leaving only an empty, aching cavity. *Never see me again?*

She continued, "They caught me on SW Eighth Street. Should have spotted them from a mile away but I was caught off guard... distracted."

"By what?"

"You, damn it! I was looking in the window of the clothing shop where we bought your calypso outfit for our trip to Cuba. Wanted to get you a present—a new outfit, so you might take me out dancing again. My head was in the clouds. I'm so ashamed of myself; I was acting like a schoolgirl overcome by puppy love. I lost my edge."

"Kat, I'm so sorry."

"I warned you, Ocean! I told you that love only makes a person weak—vulnerable and weak! And now I got Carlos killed in the bargain."

"Katarina, like I said, that was his choice, not your fault. You once told me that Carlos would give his own life, conduct a suicide mission in order to kill Nicky the Knife. Well that's what he did, suicide mission—but he failed."

"You're wrong, Eddie. It *was* my fault. Do you know how they finally broke Carlos in that prison...how they broke the invincible *el Muerte?*"

"No, how?"

"The Russian showed him his hideous collection, you know that pickle jar full of human eyeballs."

"Carlos had seen that jar before. That was not new to him. How could the Russian's sick horror show prop break Carlos's spirit?"

"Well you are right, the eyeballs had no effect on Carlos at first. Our informant Garcia witnessed everything. Carlos just smirked and spat at the jar, but the Russian told him to take a closer look.

Carlos did, and then something he saw in the jar freaked him out. Carlos began thrashing and pulled on his chains until the flesh was torn from his wrists. Then he slumped down and began to cry. He cried as they tortured him. No one present could believe that the Russian had finally broken Uncle Carlos. *El Muerte* did not even try to go into his hypnotic trance. He was broken…a broken man who took the pain until he could take it no longer. Then he died."

"I don't understand. What did Carlos see?"

"Maybe this will help you understand." Kat removed the sunglasses. Her eyes looked odd. My stomach churned. Something was wrong. I could not make out her beautiful, exotic eyes through the mesh netting. With a gasp I lifted the curtain, not believing what I was seeing.

"Oh, God!" Kat's eyes had been cut out, leaving shallow holes covered by her eyelids.

"Don't I look pretty, Eddie? Now do you know why I didn't want you to see me? The Russian said he did me a favor by not removing my eyelids too." Kat's voice sounded distant as if coming from a distant echo chamber. I felt myself moving in slow motion, floating down to the floor.

When I came to, Willard was sitting in a chair next to me. He had placed me on a sofa inside the house. Dazed, I looked around at my surroundings. Katarina was gone. "Willard, please tell me this is a nightmare. Tell me that what I just saw is not true," I said and started to sit upright.

"Wish I could have given you a warning—a heads-up—but she made me swear not to tell you, kid. She wanted to show you herself so that you would finally leave her alone. Now she's on a hunger strike. She plans on starving herself. They are not going to force feed her, so she probably has only a couple of months at best. She's already so thin."

"Willard, we've got to think of something—gotta find a way to save her!"

"Good luck with that, kid. That young woman is even more stubborn than her uncle Carlos." Willard stood up. "Come on. I'll drive you back to Islamorada. There's nothing you can do here for the time being."

We made the long drive south in total silence. Memories of Kat, strong, vibrant, and beautiful, came to me. When I closed my eyes, vivid images of Katarina and me dancing at the Tropicana and then sprinting down South Beach at sunrise filled my head. *What I wouldn't give to go back in time, to return to our old "street life in paradise." With Katarina at my side, even the hard times were good.* Then the image of her disfigured face and frail body sitting behind the mesh mosquito netting flashed before my mind's eye.

"Willard, pull over!" Just south of Key Largo, I vomited three times on the side of US 1 before we could continue the journey home.

Chapter 9

THE REUNION

Four days passed before I stuck my head outside of the boat's cabin and into the open air. In a daze, I looked around the marina; it was just after sunset. My supply of liquid anesthetics, the beer and booze, was depleted. The devil's nectar that I had been relying on to induce a mental fog to obscure from my mind the haunting and ghastly image of Katarina sitting slumped over in her wheelchair was gone. My belly was on fire; I hadn't had much to eat. *What friggin' day is this?* I was wondering when I heard someone speak to me.

"Thought you was dead, dude!" Standing on the dock was Bailey, the young evening-shift dockmaster. Next to him stood a guy wearing a tee shirt that had *OPEN SEZ A ME Locksmith Services* emblazoned across the chest.

"Say what?" I stammered.

"We thought you was dead, Ocean. Smells pretty ripe in there. We was just about to open up your hatch to check on you, dude." Bailey shrugged with his arms extended and palms turned up, his body language asking me, *What the hell, dude?*

"Smell? That's just garbage. Lots of garbage to take out of here," I said as flies buzzed around my hatch.

"Man, you look like shit, dude. You okay?"

"Yeah, sure, I'm fine. It's all about a girl." My speech was slurred, and I was wobbly.

"A girl, huh? Yeah. I've been there too, dude. Like Buffet sings, 'Some people claim there's a woman to blame!' You need to get back in the saddle, dude. You missed three or four charter bookings. That's gonna mess up your fine reputation, Captain Ocean."

"Thanks for the advice, Bailey. Think I finally got her out of my system. Hey, what time is it?"

"Six-thirty, dude. You only got thirty minutes of happy hour left," Bailey said and started to walk back toward his office.

"Yuk! Just need food, dude. A long shower and some hot food," I said. The thought of a drink almost made me puke, but my stomach was emptier than a Scottish pay toilet.

That week I booked a meager three champagne sunset cruises—barely enough to pay the bills. Business was slow. Then, late one afternoon while I was washing down the *Orion*, Bailey stuck his head out of the marina office and called to me, "Eddie! You got a phone call!" I turned off the hose and jogged over to the office.

"Some guy from Key Biscayne wants to book a cruise," said Bailey.

"Hey, great! Definitely need the work," I said as I picked up the receiver. "Hello, Captain Ocean here."

"Eddie, it's Willard."

"Willard! What's up! Don't tell me...did she...?" I wondered if he was calling to tell me that Kat had died.

"Katarina is alive—a bit better, in fact. She has agreed to eat if we let her sail with you."

"What? Why? She hates me!"

"Something's up. She's acting more rational, but I still don't trust her to be alone. She found out about your new boat, the *Orion*. It seemed to lift her spirits. Now she wants to sail with you."

"When?"

"ASAP. No telling how long this manic mood swing will last."

"It would take me a couple of days to get to you, but if you can bring her down to Islamorada I can be ready late tomorrow afternoon."

"I'll have her at your dock by five."

"Can't wait! Thank you so much! I owe you, dude!" I was ecstatic! *Maybe Kat's overcome the shock of her uncle's death and her horrible trauma. Maybe she will let me take care of her. Maybe she still loves me, too.* I hung up the phone. "Bailey, I gotta cancel my July 4th fireworks cruise. It's an emergency."

"The fourth is Thursday, the day after tomorrow."

"I know it's short notice…can't be helped. The chick needs me, man."

"You're gonna have some real pissed-off clients, dude! I hope this chick doesn't ruin your reputation, Captain Ocean."

"Tell them I'll give them a free overnight cruise as compensation."

17:35, WEDNESDAY, JULY 3RD, 1974

Since 4:45 pm I had been intermittently climbing atop the cabin and craning my neck to see Bud 'N' Mary's parking lot. I was looking for Willard's car. Fiddling with the boat all day had done little to take my mind off Katarina; the anticipation of her arrival was maddening. *Damn, 5:35! She must have backed out!* I checked my watch for the hundredth time that hour.

Expecting at any minute to hear Bailey call me to the marina office to take Willard's cancelation call, I decided to go make that call myself, but as I was walking down the dock, Willard's car came roaring in off US 1, enveloped in a cloud of white limestone dust. He had a passenger. *She's here!* I was both happy and unnerved as the image of Kat sitting in that wheelchair returned to my mind. I turned to return to the boat but then stopped in my tracks. *Maybe Willard needs help…help with her in that wheelchair.* Willard opened the passenger side door and helped Kat out of the car. She stood up and began walking. I paused and watched her, she looked considerably better than the last time I had seen her. Kat was holding onto Willard's left elbow, and he carried one small bag in his right hand. She was wearing those big, dark sunglasses under a stylish black beret. *She's still beautiful!*

Willard spotted me and called out, "Ahoy, Captain. Sorry we're late." Kat seemed to stiffen at hearing Willard address me, and she tugged on Willard's arm. Her body language told me she was just as nervous as me.

They approached me where I stood on the dock. "Welcome. Go on aboard," I said and steadied the gangplank ramp.

Onboard, the uneasiness and tension in the air was static. "Well, do you kids need anything before I go?" Willard asked, anxious to escape the uncomfortable situation. He stayed around for only about ten minutes before wishing us luck and leaving. Kat was feeling her way around the cockpit and bumped into the portside steering wheel.

"Here, let me help," I offered.

But when I tried to direct her, she became angry. "I can find my own way!" she said, and then she sat down near the wheel. It was painful to watch her struggle to maneuver about on the boat, and I didn't know what to do or say.

Finally I broke the awkward silence. "That beret looks nice." She ignored my compliment.

"So this is your new boat. They told me you named it *Orion*... named her after the stars. You always were the romantic."

"She's a fine boat, Kat."

"So when are you going to take me out sailing? I want to steer her out there in the Gulf Stream."

"How about tomorrow? It's the Fourth of July. I thought we could stay here overnight and set sail for Marathon in the morning. Then tomorrow night they'll have fireworks that we can watch from the boat."

"Yeah, *we* can watch fireworks," she said and turned her head away from me.

You idiot! Watch fireworks? "I'm sorry, Kat. I'm gonna hafta get used to our new situation."

"Tomorrow is fine. I just want to get out on the ocean again ASAP. Tomorrow night you can describe the firework show to me."

"Great. You must be tired, Kat."

"Yeah, it's been a long day."

We went below and started to settle in for the night, but a parade of motorcycles roaring in off of the highway brought me back topside. I watched as at least fifty bikers began parking outside a large houseboat. Soon heavy metal music and loud drunken voices echoed across the marina. I fetched my binoculars to take a look at the crowd gathering across the marina. *Huh, all chicks.*

"Holy shit!" I gasped when I saw Massive Mary and Big Betty rolling around on the ground wrestling just off the docks. The tall Amazon chick was screaming at them and trying to break up the brawl.

Kat came out of her cabin and was standing at the foot of the steps down below. "Eddie, normally I wouldn't mind that ruckus, but since losing my sight, my hearing has become hypersensitive. I'll never get to sleep with that noise."

"Yeah, Kat. I'm afraid there will be no peace around here for a couple of days. Those bikers are the She-Wolves, a gang of crazy-assed chicks. They must have come here for what they call the Full Moon Howling celebration. Last month I saw them in action at Captain Tony's, down in Key West. Those babes party nonstop whenever the moon is full."

"You mean they'll be doing this all night long?"

"Yeah—they haven't even gotten started yet. We can't stay here, but don't worry—I know of a sheltered anchorage about thirty minutes away. It's calm and peaceful."

Later that evening we dropped anchor in a small, secluded cove, and I busied myself with making sure the anchor was secure and that everything was shipshape, while Kat sat in silence in the cockpit. We were still as awkward as two thirteen-year-old kids at a middle-school dance.

"Well everything seems to be squared away," I said when I could think of nothing else to check.

"Okay, mister, we might as well get this over with," Kat said.

"What?"

"You and me—what was then and what is now."

"My feelings for you have not changed, Kat."

"Eddie, even before the Russian butchered me, I told you we would never be a couple…told you that I would never let myself love another because I was married to the counter-revolution. So nothing between us has really changed. We had a few good times and a few laughs together—that's all."

I don't believe you, Kat! I saw the photos of us together that you framed. I kept that thought to myself and asked her, "If that's how you feel, then what made you want to see me again, Kat?"

"I thought you deserved an explanation—why I avoided you, and why I will soon be leaving and going away." Night had fallen, and it seemed odd that she still wore the dark sunglasses. She seemed to think she was facing me, but her head was turned off to my left. *It's strange to see Katarina so helpless and vulnerable.* I had to look away.

"Thanks for that consideration," I said and stared down at the deck.

"Eddie, I think I'm ready to tell someone what happened to me in Cuba. I need someone to know what happened before I'm gone."

"Gone?" My head jerked up.

"Don't worry—just a figure of speech. Gone away."

"If you want to talk, I'm all ears, Kat. You know that. Tell me what happened."

"Okay. I was window shopping at that clothing store that you like on SW 8th Street. Wanted to buy you a present—a new outfit so you might take me out dancing again. I was so stupid. I was walking around with my head in the clouds."

I interrupted. "You already told me all of that—that it's my fault, remember?"

"No, I'm telling you *I'm* to blame...should have spotted the Commie bastards coming a mile away, but I had lost my edge. By the time I noticed their reflections in the store's windowpane coming up behind me, one guy had a chokehold on me and the other put a chemical-soaked rag over my face, tossed me into a van, and put me to sleep. They kept me drugged up. When I came to, I was in a prison cell in Cuba."

"*Modelo Presido* on *Isla de Pinos* is where we found you," I said.

"I suppose, because they never moved me. So a few days passed, and then one morning a guard told me that I was going to have a special visitor. That afternoon Rafael Cato came to my cell with his bodyguards. He told me how my treachery—as he called it—was discovered."

"The cigar, right?"

"Yeah. He was having a dinner party one evening and showing off his art collection when the power went out. Before his emergency generator came on a guest took out a small pocket light that must have been in the black-light spectrum because everyone noticed the long silver streak painted on the wrapper of the poisoned cigar. When the lights came back on, Cato removed the cigar from the glass case to examine it, but now the silver mark was gone...invisible. He ordered the light turned off again, and then they saw the mark reappear under the black light.

"He ordered his bodyguards to take the cigar to the Russians—the KGB—to be analyzed, and they discovered the deadly poison inside. Cato said that my betrayal of his trust and affection put him into a state of depression that lasted for days. He was devastated that his 'Flamingo Princess,' his muse, would try to harm him. He ordered the KGB to find out my true identity and to locate me. When the Russians reported that I was a dissident working with Brigade 2506 and not a Canadian Communist sympathizer, his depression turned to rage, and he ordered his minions to bring me back to Cuba alive. He also found out your true identity, Eddie. That means that you are in grave danger—again that's my fault."

"No, you're not to blame, I would do it all over again—for you, Kat, all over again."

"Then you truly are stupid. How many times must I tell you that caring for another person—you call it love—brings nothing but weakness and vulnerability into one's life. If *I* had it to do all over again, I would want to have never met you, Eddie Ocean!"

"I don't believe you, Kat. I saw your apartment and the pictures of us together in Cuba. You framed them, and I saw your lip prints above my heart."

"You bastard! You had no right to go in there...to look through my things!" Katarina began making gasping sounds, and her chest was heaving. She seemed to be crying. *Can you cry without eyes?* I put my arm around her. She seemed startled and then violently knocked my arm away and stood up.

"Don't touch me, Eddie! Don't you ever touch me! Why can't you learn? I don't want you! I killed Uncle Carlos, and I've probably already signed your death sentence too, you idiot!"

"Okay, calm down, Kat."

She sat down, and several minutes passed before she regained her composure. Then she asked, "Do you want me to finish?"

"Yes."

"The next day after Cato's visit, the Russian butcher Nikko Nikonov came to my cell. He said that he had put me on his schedule for the following morning—set aside a two-hour session just for me. He said that he would need only two hours to put me into the right state of mind. He opened his leather jacket and showed me the instruments of torture that he carried sewn into pockets on the inside lapel. He suggested that while I slept I should imagine what fun we would have together come morning."

"I've gotta kill that sick bastard!"

"Get real, Eddie. You would have about as much chance of taking down Nicky the Knife as a mouse would have going after a mountain lion."

"You underestimate me, Kat, but go ahead—continue."

"They came for me in the morning. That first day they took me to the dungeon, strapped me to an autopsy table, and gave me a drug that caused severe pain. It was like having a cramp, a charlie horse, in every muscle in my body. The pain was excruciating, and I could barely breathe when my chest muscles constricted."

"Bastards! What did they want from you?"

"They wanted me to tell them your real name. I didn't tell them anything, but later I discovered they already knew who you were; they were simply testing me to see if I would lie to them. Then they wanted to know everything about 2506—the people involved, and how and where we operate. They knew about our CIA connections. They wanted the locations of the safe houses. I denied everything. On the second day they waterboarded me. It felt like drowning. The third day they spent beating me with a rubber hose. On the fourth day they did not come for me. They left me in my cell with a warning that if I did not cooperate that the next phase of my interrogation would leave my body and mind permanently damaged and scarred. 'Think it over, pretty girl. We will come back for you in the morning,' they said."

"Carlos was right. We should not have waited to come for you! The CIA made us wait. They tied Carlos up and disabled the boat...."

Kat interrupted, "I'm the only one to blame. I let myself be distracted by silly, misguided emotions."

Yeah, because we were in love, Kat!

She continued. "So I still refused to cooperate, but then after three days of sleep deprivation, having my flesh burned with cigars and my toenails torn off my feet, I was about to break. I could no longer stand the torture, but before I could beg them to stop...*it* happened." She paused as if she was at a loss of words, and we sat in silence.

Finally I asked, in a soft voice that I could not keep from quavering a little, "*What* happened?"

"I don't know. I must have fainted in the dungeon before I could surrender to make them stop. I was going to give up, but when I came to I was back in my cell in excruciating pain and darkness. It took me several minutes to realize that my eyes were gone." She removed her sunglasses. "Now see how pretty I am, Eddie? Do you still love me?"

The description of her suffering and her disfigurement made me feel nauseated. But I managed to hold myself together. "Yes, I do."

"Oh, really? To me you sound sick to your stomach. That's right, since losing my sight I've become very perceptive in other ways."

"Katarina, many blind people live good lives. Take Stevie Wonder, Ray Charles, and heck, Helen Keller was not only blind, she was also deaf and mute...."

Kat interrupted me. "Yeah, Eddie, but I don't sing, and I sure ain't no Helen Keller."

"You can still have a good life."

"Shut up, Eddie! Like I was saying, the Russian had broken me, but after he popped my eyes out and put them in his jar, I only wanted to die. I no longer cared to survive, so I never gave them a thing after that. Eventually they left me alone, left me to wither and die in my tiny, cold prison cell, which is what I wanted to happen. Then you and Carlos had to screw that up by rescuing me." She slumped forward and began gasping again.

"Let's get some sleep, Kat. It's been a long day. You might feel better in the morning." I could not take any more of her horror story.

She straightened up. "No, I'm not done yet, *chico*. The worst is yet to come."

The worst? How's that possible?

"An informant named Garcia poses as a prison guard where I was held. After you rescued me, the Cubans captured Uncle Carlos, and the Russian went to work on him. The Russian broke the unbreakable *el Muerte* in one short session. Do you know how that happened Eddie?"

"Yeah, you already told me. In Key Biscayne, don't you remember?" I was beginning to wonder if Katarina was losing her memory, or losing her mind.

"My unmistakable eyes were looking back at Carlos from that jar. That broke him, and Nicky the Knife tortured him to death— once again, my fault."

"Kat, I can't take any more of this."

"That's the end, Eddie, the end of everything. Just wanted you to know what happened and to be aware of what is in store for you if they catch you. Don't do what I did; don't let your guard down even for a moment. Now lead me down below. I'm tired."

We went to separate cabins, but I did not sleep in mine. Her talk of wanting to die, the end of everything, and going away was disturbing, so I snuck up to the deck and sacked out in front of the hatch to make sure that Kat did not try to jump overboard during the night. Now I understood why Willard did not want Katarina left alone. I stared up at the stars as I fell off to sleep. *There must be something I can do for her.*

Chapter 10

OVERBOARD

Morning came, and the first light of day woke me. My body ached from sleeping outside on the hard deck near the hatch. I went below to make eggs and coffee for Katarina. The clanging of pans probably woke Kat, and she came out of her cabin but immediately bumped her head on the staircase.

"Ouch, shit! See what a useless piece of crap I've become?"

"Here, let me help." She let me guide her to a seat at the table. "Happy Fourth of July, Kat! After breakfast we'll go sailing together. It's a beautiful, clear day with a nice southeast breeze."

"Why are you always so cheerful? It's annoying as hell, especially early in the morning."

"Just a curse I suppose." I thought I saw a smile flash across her face for just an instant.

"Hey, where are my sunglasses?" She held her arm up to hide her face while I got the sunglasses from her bunk.

"Here you go, Kat." She took the sunglasses. "Want some coffee?"

"Ahhh, that's better." She relaxed once her sunglasses were in place, covering her scars. "Sure. Just black, please."

After breakfast I pulled the anchor, and we set sail, heading for the Gulf Stream. Katarina was sitting near the starboard steering wheel while I drove the boat with the portside wheel.

"Kat, stand up and take that steering wheel in front of you." She did, and I released mine. "Okay, she's all yours now," I said and went to stand beside her at the helm.

"But I can't keep the heading. Can't see the compass."

"Feel that sunshine on your face? Try keeping it at the same angle."

The boat began drifting off to port, but Kat lifted her face skyward and then turned the wheel slightly and corrected our course. "Hey, that works. The sun is helping me steer the course. Hope those clouds don't come back." For the first time since Cuba, I saw Katarina smile.

"Look! Uh…oh sorry, Kat, anyway there's a nice weed line."

"Put out a trolling feather," she said.

I brought a spinning rod up from below deck and dropped a yellow-feathered lure off the stern as the sailboat traveled parallel to a long stretch of floating Sargasso weed. Within five minutes I had an eight-pound dolphin fish hooked up.

"Kat, he's jumping around like a Mexican jumping bean," I said as the dolphin repeatedly jumped from the water and thrashed its head from side to side.

"We gots ourselves some dinner, babe," I said and brought the fish onboard, then tossed the lure back out as the dolphin thrashed around on the deck.

"I love the neon colors of those dolphin. Don't let him suffer, Eddie." Kat looked down toward the thumping sound that the fish was making as it slapped the deck with its tail. The distraction caused her to lose course and the boat ran straight into the weed patch. Just before the weeds fouled the lure, a big bull dolphin took it and began running and peeling off fishing line. I handed the rod to Kat and took the wheel. "Here, you take the rod this time."

"Wow, it feels like a monster!" She gasped as the reel screamed, *Zzzzzz!*

"It's a big bull. I saw him come out of the water to hit that feather." Kat began stumbling forward and almost fell, so I sat her down in the portable fighting chair in the stern. Fifteen minutes later she had the fish alongside the boat.

"He's got to be 25 pounds at least!" I said as I watched the exhausted fish look up at me with a big round eye as he swam along on his side beside the boat.

"Let him go. You're not gonna keep him, are you?" Kat asked.

"We could sell him for a pretty penny at the docks."

"But I caught him, so I get to decide," she insisted.

"Okay, that eight pounder is plenty of fish for us. I'll release this big guy so we can meet another day."

"Goodbye, fish. I have a feeling we *will* meet again real soon," Kat said with a grin as her fishing line went limp.

When we made it as far south as Marathon, I aimed the boat back toward shore, and we found an anchorage near where the locals were going to have a modest fireworks display later that night.

"I'll grill up some dolphin on the hibachi. What kind of wine do you want, babe?" Things were finally beginning to feel normal again, and Kat seemed to relax for the first time.

"Do you have Pinot Grigio?"

"I think so. Hey, you got some sun today. You're getting your color back, babe."

"Thanks, Eddie. I had a nice day with you." Her pleasant demeanor renewed my hope that we still might have a future together.

That night as we sipped more wine, I described Marathon's modest fireworks display to Kat as she listened to the booming explosions. It was definitely no Key Biscayne Fourth of July extravaganza, but I embellished the description of the colorful light show and showering sparks to her great satisfaction.

Then to my surprise, when it was time to turn in for the night she asked if we could sleep together. "One last time before I'm gone, Eddie. Just to cuddle, nothing more," she said.

"I would love that, Kat," I said as I guided her to my cabin.

"Good, and in the morning you will take me back, but I would love to sail home during the night."

"That can be arranged." I said as we cuddled in the master cabin and drifted off to sleep.

The next day we went ashore and had lunch at a quaint tiki hut restaurant at the foot of the Seven Mile Bridge. On the way back to the boat we stumbled upon a place on the Gulf side where a fellow was in the process of establishing an animal rescue center. He had some injured pelicans and several sea turtles that were undergoing rehab. I enjoyed watching Katarina happily comforting the critters, and they seemed to respond in kind, bringing another rare smile to her face.

"Soon I will be right at home where you live, my little darling," Kat said as she held a small, very young green sea turtle.

"What do you mean by that, Kat—at home where he lives?"

She seemed surprised by my question, as if she had forgotten that I was there with her. "Ah, well, you know—in some rehab center."

"Oh."

At sunset I pulled anchor, and we sailed out into the Gulf Stream. The moon was still nearly full as it oozed out from the depths of the ocean, coloring the horizon in hues of red and orange.

"The moon is coming up, big and bright, but the stars are just now starting to burn through."

"Do you see your old friend Orion?" Kat tilted her head skyward.

"No, not yet...still too bright." It was about ten o'clock, and the moon was high in the sky when Kat asked for some wine.

"What kind?"

"I don't care. You pick." I went below, chose a bottle of red, opened it, and grabbed two glasses before heading back up. When I got back on deck, the cockpit was empty. I turned to see if Kat had gone up to the bow of the boat. She was not there. When I realized that she was gone, I felt the glasses slip from my hand and shatter at my feet.

"Kat!" I screamed. Feeling panic spread through my body, I looked into the ocean behind the boat. The long shimmering reflection of moonlight stretching hundreds of yards behind *Orion* revealed no sign of Katarina.

"Oh shit! She fell overboard!" I sprang into action, trying to remember the man-overboard drill.

Okay, get yourself under control, dude! You know what to do.

"Damn, I can't remember! Just relax, dude," I said aloud. Then I looked to the heavens and saw Orion directly above me. "I need help, my friend."

Change course to a beam reach and count to fifteen...fifteen seconds

Good, okay, now head into the wind and tack! Let the jib flutter.

Now veer off on a broad reach.

Okay, turn upwind on a close reach! Katarina should be somewhere ahead of you now, dude.

"I'll never spot her black hair in this dark water." I started the engine, grabbed a handheld searchlight from the console, and scanned the water ahead of the *Orion*.

"What's that?" Something white was floating up ahead.

Slacken the mainsail!

I put the gear into neutral, and the *Orion* slowed drastically as I neared the floating object. Now I could see a pair of hands reaching up. Katarina was floating on her back with her hands raised.

"Kat! Hang on!" Thankfully the boat was moving slowly and coming to a stop as Kat floated close on the leeward side. I ran to the stern and leaned out over the water from the stern platform just as Katarina came within reach. We clasped hands, and I pulled her up onto the boat.

"Thank God! I thought I lost you, my darling Katarina!"

"I'm so sorry, Eddie. I don't want to die!" Katarina was sobbing again.

"Kat, I should never have left you alone. It's my fault you fell overboard." She was as light as a feather as I carried her up to the deck. Broken glass cut my feet, but I barely felt any pain.

"I didn't fall...I jumped. I've planned it all along, back in Key Biscayne, even before Willard brought me to you. I wanted to die and be buried at sea. But now I want to live."

"Jumped overboard?"

"That's right. I didn't want to live like a helpless child, an invalid. I tried to sink to the bottom of the ocean. But when I was in the water something happened...I wanted to live." I clutched her tight, close to my chest, as she sobbed and begged forgiveness. Her sunglasses were gone, lost overboard, and the pitiable look on her disfigured face broke my heart.

"What are we to do?" I asked and looked up to Orion as if the constellations held the answer. Then a voice filled my head. A familiar voice said, *Bring her home, Sunchaser Eddie Ocean. Bring her to the Whatchacallit people and to me.* It was the familiar voice of Weeping Willow, the old Whatchacallit witch woman.

"Eddie, if death is not the solution to my dilemma, then what is? I won't go back to my insipid and tedious existence in Miami, and I can't stay here with you...being waited on by you, helpless as a baby. If I must continue living, what will be my fate? Where is my place in this world of darkness?"

"Katarina, let me take you to the Whatchacallit people. They have great wisdom—ancient wisdom and magic. Maybe they can help us."

"Okay, Eddie. I have nowhere else to go."

I spun the wheel of *Orion* and jibbed, then set a course for the Gulf of Mexico and the Big Cypress Preserve.

Chapter 11

THE WHATCHACALLIT VILLAGE

Our journey from Marathon to the Ten Thousand Islands had consumed two and half days, and Katarina's depression had returned with a vengeance. Her manic phase had reverted to a dark and cynical sadness, and I feared that if I left her alone above deck she might once again jump overboard.

It was early in the afternoon when I caught sight of land in the distance and called to Katarina. She had stopped sulking in the darkness below deck and was now tying knots in a piece of rope at the bow of the boat. After losing her sunglasses she had begun tying a red bandana around her face to cover her eye sockets.

"Kat, land ahoy! Soon you will meet my Whatchacallit Indian friends," I said.

"Why are they called such a stupid name—Whatchacallits?"

"For many years, the tribe was known as the 'Invisible People.'"

"Another dumb name," Kat said and whipped the rope against the deck beside her.

"Those Indians are the remnants of the once-mighty Calusa Indian Tribe. They lived in seclusion for hundreds of years in that remote area of the Everglades that lies just ahead." I pointed at the landmass in the distance. Kat lifted her head.

"I wish I could see it," she said.

"It's just a tree line in the distance, Kat. The area is now called the Big Cypress National Preserve, but hundreds of years ago it was the empire of the mighty Calusa. By 1700, only about 1000 of the Calusa people remained in Florida."

"What happened to them?"

"European invaders began killing and enslaving them."

"Then they must not have been all that mighty," Kat said as she stood up and threw the strand of rope down at her feet.

"They were outgunned by the Europeans' firearms. The Calusa warriors fought hard and were the last tribe in Florida to be conquered by the invaders. Many escaped by fleeing to Cuba. Others survived by retreating into the swamps and finding refuge on a couple of hundred acres of secluded land located just east of the Ten Thousand Island chain. The remaining Calusas developed the ability to become 'invisible.' When outsiders approached, they vanished into the forest and swampland. That's how the tribe became known as the Invisible People."

"Calusas, Invisibles, or Whatchacallits—make up your mind."

"They are all the same people, renamed time and again by the white invaders. In 1949, in order to study the indigenous Native Americans, missionaries established a temporary camp near the Invisible People's village, and a close friendship between the two groups was quickly established.

"The missionaries were in the process of compiling a dictionary of Native American Languages. In order to learn the native people's vocabulary, the whites were constantly pointing to objects and asking the Indians, 'What do you call that?' To the Indians, the phrase 'What do you call that?' sounded like one word, 'whatchacallit.' As a consequence, the first English word the Indians learned to speak was 'whatchacallit.' To them, this first communication was a great discovery.

The Indians repeated the word, 'whatchacallit,' while pointing to an object and were thrilled when the white people responded with an English word. The people repeated 'whatchacallit' often; they would smile and point at one another and for no good reason say, 'Whatchacallit!' Those who called out 'Whatchacallit!' were considered sophisticated, the enlightened elite.

"Now that the people were no longer in hiding, the missionaries decided that documenting them as the 'Invisible People' was no longer appropriate. They went to the chief and asked him by what name should his tribe be identified in *The Dictionary of Native American Languages*. The chief didn't understand their question, so he immediately responded, 'Whatchacallit.' Thus in the year 1950, the missionaries documented the people living in the region of Big Cypress and the Ten Thousand Island chain as the Whatchacallit Indian Tribe."

"So how did you find them?" Kat's mood seemed to be lightening.

"I had come to know these kind people in 1973 after being critically injured by a mutant bull-croc on Crocodile Island. Three Whatchacallit fishermen rescued me and took me to their medicine man, Night Owl. He, along with his beautiful young assistant, Little Hooters, nursed me back to health. Later I learned many things from the wise elders of the tribe, and they even adopted me as one of their own and trained me to be a warrior. The tribe gave me my Indian name, 'Sunchaser Eddie Ocean,' and soon I fell in love with Little Hooters. We became engaged, but as fate would have it she was destined to marry another: my best friend, Jumping Jack."

"So now you are going to show up unannounced with a pathetic blind woman. Awkward!" Kat said as the breeze ruffled the red bandana tied around her face.

"They will like you, Kat."

The west coast of Florida grew larger on the horizon, and I scanned the coastline, looking for the landmarks that would lead me to a secret unmarked channel that was the only navigable passage to the shores of the Whatchacallits' village. My mind was racing, my thoughts bouncing back and forth like a ping-pong ball between my two loves, Katarina and Little Hooters. My concern for Katarina's well being gave way to my nervous anticipation of being reunited with Little Hooters; and then my thoughts went back to Katarina. *Katarina's depression worries me. I fear she will try to hurt herself again. How will Little Hooters and Jumping Jack react to my surprise visit? Will the Whatchacallit people welcome my return after such a long absence?* My mind was racing.

"I smell land…mangroves, muck, and poinsettia trees with a hint of jasmine." Katarina stood facing the bow, her held tilted back, breathing in deeply. The offshore breeze lifted the red scarf tied around her head like a blindfold and exposed the sunken sockets that once had held her beautifully exotic eyes.

"Yeah, Kat, we are about to enter the secret channel that will take us to a creek that leads to the Indian village." I started the motor and dropped the sails.

"Won't your friends be thrilled that you are bringing them a helpless woman to babysit, a woman who's blind as a bat?" Kat's voice was dripping with sarcasm as she pulled the bandana back down to cover her scars.

"They are a kind and generous people, Kat, but I don't know how they will react to my return—especially Little Hooters and Jumping Jack. They must be married now." We entered the mouth of the winding creek, the last leg of our journey home.

Katarina was looking agitated again. "Oh yeah, Little Hooters, the girl that you said you dumped and left crying on the beach. She should shoot you with a poisoned arrow! You deserve it!"

"It didn't happen like that, Kat. I didn't just dump her. It was our fate." We came around a tight bend in the creek, and I saw the white, sandy beach at the foot of the Whatchacallit village, the very beach where I had left Little Hooters.

"Kat, people are coming out of the forest and gathering on the beach. They must have seen our sails approaching."

"Do they look friendly?"

"Yes. They have flowers and gifts."

"I hear drums!" Katarina said as the drummers began that familiar rhythmic Whatchacallit beat that I had not heard for well over a year.

"They'll probably give us a welcoming feast tonight, Kat."

"I'm in no mood for a party," she said as she nervously adjusted the red bandana to make sure it was covering her face.

The *Orion* drew more water than my old *Watermelon* boat, so I was not able to reach the small dock at the beach. "Kat, my new boat has a 6' draft, too much for these shallows. We will have to anchor just off shore and take the dinghy to land."

"Okay. What should I bring with me?"

"Nothing until I talk to Chief Thunderbutt. It would be rude to make ourselves at home without being invited." Over a hundred smiling people of all ages greeted us on the beach offering flowers and fruit baskets. My friend Running Deer led the group. He grabbed Katarina's arm to help her out of the inflatable dinghy.

"Welcome, Sunchaser Eddie Ocean. Is this blindfolded woman your prisoner?" Running Deer asked.

Katarina pulled her arm away, "No, stupid, I'm blind."

Running Deer's eyes widened, and he said, "Sunchaser's squaw very feisty woman. Is she Sunchaser's new woman?" He bent down at the waist to look Kat over, bobbing up and down with an animated motion. "Woman skinny, but still good-looking woman."

"I'm not a squaw and I'm nobody's 'woman'! I'm Katarina Romero. Who the hell are you?"

"Me Running Deer, Whatchacallit Warrior and great hunter."

"You're a great chauvinistic ass as far as I can tell!"

I intervened in the little spat, "Running Deer, I need to speak with Chief Thunderbutt to ask him a favor."

"Chief Thunderbutt dead. He go to afterlife. Now Jumping Jack be Whatchacallit chief."

"Dead? Oh, I'm sorry. What happened to the chief?"

"At grand feast on cold, clear night, Chief Thunderbutt came down from royal platform to warm his hands at bonfire. When he turned to warm his back the people heard a rumble of thunder and then a great fireball appeared behind Chief's back. Chief's pants caught on fire. Before warriors could react another rumble of thunder was heard and then a bolt of lightening shot from the sky and struck behind Chief Thunderbutt. Chief exploded and vanished. Only Chiefs smoking moccasins where left where he was standing. Elders say that he was summoned by the Ancients and taken to the afterlife."

"Huh, but you said it was a clear night. I think there may be a more scientific explanation for that explosion dude. The Chief was a human...you might say a walking methane gas tank. The rumbling thunder was probably the sound of the Chiefs flagellation. I think his ass exploded dude."

"That what Night Owl say, but Elders became very angry. They say the Ancients summoned Chief Thunderbutt to Meadow of Tranquility."

"So they made Jumping Jack chief? That's great! Did he marry Little Hooters?" I asked.

"Yes. Now she chief's wife. She have one baby boy. You come and see Jumping Jack now."

Running Deer led us up the winding pass, through the forest, and toward the main village as the large crowd of curious people followed closely. Katarina stumbled and then grabbed my hand for guidance; the murmuring of the excited crowd seemed to make her nervous.

"Don't worry, Kat. These are kind people. Running Deer may be a bit crude and not much for etiquette, but he is a very honorable fellow," I said as we walked under the dense canopy of giant, ancient cypress trees. Katarina tilted her head back and began sniffing the air and listing to the cacophony of chirping and squawking birds perched in the trees above us. "This place sounds and smells beautiful," she said.

"Yes, right now we are walking through a forest of giant cypress trees."

"A-ha, that's what I've been smelling. Spanish moss must be hanging from the cypress!" She breathed in deeply.

"That's true. Very good, Kat!"

Running Deer led us out of the forest and into the open area of the main lodge, the home of the new Whatchacallit chief, Jumping Jack. We entered the expansive hall, where Jumping Jack was seated in former Chief Thunderbutt's large bamboo throne. He was holding a long spear and was surrounded by several warriors. Jumping Jack greeted me. "Welcome home, my brother Sunchaser Eddie Ocean. Sorry I no greet you at boat. It is custom for guests to be brought up before the chief."

"I know that ritual well, my old friend. How are you, Chief?"

"Jumping Jack good."

"I want you to meet Katarina Romero," I said and guided Kat forward.

"Hello Chief." Kat said and bowed at the waist.

"Hello Kata...arina. Why bandage on face? You burn eyes?"

Kat stood upright, "No Chief, a very evil man poked out my eyes."

The chief's jaw dropped and his eyes widened. He stood up. "Man poke out woman's eyes? Why crazy man do this?" In disbelief, Jumping Jack directed his question to me for confirmation.

"It's true, Chief. He is an evil man. The man is our enemy. He works for a Cuban dictator."

"Any enemy of Whatchacallit warrior Sunchaser Eddie Ocean also enemy of the entire Whatchacallit Tribe. Where this crazy man be?"

"Cuba," Kat said.

"We take warriors of ten ocean canoes to Cuba to kill this evil man, *hoka hey!*" Jumping Jack pumped his spear into the air and the warriors surrounding him followed suit. "Hoka hey! Hoka hey! Hoka hey!"

Jumping Jack was still living in the past and had no concept of Cuba's modern army and navy, but I did not want to insult the Whatchacallit warriors.

"Thank you, Chief, but the Cuban tribe is very large and powerful.

"Great planning will be needed before we attack them. What we need most right now is Weeping Willow's wisdom. The great witch woman came to me in a vision and told me to bring Katarina Romero to her lodge. Katarina has suffered greatly, and her spirit is in deep despair."

"Very good, Sunchaser. You both will stay with tribe till blind woman get better. Sunchaser stay at lodge of Night Owl, and blind woman stay with Weeping Willow." He pumped his spear in the direction of Running Deer and said, "Now Running Deer, take blind woman to lodge of Weeping Willow. Sunchaser, you come with me. Time for Sunchaser to see Little Hooters and my son Jumping Owl."

We went from the porch and entered the lodge. Little Hooters was breast-feeding an infant with her back to me.

"Hello, Little Hooters," I said. She turned to face us. She had gained some weight but was just as beautiful and even more radiant. Her long, dark hair fell over her baby's body, covering the infant and her right breast from view.

"Hello, Eddie. You look well. You have filled out. You look strong." The ever-jealous Jumping Jack whacked me hard on the shoulder and yelled, "*Whatchacallit!* See, Jumping Jack strong, too. Now maybe Jumping Jack get wrestling rematch with Sunchaser Eddie Ocean."

He stood staring at me with that broad, toothy smile I knew so well as I tried to rub the stinging from my left shoulder. I knew what he was waiting for. "Okay, whatchacallit!" I yelled and smacked his shoulder hard with an open hand.

Jumping Jack didn't flinch and pretended that the whack didn't hurt. "Huh, maybe Sunchaser not as strong as he look. We must wrestle again to find out."

I started rubbing my shoulder again. "You already won the grand prize, Jumping Jack," I said and nodded at Little Hooters, holding his infant son.

She blushed, and Jumping Jack said, "Sunchaser still very smooth talker. Sunchaser not change much."

Then Little Hooters said, "The people say you brought a woman with you. Is she *your* woman, Sunchaser?"

"She's my friend. Her name is Katarina Romero. She needs help—Weeping Willow's help."

"Why does she need a witch woman? Is she under a spell—a curse?"

"No, but she needs spiritual help. A lunatic cut out her eyes. Now she is so depressed that I'm afraid she is suicidal."

"Eyes cut out! No wonder she is in despair. What would I do if someone did that to me?" Little Hooters clutched her baby tight to her chest and looked at his face, then moaned. "I just don't know if I could bear blindness."

Jumping Jack stepped forward with authority, "I know what to do! We have big feast tonight, then Little Hooters meet your blind woman. Everyone meet your blind woman."

"Jumping Jack, call her 'Katarina,' not 'blind woman.' Her self-esteem is already badly damaged."

"Okay Kata…arina," he said awkwardly.

I realized he was having trouble pronouncing "Katarina," so I said, "Let's just call her 'Kat.' That's what I call her, Chief."

"Good. Cat much better name. 'Blind Cat' good Indian name," Jumping Jack said with a look of satisfaction.

Well I guess "Blind Cat" is better than "Blind Woman," dude.

Chapter 12

THE MASK

"Hey, hey, hey, Night Owl, are you home?" My call went unheeded; the mysterious old medicine man was not home. I had come to tell him that I planned on living aboard my sailboat during my extended visit, and not at his lodge. *Maybe he's in the garden.*

After searching for him in the expansive herbal garden surrounding his modest lodge, I decided to leave him a note, so I entered the medicine hut and called again, "Hello!" There was still no answer. *Wow, look at all the concoctions...so many potions!* The main room was very large, and many containers marked with hieroglyphic sketches lined the shelves that covered all four walls. An elevated bamboo-frame bed, its mattresses overstuffed with sphagnum moss, was in the center of the room. *This is the medicine room where Night Owl and Little Hooters treated the wounds that I suffered on Crocodile Island.*

After walking to the bed, I placed my hand on the mattress and closed my eyes. *This bed gave me great comfort for several weeks.* The memory of Little Hooters' angelic face hovering above me came to mind. *She is still just as beautiful as the day I first I saw her.* It was on this bed, where I had lain so close to death, that I fell in love with Little Hooters. The memory of her gentle smile, her warm, tender touch, and gentle kiss brought a warm flush to my face but an empty sickness to my heart. *The first time I saw Little Hooters, I thought she was an angel coming down to take me to heaven, and I knew then that I loved her…love at first sight.*

Okay, snap out of it, dude. That's all in the past. My eyes opened, and then a new image came to mind: my first meeting with Katarina Romero. The image of Katarina standing high above me on the deck of the *Third Wish* on that lovely morning in Miami filled my head. Again I closed my eyes to better remember that first meeting. The vivid image of Kat, mysterious and beautiful, cold and calculating—Kat clad in her white bikini, standing silently in the morning glow, staring right through me with those exotic, penetrating blue-grey eyes—filled my mind. *How can these two women who are so starkly different hold the same place in my broken heart? Katarina is so strong, independent, and aloof, her cold exterior only a façade designed to disguise her vulnerability and tenderness. On the other hand, there's Little Hooters, with her heart an open book, so beautiful through and through, always gentle, compassionate, and kind. The Ancients forced me to protect Little Hooters by rejecting her to save her from a terrible fate, and now in turn I'm being rejected by Katarina Romero!*

"This is a cruel world." I lifted my head and spoke to the heavens. "Ancient ones, I have done all that has been asked of me only to lose or be rejected by all those I love. It is clear that here on earth there is no soul mate for me." I closed my eyes and prayed, *Great Wanaka, maybe in the afterlife you will let me find a woman whose spirit is as strong as Katarina's and as tender as Little Hooters'.* I opened my eyes. *Stop feeling sorry for yourself, dude.*

In the back of the lodge, I found two separate windowless sleeping rooms, each with a moss-stuffed mattress lying directly on the dirt floor. One room contained some personal items and clothing. *This must be where Night Owl sleeps. I'll leave him a note and then go to the boat to gather some clothes for Kat.* Dejected, I walked through the village toward the beach, rudely ignoring the smiles and greetings of the curious villagers.

After collecting some clothes and Kat's toiletry bag from the boat, I stuffed them into my backpack, returned to shore, and walked to Weeping Willow's lodge to deliver Kat's belongings.

"Hey, hey, hey! I have some things for Kat!" I called out after knocking on the wooden door. Weeping Willow's creepy grandson, Horny Owl, opened the door and snatched the bundle from my hands. The pale waif of a boy began to close the door in my face without speaking a word, but I used my foot to block the door and said. "Hey, wait, Horny Owl! I want to see Katarina."

"She no see anyone now. She in healing trance," he said and tried to push me from the doorway.

"Healing trance? Well, let me see Weeping Willow, then."

"You no see Weeping Willow either. She in healing trance with Blind Cat woman." The kid managed to shut the door and latch it. Just as I was about to pound on the locked door someone behind me spoke.

"Sunchaser Eddie Ocean, you must leave your friend alone with Weeping Willow." I turned to see the wrinkled old face of Night Owl, the wise old medicine man.

"Hi, Night Owl, I stopped by to see you...left a note for you. How are you, sir?" I bowed to the tribal elder.

"I good. Girl you brought here not good. Girl in need of much medicine. Not my herbal medicine. Girl need Weeping Willow's strong *spirit medicine*."

"Spirit medicine?"

"Yes, I give girl some calming potion, but only Weeping Willow can heal her soul. Good that you bring girl...girl very sick. Now you come with me and leave girl alone. We will help the people prepare for tomorrow night's grand welcoming feast in honor of you, Sunchaser Eddie Ocean." Night Owl turned and walked away toward the central lodge, so I followed him.

After spending the day helping the people prepare the area in front of the main lodge for the upcoming bonfire celebration, I went to the entrance of the grand lodge to find Jumping Jack. He was not home, but Little Hooters was.

"Hello, Eddie. Come in." Little Hooters stood before me, smiling; the glow of the magical aura that I had witnessed many times before framed her lovely face. *She must be very happy today; she is exuding that mystical aura.* Her jet-black hair accentuated a bright yellow hibiscus flower that adorned the left side of her head. It took me a moment to speak as I resisted my urge to kiss her and to tell her how much I had missed her.

"Hello, Little Hooters. I've come to see Jumping Jack."

"He is out hunting boar and deer with Running Deer...obtaining fresh meat for the feast." We were alone, and I realized it would be wise to leave before my desires got the better of me.

"Okay, I'll come back later."

"They will be on the hunt all night."

"Oh, well—I must go now." I turned to leave.

"Wait, Eddie, I want to show you something...something I'm making."

"What is it?"

"Let me show you." She turned and walked to a table in the corner and picked something up. Two patches of green and yellow cloth were hanging down from a long, thin leather string.

"What is that? A bra?" I asked.

"A bra? Ha ha, you are funny, Eddie Ocean!" Little Hooters began laughing; she clutched her hands to her stomach and doubled over in uncontrollable laughter as her long, silky hair thrashed through the bright aura surrounding her. I wanted to take her in my arms, pick her up off the ground, and kiss her. She finally stopped laughing, but when she looked at me the laughing started up again.

"Okay, you made your point! I'm an idiot. So it's not a bra," I said.

"Ha, a bra? Whatchacallit women do not wear the bra of the Wasichu woman. These patches...would be...even too small...for me," she gasped out as she tried to catch her breath between laughs and held out the string with the small, colorful patches.

"So what is it, then?" I asked.

"This is a mask for your friend Katarina. That dirty red bandana that she uses to cover her face is not very becoming. This will be much better, I hope." She held the mask by both ends of the string so that it was displayed horizontally, and now I could see that it was a beautifully handcrafted mask. The patches were painted to resemble exotic green and yellow eyes shaped like tear drops.

"Those look like the eyes of an ocelot," I said, amazed by the beauty of her creation.

"What is an ocelot?"

"It's an animal—a big cat that resembles a small leopard. They live in South America."

"That's what I wanted for her...to have the eyes of a cat." Little Hooters smiled with approval and admired her handiwork.

"It's very beautiful, Little Hooters, but Kat's eyes were round... round and colored grey-blue. The look in her eyes reminded me of the eyes of a wolf."

"Eddie, her eyes must have been beautiful. I will make her those wolf-eyes next time."

"No, I think this mask is perfect for her now, Little Hooters. Did you know that the people are calling her the Blind Cat Woman?"

"Yes, I know. So if you approve, I will give her the mask before the feast tomorrow night."

"She might not be attending. Weeping Willow has her in something called a 'healing trance.'"

"The healing trance? That is wonderful, Eddie. If Katarina was able to go under Weeping Willow's spell, I think she will be helped greatly. I think your friend is going to be all right Eddie!"

"I hope so." I reached out to touch the beautiful mask. "Thank you, Little Hooters. You are always so kind. Now I should return to my boat for the night. Tell Jumping Jack that I will visit him in the morning."

Chapter 13

WELCOME HOME FEAST

After spending the afternoon doing routine maintenance on my sailboat, I sat down in the stern with a bottle of warm Kalik Beer and watched the seabirds returning to land as the sun began to set into the Gulf of Mexico. At the whim of the wind and tide, my boat, which was moored in eight feet of water in the middle of the narrow access channel, swung gently to and fro on her anchor line. The cacophony of chattering birds settling in among the surrounding mangroves was surprisingly soothing—at least the racket let me know that I was not all alone. The land had just begun to grow dark; the silhouette of the green cypress forest to the east resembled a towering black picket fence against the evening sky. The sound of drums arose in the distance. *The feast has begun. I wonder if Katarina will come tonight?*

After taking the last swig of beer, I rode the dinghy to shore, tied it to a mangrove root, and then began walking toward the main village. The sound of the drums grew louder as my path merged with two other pathways, one that led east to the farming village and the other west to the fishing lodges. Here I joined a large group of excited people as we walked together along the main pathway toward the central lodge. The men were chanting, Hey, hey, hey, yo!" And many of the women made a trilling sound, calling out with long, loud ululations as they walked.

Near the end of the path, the evening sky was illuminated by a bright orange glow being emitted from a bonfire. When we emerged from the forest and into the clearing of the celebration square, I saw Chief Jumping Jack seated high up on the elevated bamboo platform in his oversized wooden chair. Four warriors stood guard on the ground below the chief, two on each side. Jumping Jack was shirtless but had a vest made of animal bone hanging down from his neck, and he was wearing only a simple breechcloth and a pair of colorful beaded moccasins. His muscular body glistened in the glow of the fire as if it had been oiled, and on top of his head was a large feathered headdress. He was a very noble and imposing figure.

Next to him sat Little Hooters. She was stunning, dressed in colorful Native American powwow regalia. On her head was a much simpler headdress, made of blue heron and white egret feathers and held in place by a yellow and blue headband. I found a vacant spot and sat down on the grassy embankment that bordered the fire pit on three sides. The open side faced the chief's platform. The drummers increased the tempo of their beat as the last of the villagers entered the square and took a seat.

Then a long line of Whatchacallit warriors came trotting out from behind the central lodge chanting, "Hey, hey, hey, yo!" They trotted in single file and circled the fire pit. After circling twice, they stopped and then stood with their backs to the fire and raised their spears toward the sky. They pumped the spears skyward in rhythm to the chant and drumbeat three times more.

Suddenly the drumming stopped, and the warriors stood in silence. I scanned the crowd, looking for Katarina and Weeping Willow, but they apparently had not come to the feast. The crowd was silent as Jumping Jack rose from his chair and walked to the edge of the platform holding a carved ironwood scepter that resembled the head and body of a serpent.

"Greetings, people. We have come together to welcome home our adopted son, Sunchaser Eddie Ocean." Jumping Jack pointed the scepter at me and made a motion for me to stand up. I stood and then bowed toward the chief.

"Sunchaser, what have you come to tell to your people?"

"Ah...well, hello everyone." I rotated my body and waved to the crowd as I felt my face turning red, embarrassed by my stage fright. I didn't know what to say.

"Sunchaser, tell the people about the blind woman that you brought to us—the Blind Cat woman."

"Okay. Her name is Katarina Romero. She is my friend. Katarina was not always blind. An evil man tortured her. The man took out her eyes with a knife." A collective gasp was followed by a low murmur passing through the crowd.

"What kind of man would do such a thing, Sunchaser?" the chief asked with an angry scowl of disgust.

"He is a very evil man. Some people call him 'Nicky the Knife.' He is a Russian—a Northman—but he lives in Cuba. He is Katarina's and my greatest enemy. Our burning desire is to one day kill him. But he is protected by a powerful army that carries many Wasichu thunder sticks."

Suddenly the murmuring from the crowd ceased, and everyone began looking and pointing at something off to my left. When I turned to see what it was, there was Weeping Willow standing on the elevated, crushed-shell speaking mound. People near where she stood cowered and hid their faces from the intense, intimidating gaze of the wrinkled old witch woman.

Jumping Jack noticed her standing on the mound and announced, "Weeping Willow wishes to speak to the people." Then he sat back down on his throne.

Weeping Willow's wandering right eye glared at the cowering people sitting to the right of the speaking mound as she faced me, pointing her dreadful, crooked finger in my direction. She spoke,

"The Ancients from our past have spoken to me. They say Sunchaser has prayed to them for help—help for the blind girl. The spirits came to me in a dream and say to me that I—*we*—must help the woman." Weeping Willow turned toward the dark pathway that went off into the forest and spoke. "Come now Katarina. Come toward my voice." Out from the shadows came Katarina. Her head was tilted toward the sky, and she wore the mask with the green and yellow ocelot eyes that Little Hooters had made for her.

"This woman is Katarina Romero," said Weeping Willow. Katarina stood before us, straight and tall, towering over the little hunchbacked witch-woman. She looked stunning in her new mask, like a comic book superhero or what a Hindu might see as an avatar.

Weeping Willow continued, "This woman is in a trance and has been under my spell for two days. She is in a healing trance. When she came to me, a black aura of negativity surrounded this woman. Anger, hate, rage, and revenge had consumed her spirit for many years, but much has been learned. Katarina and I together have visited with the Ancients who reside in the great teepee in the Meadow of Tranquility. The wise ones have told me that this woman is a descendent of our ancestors. She is a descendent of the great Calusa Nation, and because of that we must help her." A gasp went up from the crowd. And Chief Jumping Jack stood up with a perplexed look on his face.

"Weeping Willow, how can this be? Sunchaser say that this woman is from the island of Cuba," said the chief.

"Yes, that is true. But when the white warriors began killing and enslaving the ancient Calusa people, many of our ancestors disappeared into the swamps and forest to become invisible and hide, but others left our native land by escaping in long boats to the island of Cuba. Katarina's Calusa ancestors hid and settled in the eastern mountains of Cuba—so say the Ancients. One Calusa woman married a Spaniard settler—a farmer named Juan Pedro Romero."

Romero? I felt my jaw drop open. Katarina's heritage was not only Cuban and Ukrainian; she also had the blood of the ancient Calusa people.

Jumping Jack raised his scepter. "Weeping Willow's wisdom has never failed the tribe. Hey, hey, hey, yo! By the blood of the Calusa, it is revealed that blind cat woman is one of our Whatchacallit people! Bring blind woman to me."

"Call her name, Chief, and she will come to you," said Weeping Willow.

"Come to me, blind cat woman!" the chief said. Katarina did not move; she stood in place, moving her head around in a manner that reminded me of the singer Stevie Wonder.

"You must call her real name, Chief."

"Come to me, Kata..arina," he said. Kat just stood with her head tilted to the sky.

Weeping Willow walked over to the stage and stood below the chief. Apparently Jumping Jack could not pronounce Kat's name. "Come to me, Katarina."

Kat slowly walked to Weeping Willow. She was clearly in some kind of a hypnotic trance. She stood with her head tilted up toward the chief, and he gazed down at her.

"Blind woman very beautiful. Mask that my wife make look very good on her." The chief turned his head toward Little Hooters, and they smiled at one another. Then he turned back toward Kat and held the serpent scepter above her head.

"I will give blind woman good Indian name. She will be called 'Blind Cat Woman.' Blind Cat Woman Kata...arina Romero! She is welcome to live among the Whatchacallit people! Hey, hey hey, yo! All hail Blind Cat Woman!" The chief shouted with his scepter raised.

"Hey, hey, hey, *yo*! All hail the Blind Cat Woman!" the crowd repeated. Then the drumming commenced again, and the warriors danced and hopped to the rhythm while circling the fire as cooks began placing clay wet-ovens onto the hot coals and roasting whole pigs that had been skewered on long spits.

Jumping Jack stood and said, "Now Sunchaser, you must once again show us the Wasichu warrior chicken fighting dance. I forgot how you do that." Reluctantly I walked to the fire pit and asked, "Where is my old partner, Dancing Bird?" I looked at the crowd, searching for the old man who had been my dance partner the last time I was at a feast.

"Dancing Bird die three moons ago," said Night Owl.

"Oh, I'm so sorry," I said.

"Sunchaser no worry. Dancing Bird dances in the Meadow of Tranquility each night," said Weeping Willow.

Katarina raised her arms over her head and smiled. "Yes, I met Dancing Bird. He dances in the green meadow right now." I looked to the sky to where Kat was pointing and saw the Orion constellation shining brightly through a thin, wispy cloud cover.

"Hey, she can talk!" I said.

"Yes, but Blind Cat Woman must go now to rest. She is coming out of the healing trance. It is almost complete. Soon you can talk with her, and we will know if her spirit has been healed." Weeping Willow began leading Kat away down the path toward the witch's lodge. As I watched her disappear into the shadows, a young woman grabbed my arm. "I will dance with Sunchaser Eddie Ocean! I know the chicken dance," she said.

"Hey Little Hummingbird! How have you been?" It was Little Hooters's best friend, Little Hummingbird. We began doing the chicken dance, and the crowd began laughing at us. Then many people got up and joined in on the nonsense, which lasted quite a while.

Finally Jumping Jack stood and said, "Okay, enough of the crazy Wasichu war dance. Now we do Sunchaser's disco fighting war dance!" The drummers remembered the Latin rhythm beat that I had taught them on my last visit, and they began playing it with a vengeance.

The faster tempo excited the Whatchacallit warriors ringing the fire pit, and they erupted in a chant. "Hey, hey, hoka hey!" Then they paired off and began performing their wild disco fighting kata movements. I began disco dancing with Little Hummer. She laughed as I spun her around until she was dizzy, and then Jumping Jack and Little Hooters came down from the platform and joined the fun.

Once again I could not believe my eyes as they and fifty warriors flew through the air, inventing new and impossibly athletic disco moves, while Jumping Jack, with the feathers of his full Indian chief headdress pulsing to the disco beat, danced with his beautiful Indian princess wife. It might be fickle of me, but since being rejected by Katarina and my return to the village, my feelings for Little Hooters had been reignited.

With envy, I watched my good friend Jumping Jack dancing with his lovely wife. *That should have been me.*

Chapter 14

KATARINA'S TRANSFORMATION

The heat and brilliant light generated by the late morning sun were a rude wake-up call. I climbed down from my roost atop the cabin of *Orion*, where I had spent the night, and looked at my watch. *Dang, already eleven o'clock? That was a heck of a party last night. But now I'm starving!*

I walked back to the central lodge to see if there were leftovers from the previous night's feast and found dozens of people lying peacefully in shady spots, asleep on the grassy areas surrounding the perimeter of the open square. Some of the clay wet-ovens were still nestled in the warm embers that filled the fire pit. I pulled one out with a long forked stick and then sat on the steps of the central lodge to eat a delicious breakfast of tender root vegetables.

"Good morning, Sunchaser. That feast big fun for our people."

I turned to see Jumping Jack standing in the doorway. "Yes, it was fun, my friend. Best of all was to see the transformation of Katarina. My hope for her well-being has been renewed. Thank you, Chief."

"No thank Jumping Jack. Thank Weeping Willow and Little Hooters. They help Blind Cat Woman, not me."

"I want to see if Weeping Willow will let me talk with Kat today."

"Good. Your woman is blind, but she still very beautiful woman. You go to her now," Jumping Jack said as Little Hooters emerged from the doorway to stand beside him.

"Did you leave any food for us, Sunchaser Eddie Ocean?" she asked.

"Yeah, but you'd better hurry." I nodded toward the people pulling the remaining clay ovens out of the coals.

"Uh! I go now. We see Sunchaser later," Jumping Jack said as he leaped off the porch and jogged to the fire pit to claim a pot.

"Little Hooters, thank you for making that beautiful cat mask for Katarina. I think it has helped her confidence. She did not seem to be so self-conscious of her scars last night."

"Go to her now. She needs you," Little Hooters said.

"Thanks again," I said and then left to go to the witch woman's lodge.

Weeping Willow was hunched over in front of her lodge, sweeping fallen leaves from the front of her door with a short-handled straw broom.

Hello, Weeping Willow. May I see Katarina today?"

"Yes. She is almost out of the healing trance—maybe in an hour. You come back."

"Great! Can I help—maybe do something for you?"

"Bring me three pails of water from the river. That will pass an hour," she said with a scowl on her wrinkled old face as she went back to sweeping.

After the last bucket was dumped into the witch's cistern, I knocked on her door.

"Come in, Sunchaser." The witch opened the door, and I entered the room, where a strong odor of burning incense and herbs filled my nostrils. Weeping Willow's strange, hand-carved gargoyles leered down at me from the rafters where they were perched, guarding the jars of medicines and potions that lined the walls. Her displays of animal bones and bird feathers always captured my attention, and the thought of her black magic made me ill at ease.

"How is Katarina today?" I asked.

"You should call her by her Indian name so that she will grow to know it. Very important for her to accept her new identity. Call her 'Cat Woman.'"

"Okay, how is Cat Woman?"

"You see her. Then you decide for self." Weeping Willow pulled back a blanket covering the opening to a back room and used her hand to direct me to go inside. Katarina was sitting in a chair with a broad smile on her face, petting a baby raccoon.

"Hi Katarina...uh, I mean Cat Woman. Who is your little friend?"

"Call me Cat, just like you used to, Eddie...only 'Cat' with a 'C,' not a 'K.'"

"Okay, Cat," I said.

"This little guy is Ringo Raccon. They tell me he has many tan-colored rings around his tail. That's why they call him Ringo. Isn't he adorable? Eddie, you won't believe how smart he is." She laughed as the critter used his little hands to unbutton the top of her blouse, searching for a turnip root that Cat had hidden in her bra. "Ha, that tickles." She pulled the root out and let Ringo have his prize. He took it with his little hands, jumped off her lap, and scurried away.

"You are looking much better," I said.

"Weeping Willow is magical...a miracle worker."

"What did she do?"

"It would be a waste of time to try to explain, Eddie. You would not believe me—no one would believe me."

"Give me a try."

"Well, Night Owl gave me some medicine, and then Weeping Willow gave me a potion that tasted like muddy water seasoned with Tabasco sauce. Then she used her voice—chants and incantations— to put me into a deep trance. She called it a healing trance. Many visions came to me."

"What did you see?"

"Not much at first. Just felt peaceful, my body seemed to dilate as soothing warmth flowed through my veins. My body seemed to float—float supine among fluffy white clouds. It was very relaxing. All my pain and worries melted away. Then Weeping Willow appeared beside me. She took my hand, and I stood up. She took me to a strange place." Cat stopped talking.

"What place?"

"You won't believe me anyway. You'll just think I'm crazy."

"Well, maybe I'll think it was just a dream—a hallucination from the potion—but so what?"

"Okay, then I'll tell you. It was nirvana...heaven." Cat tilted her head back, anticipating my reaction.

"Huh? You went to heaven?"

"She called it the Meadow of Tranquility."

"Holy crap! I *do* believe you, Cat. I've been there too—once when I almost died from the crocodile bite, I walked in that meadow."

"Eddie, you're not just humoring me, are you? You don't have to protect me. I'm no longer so fragile."

"I swear, Cat, I was there too."

"Okay, prove it, then. What did you see?"

"A vast green meadow where animals of every kind roamed the plain together in peace. Predators were friendly with their prey. Then I found a great teepee, where I met and communed with ancient spirits, who taught me many things about life and death...."

Cat interrupted me and leaped to her feet. "Oh my God! That's what I saw! So it *was* real—and you've been there too! It was not just a dream! I *did* meet those ancient spirits.... So then the things they told me must be true!" Her body began shaking, and she appeared to be light-headed. I grabbed her by the shoulders and forced her to sit back down.

"You seem upset. What did the Ancients tell you, Cat?"

"No, I'm not upset—I'm happy. The Ancients told me that I would have a good life, marry, and have children...that I would be happy and would see again! But that I would see the world in a very different way."

"That is great news, Cat! Please believe them. Believe what the council in the Great Teepee told you. They were right about me— right about my fate—what they said would happen to me became true."

"What did they say to you, Eddie?"

"Bad news, not good news like yours. My fate was not good. The Ancients showed to me in a vision that if I married Little Hooters her destiny would be altered...her fate would be that she would die young...die of malaria in Africa. However, they said that I could prevent that horrible fate if I left her and went away. With me gone, she would live a long and happy life among her own people and marry Jumping Jack. Everything that they predicted has come true."

"That is amazing! I've been hoping my vision was not just a dream."

"Cat, did they tell you where you would live and who you would marry?" *Please let it be me, Great Wanaka.*

"No, none of those details. They just gave me hope for my future. I no longer feel like my life is over."

"That's great, Cat!" I could not help feeling disappointed that the Ancients hadn't given her details. I held her hand and looked at her beautiful face. The bizarre ocelot mask somehow made Kat look even more exotic and beautiful than ever, not at all comical. I wanted to kiss her supple lips but refrained out of the fear of not knowing how she would react to my advances.

"Go ahead. I *want* you to kiss me, Eddie," she said, as if she could read my mind. I embraced her, and we kissed—a long and passionate kiss.

I drew my head back and said, "Welcome back, Cat." Then I kissed her again.

"Okay, lovebirds. That is enough excitement for one day." Weeping Willow was standing in the doorway with the blanket pulled back, pointing her gnarled and crooked finger at me. I sensed that she had been eavesdropping on us the whole time.

"I will see you tomorrow, Cat," I said and stood up to leave. The little raccoon scurried across my feet and jumped up into Cat's lap.

"Sunchaser, I need to talk with you outside," Weeping Willow said with a sullen expression. We went outside of the witch's lodge.

"Thank you, Weeping Willow. Cat Woman is much happier now."

"Sunchaser, I suggest that you and Cat Woman take things very slowly. In the Meadow of Tranquility I was told much by the Council of the Ancients. They gave me a vision into the future. I have learned things that I must not reveal to you or anyone else. But I can tell you that soon you will be going on a quest."

"A quest? A quest for what?"

" A quest that will benefit your Cat Woman girlfriend. You must find the Cave of Perdition, located in the mountains on the far away Isle of Haiti. There you must slay and bring to me the body of one Great Vandalic vampire bat."

"Vandel what bat? Vampire bat?"

"It is the giant, iniquitous, flying vermin that exits the underworld each night to wander the sky, searching the land for a victim, lusting for blood. I must warn you! Sunchaser Eddie Ocean will be in great peril and very likely will not survive this impossible quest."

"Not survive? Why do you need to have this bat?"

"With the body of the bat, I will be able to make strong medicine and conjure a spell that will help Blind Cat Woman see the world again. Weeping Willow knows that you love the Cat Woman, but you must guard your heart. Your fate is uncertain—your fate with her is uncertain."

"For Cat, I will bring you this bat on a silver platter, Weeping Willow. When will I leave?"

"You come to see me tomorrow morning, and I will tell you what you must do to prepare for the quest. Now you go and do whatever a Wasichu man does to strengthen his spirit. You will need a very strong spirit. You must be both mentally and physically strong to survive this quest."

Chapter 15

KEY WEST

MONDAY, OCTOBER 28TH, 1974

For the past three weeks, we have been making preparations for our voyage to Haiti. The composition of my crew has become an issue of debate among the tribal leaders. Jumping Jack has been insisting on joining my expedition, but many of the tribal elders have stated that sending the Whatchacallit chief on such a perilous quest would be reckless and inappropriate. Yesterday Jumping Jack stood before the Council of Elders to plead his case as Full Moon and I watched the proceedings from the bleachers.

"Jumping Jack grows soft," Jumping Jack said and pulled on the flesh around his midriff. "Jumping Jack get fat. He need to rekindle warrior spirit to stay strong. Jumping Jack need to go with Sunchaser Eddie Ocean and Full Moon on voyage to Haiti."

The council members huddled together, whispering. Then Golden Tortoise spoke. "We will consider this request, Chief. You may go now," said the elder. Jumping Jack gave us a closed-fist salute and left the lodge to await his verdict. Then Night Owl and Weeping Willow took the floor to make closing arguments before the panel of three senior tribal elders.

Night Owl spoke first. "Who will be acting chief when Jumping Jack gone? If he die, then who will become chief? I say Running Deer should go with Sunchaser, not Chief Jumping Jack. Running Deer should be third warrior, not our chief."

Weeping Willow disagreed. "If Jumping Jack die, the elders then choose new chief, maybe Running Deer. My visions show me that Jumping Jack is needed for this dangerous quest. Jumping Jack must go with Sunchaser." Weeping Willow pointed her dreadful crooked finger at the council of elders. "If Jumping Jack no go on mission and mission fail, then Ancients will hold these elders responsible."

After a short discussion the elders acquiesced to Weeping Willow's demand. Golden Tortoise announced the verdict. "It has been decided. Jumping Jack will go with Sunchaser, not Running Deer. Running Deer will stay at village to provide the people with fresh meat and his leadership. Chief Jumping Jack will join the expedition to search for the giant Vandalic bats. So be it!"

"Ola, ola, hoka hey!" the other elders chanted and then disbanded their meeting.

"I'm happy for Jumping Jack, but Running Deer will be very disappointed," I said to Full Moon as we stood to leave the lodge and deliver the good news to Jumping Jack. He was waiting for us outside.

"Chief, you will be coming with us," I told him.

"Yes, Weeping Willow just told me. She has summoned us to her lodge for a final meeting. Hoka hey!" Jumping Jack yelped with a broad smile, and with a skip to his hitch, he led the way to the old witch's lodge. Inside, we gathered around her as she sat cross-legged on a woven rug that was adorned with the images of many animals. Upon our arrival at her lodge she began to chant.

"Hey, hey, yo, hey! Hey, hey, yo, hey!" Her eyes were closed and her head tilted up and back. Jumping Jack sat down at the edge of the rug and used a hand motion to signal Full Moon and me to sit. As we sat crossed-legged in a semi-circle around the old witch in the dimly lit room, a strange glow began to emanate from the ceiling above us. Full Moon pointed to the bluish hue, but Jumping Jack put a finger to his lips, signaling for us to remain silent. The witch stopped chanting and opened her eyes to look straight at me. From her wrinkled, leathery face a pair of glazed eyes burned intensely with that same surreal, bluish glow, causing me to look away in fear. *She is creepy, dude!* I looked down at her twisted, gnarled hands, deformed by arthritis and age. Her clenched right fist began to pump in an up-and-down motion, and then she scattered a handful of small animal bones across the rug and began to read them.

"The animal spirits warn me that you three Whatchacallit warriors will be in grave danger," she said, and then one by one looked into our eyes. The bluish glow from her eyes had diminished; she seemed to be coming out of her trance.

"I have very bad news. The spirits say that one of you will not return home. I see only two men returning, but I cannot tell which two. The Ancients say that something very evil guards the mouth of the cave where the giant Vandalic bats reside." We all looked at one another wondering which one of us would not survive.

Then Jumping Jack asked, "How will we know this evil spirit? What form does this devil spirit take?"

"The form that the devil takes is not clear to me. I cannot tell if it is a vertebrate or an invertebrate…maybe it can change its form. The entity does not appear to be a mammal or a reptile, and it cannot be a fish. Maybe it is amphibian, but it is clearly not human. I can see only that the demon is clever and deadly, a very formidable opponent."

Then she looked back down at the bones and continued to speak, "I have communed with the Ancients in the Meadow of Tranquility and have asked them to guide you. I have asked that they give our warriors protection, but the Ancients say that your fate will be in your own hands. You must depend on your own will, wits, and prowess to survive and to vanquish the evil that you will encounter."

"Hoka hey, Weeping Willow! We will prevail over the demon creature and bring to you the body of one giant Vandalic bat!" Jumping Jack proclaimed with great bravado.

Weeping Willow began collecting the animal bones. "I have also conjured forth the spirits of many predatory animals to provide you with their powerful medicine." She stood and began collecting containers of potions from a shelf. "The spirits have helped me devise a plan of attack so that you might enter the bat cave and survive."

"What plan, witch woman?" Jumping Jack asked.

"They have revealed the location of the great cave." She presented Jumping Jack with a rolled-up parchment paper made from the bark of a melaleuca tree and said, "I have sketched a map from the directions given to me by the spirit of an ancient seabird. This map will guide you to the bat cave. As you can see, the cave is located high in the mountains on an island called Haiti."

Jumping Jack examined the map as Full Moon and I leaned in for a look. "Brothers, I know of that island—Haiti. I have sailed past that land several times in the past, but I have never gone ashore," I said.

Then Jumping Jack spoke, "Good, Sunchaser knows way to island. My brothers, we must travel many miles to reach this faraway place. Such a journey will be very difficult in our ocean-going long boats."

"It's too far for the longboats. We must travel to Haiti in my sailboat," I said.

"That is good, but we will need a smaller boat—a longboat—to navigate these shallow streams on the island of Haiti. The streams are the only way to penetrate those swamps and dense forests leading to the mountain cave," Jumping Jack said as he pointed out a web of tributaries snaking across the map. A look of concern crossed the faces of my friends as we all examined the map and calculated the great distance.

I spoke. "Huh, it's 638 nautical miles from Key West. Jumping Jack, may I make a suggestion?"

"Speak, Sunchaser."

"Jumping Jack, we must take my sailboat, but we can tow one longboat behind us on a painter line. First we will go down to Key West for fuel and supplies, and then cross the Florida Straits and sail non-stop to Port Au Prince, Haiti to rest. After we are refreshed, we will sail farther south to the *Massif de la Hotte* Mountains." I pointed to the area on the map that is southwestern Haiti. "Here is where we will battle the demon guarding the cave and then kill the bat."

"That good plan, Sunchaser. We prepare boat tonight and leave with the morning tide," Jumping Jack said, and then he rose to his feet.

"Wait, Chief. You must take these potions with you," said Weeping Willow, as she held out four containers carved from wood. Each container had hieroglyphic images painted on it. One had images of lions and panthers stalking prey, another a crocodile with its mouth agape, the third one depicted a lone fox, and on the fourth a pack of wolves.

She gave one container to Jumping Jack and said, "The jungle cats give you speed and agility." Jumping Jack took the container, and then she turned to Full Moon. "The crocodile provides power and strength." Full Moon took the wooden jar. Now she faced me. "Here is the fox, so that you may have stealth and be clever." Then she gave Jumping Jack the last potion and said, "You are the chief— the leader. This potion will help you all work well together as a pack of wolves. You all must share this one."

Jumping Jack again glanced at the hieroglyphics painted on the containers and said, "Okay, Weeping Willow, we go now."

When we went outside, I saw Katarina walking on the path leading toward Weeping Willow's lodge. She was wearing Little Hooters's ocelot mask, and Horny Owl was walking with her.

"Hi, Cat."

She smiled and said, "Hi Eddie. Horny Owl has been teaching me the pathways surrounding the village."

"Blind Cat Woman fast learner. She walk home by self. Horny Owl no guide her. Cat Woman already know way home," Horny Owl said in his emotionless, deadpan voice and thousand-yard stare.

"That's great!" I said.

"Eddie, you are going on a dangerous voyage that is somehow supposed to benefit me. You don't need to do that. I'm very happy now, and I don't want you to leave."

"It's a done deal, Cat. We leave in the morning."

"Then please be careful, take care of yourself, and don't be a hero. I don't want another Uncle Carlos on my conscience." Kat extended her arms.

"Don't worry, Cat, I ain't no hero." We hugged, and I kissed her forehead. "Goodbye, Cat," I said, wondering if I was the one who would not be returning and if this was our last embrace. The following morning we set sail for Key West.

WEDNESDAY, OCTOBER 30TH, 1974

After a voyage of a day and a half, the coast of Key West came into sight. Our voyage across the calm waters of the Gulf of Mexico had been uneventful, and it was dinnertime when we arrived at the Key West Bight Marina. The sun was burning a fiery hole through a bank of dark cumulus clouds drifting across the gulf waters as we docked the *Orion*. Our approach to the island had been from the northeast, but to our west we could hear loud drumming coming from the sunset celebration at Mallory Square.

"Listen! Hoka hey! We no welcome here, Sunchaser! Key West warriors sounding war drums!" Jumping Jack said with a scowl.

"Hoka hey! Hoka hey!" both of my friends chanted as they picked up their long spears, preparing to defend themselves from the hostile inhabitants of Key West.

"Relax, my brothers. Those are not war drums. They are the Key West people celebrating the setting of the sun."

"Why the Wasichu people so crazy? Sun sets every day. No big deal," Full Moon said.

"Many of the people are tourists enjoying vacation."

"What is vacation?" Jumping Jack asked.

"Time off from work."

"What is time off?"

"Forget about it. Never mind that drumming. Bitter root water and ganja weed may have something to do with those loud festivities," I said.

"Bitter root water? Yum yum. We eat meat and drink the Wasichu's bitter root water now," said Jumping Jack.

It was the day before Halloween, and Key West was packed with visitors who had arrived for the annual Fantasy Fest celebration.

"Let's take the back streets to avoid this crowd," I said and then walked my friends to a nearby restaurant. After eating, we walked toward Duval Street to have a beer and watch the crazies' party. The Native American attire worn by my Indian friends drew quite a bit of attention and smiles from people as we walked along the streets.

"Nice costumes, dude!" a young guy with long, curly hair, who was leaning against a red brick wall, said as we passed him. The sweet smell of ganja in the humid air mingled with the tart smell of Key Lime blossoms.

"Want a hit?" The hippie held out a small pipe and offered it to Full Moon. I intervened.

"Maybe later, dude," I said and pulled my friends along by their arms.

"Why we no smoke peace pipe with nice Wasichu fellow?" asked Full Moon.

"That peace pipe smelled like ganja—maybe hashish."

"What that—ganja?"

"Ganja's a weed that makes you act silly. I need you guys fresh and clear headed in the morning. We must provision the boat. Maybe a few more beers before we get our butts back to the boat. We need to stay out of trouble!"

"Okay, more bitter root water before bed. That good idea," Jumping Jack said.

"Let's go to the Green Parrot Bar. Not as many tourist hang out in that part of town," I said and turned left on Duval Street.

"This Wasichu village very crowded," Full Moon said as we wormed our way through the meandering horde. The sidewalks were packed with people who had arrived early for the Halloween Fantasy Fest parade that was scheduled for the following night. Like multicolored ants fleeing an ant mound, a throng of tourists poured off a massive cruise ship that had recently docked. Most were headed in the opposite direction, toward the bars on Duval Street.

"Tomorrow night is Halloween," I said.

"Jumping Jack remembers Halloween. Halloween good fun. Halloween in Miami with Nick Dagger plenty fun," said Jumping Jack, referring to our visit to Miami after leaving Crocodile Island in 1973.

"Maybe I'll lay over one more day here in Key West so you fellows can see the big parade tomorrow night," I said as the sweaty, raucous crowd of tourists mixed with local misfits, adventurers, hippies, excitable Cubans, and deadbeat losers began to thin out. The farther we got from the main drag, the less crowded were the streets. We turned off onto White Street in search of the Green Parrot Bar.

"That's it, the Green Parrot. Let's go." We entered the open-air pub that resembled an oversized, white-clapboard garage. Toward the back, a live band was playing an odd rendition of "Mamas, Don't Let Your Babies Grow Up to Be Cowboys" with a reggae beat. The main bar was located in the center of the room, and every bar stool was occupied. The bartender did not see me as I waved to get his attention, so I turned sideways and nuzzled up to the counter, trying to order beer. I found myself sandwiched between two girls perched on bar stools. They were both barefoot and wearing identical cut-off blue jeans and white tube tops, and were speaking loudly with a distinct southern drawl.

"Hello, ladies. Mind if I squeeze in here? I can't get that bartender's attention."

"I know. He's busier than a long-tailed cat in a room full of rocking chairs. Come on in, cowboy," one girl said.

"Thanks. Oh, sorry, miss," I said as my back brushed the chest of the girl behind me.

"Not a problem," she said as I felt a pair of ample breasts press hard against my scapulas.

Out of nowhere, a country expression I had learned when growing up in Kentucky came to mind, "Well, don't those feel prettier than two globs of butter melting on a stack of wheat cakes!" I said to her over my shoulder.

"Ha! Good one, cowboy. I like that expression!" The voice came from behind me. The gal in front pointed at my friends and asked, "Are those wild savages with you?"

"Yes ma'am—they're real Indians. Hey, bartender, three Buds, *por favor*." After I ordered, I felt the chick behind me grab my ass and then say, "Hoo-whee! Lord, Tawny, this cowboy's ass is so tight that if he farted he'd blow his boots off."

"Uh-huh. Briana, check out his Indian friends. Those bare-chested boys are hotter than a Laredo parking lot on a summer afternoon!" Tawny said, exaggerating her southern drawl.

"Hey, you girls are not from around here, are you?" I asked as I squeezed back out with three bottles of beer.

"We're from Dallas. Texas cowgirls through and through."

"Huh, well, how about that? Two cowgirls and two Indian boys." I said.

"Are you gonna introduce your friends to us, cowboy?" Tawny asked as she eyed Jumping Jack.

"This fellow is Chief Jumping Jack, and that is Full Moon."

"Well, well—a chief, no less!" Tawny said as she reached out to shake his hand.

"Yeah, and Chief Jumping Jack is married," I said.

"Full Moon no married," said Full Moon as he stepped forward to shake Tawny's hand.

"Well, you not only dress the part and walk the walk, Indian boy, you even talk the talk," Tawny said, mocking Full Moon's broken English. She let her handshake with Full Moon linger.

"I told you, ladies, they're not fake. They're real Native Americans."

Both girls giggled. "Yeah, and tonight we're queens of de Nile, but tomorrow we'll be Dallas Cowboy cheerleaders."

Suddenly someone nudged me hard from behind and spoke in a loud and angry voice. "Hey, what's up? I leave for a minute to drain the lizard, and you two sluts pick up other guys?"

"We was just talking, Otis," said Tawny.

"Oh no! Not after I bought you girls two rounds of drinks! Hell, no!"

I turned around, prepared to punch the guy in the nose for calling the girls sluts, but found myself staring at a big, silver belt buckle. At eye level, a silver eagle glared at me with an open beak, ready to attack. I tilted my head back to see where the voice was coming from—up, up, up. Finally, near the ceiling, a big round face came into focus. Wispy, cirrostratus clouds of cigarette smoke being circulated by a ceiling fan swirled around the guy's enormous head.

"Holy crap! Is this guy your boyfriend?" I asked no one in particular.

"Hell, no! We just met him. His name is Otis," Tawny said. *Otis? I would need an Otis elevator just to punch him in the friggin' nose!*

"Scram, and take your two trick-or-treat butt-buddies with you, punk!" Otis said and shoved me.

"Sure thing. No problem, dude. I was just buying a few beers for my friends," I said. A crick was forming in my neck from looking up at the behemoth.

"We no leave. You leave instead. Full Moon like Tawny girl," Full Moon said as he stepped between Otis and me.

"Well then, it looks like me and you need to go outside for a little powwow," said the giant.

"Hey, Full Moon, we don't need no trouble tonight, dude," I said as I tried to guide him away toward the pool tables.

He pulled away from me. "Full Moon no want trouble either. Full Moon just want to look upon girl with eyes like blue sky and sunshine hair."

"My hair? Sunshine hair?" Tawny said with a smile and seemed to swoon on her barstool.

"That's it, Cochise, I warned you!" Full Moon saw the roundhouse sucker-punch coming and ducked, but I didn't. The last thing I remember seeing was a big meaty fist the size of a football flying at my face.

"Hey, he's awake." I opened my eyes and saw Briana looking down at me. She was holding a bag of frozen peas to my left eye.

"Hey, what happened? Where are we? Ouch!" A burning pain shot across my cheek.

"We are on your boat, Eddie. The big guy knocked you out, and we carried you here from the Parrot Bar."

"Are my friends okay? Did the giant kill them?"

"Kill them? Hell, no! Full Moon kicked the big guy's butt. He made Otis get on his knees and beg Tawny to forgive him for being such an A-hole," Briana said.

"He kicked that giant's butt? Full Moon's not known for his fighting skills. Jumping Jack must have helped him."

"No! Full Moon used some kind of advanced disco karate fighting style. It was amazing. He said that you taught him how to disco fight."

"Where are they now, Briana?"

"Tawny and Full Moon are sitting up on the deck, watching the moon rise. Jumping Jack is across the dock having a beer at the Half Shell Raw Bar."

"Oww." I repositioned the frozen peas.

"Eddie, do you mind if we spend the night on your boat? It's a long walk back to the Southernmost Point."

"Sure, the *Orion* sleeps eight people, no problem." I sat up. "Oww! I need some aspirin."

"You got a real nice shiner, Eddie. You should learn how to duck."

"Thanks for the advice, babe. Pick a berth. I'm turning in for the night." I went to my captain's cabin, and Briana followed me.

"Hey, what a coincidence! That's the same bunk that I picked out!"

Chapter 16

FANTASY FEST

OCTOBER 31ST, 1974

*S*omeone's cooking. Loud sounds coming from the galley woke me. For a moment I listened to the sound of the pots and pans clanking together and then glanced at my watch; it was six o'clock, and Briana was lying on her back next to me.

"You awake, cowgirl?" I whispered.

"Huh?" she mumbled.

"Briana, you still sleeping? It's six o'clock." I nudged her, and she rolled to her side to face me.

"Asleep? Hell no! I was just lying here checking for holes in my eyelids!"

"Sorry, babe, but we gotta get up. Me and the boys have a lot to do this morning."

"Okay, give me five," she said and rolled away to her other side.

I found Tawny and Full Moon in the galley. Tawny was fixing breakfast while Full Moon watched her; they were fixated on one another and didn't notice me standing in the doorway. Tawny turned to smile at Full Moon, and the couple looked at one another with goo-goo eyes like a pair of love-struck teenyboppers.

"Good morning." I interrupted the enamored couple.

"Hey, hey!" Full Moon said without taking his eyes off of Tawny's posterior.

"Want some eggs, Eddie?" Tawny asked.

"Sure. Where's Jumping Jack?"

"Jumping Jack took longboat to catch fish. He go fishing, not sleep last night," Full Moon said.

Jumping Jack must be homesick…missing Little Hooters, I bet.

Tawny put four plates on the table and asked me, "Is Briana getting up?"

"Yeah I'm up, I'm right here, bright eyed and bushy tailed. You got some grub for me, girl?" Briana was standing in the doorway of my cabin, brushing her hair.

Tawny pointed her spatula at me and said, "Eddie, I'm warning you, that girl thinks the sun comes up every morning just to hear her crow!" Then she looked over her shoulder at Briana. "You want scrambled or sunny side-up, darling?"

"Sunny side up—and extra grits."

"Honey, these cowboys don't have no grits."

"What? No grits? That's criminal."

"You know it, girl! We gotta settle for mush. Only oatmeal today," Tawny said as she cracked two eggs over the skillet and then began dishing oatmeal onto the plates.

"Last hog to the trough gets the rotten egg!" Briana said as she shoved me to the side and grabbed a seat. Shortly after we had finished eating we heard the thumping sound of the longboat being tied to the stern of *Orion*, then Jumping Jack's voice; "Hey, Hey, Hey! Jumping Jack got fish!" We all went topside to see his catch.

"Those are nice groupers, Chief," I said as he tossed three eight-pound gag groupers up to us.

"We eat one for lunch," he said as he climbed out of the longboat.

"You want some breakfast, sweetie?" Tawny asked.

"Jumping Jack already eat." He held up the remains of a small sea trout that had the flesh stripped from one side.

"Eww! Did he eat that fish raw?" asked Briana.

"Sure. He slices it micro thin. Didn't you ever have sashimi?" I asked as Full Moon began cleaning a grouper and throwing fish guts overboard.

"Eat raw fish? No, that's gross!" Briana wrinkled her nose in disgust.

Tawny seemed to gag as fish guts spilled out of the second grouper. "Briana, let's gather our stuff so that we can leave these boys to their chores." Both girls went below deck to gather their belongings.

"Those gals are a bit squeamish. They must be *urban* cowgirls," I said with a chuckle. "After they leave, we need to stock the boat with provisions for our voyage."

The girls came topside with their oversized purses. "Well, we should be on our way, fellers. It was real fun," Briana said and began stepping off the boat.

Tawny paused and walked over to Full Moon. He grabbed her under the armpits and picked her off the ground, looked into her sky-blue eyes, and then kissed her. "Full Moon, do you want to meet up at the parade later?"

"Yes, Full Moon meet cowgirl at front of Sloppy Joe Bar tonight," said Full Moon.

After the girls left we went to work. We used four oars from the longboat and two small tarps to build a pair of pony drags as a means to haul provisions from town to the boat. It was one o'clock when we finished shopping and hauling supplies, and then Jumping Jack grilled one of the groupers on my hibachi.

"Damn, this is good eatin', Jumping Jack! Pass me another Kalik," I said. After lunch we spent the rest of the afternoon cleaning and performing routine maintenance on the boat.

At five o'clock, Jumping Jack said, "Jumping Jack hungry again. We eat more fish while still fresh."

As we ate dinner, I pondered our plans for the evening. "You guys have your Indian garb—people think those are Halloween costumes—but what should I wear?"

"Sunchaser Eddie Ocean be Indian too. We all dress up for pow-wow. We go below now and prepare." Jumping Jack stood up and took his empty plate below deck.

Jumping Jack and Full Moon each brought a duffel bag out into the galley and began handing me articles of clothing.

"Here, you wear nice bone breastplate." Full Moon handed me a vest made of animal bones and then held out a buckskin breechcloth. "My breechcloth too big for Sunchaser. Sunchaser very skinny," he said to Jumping Jack.

"Sunchaser, you wear one of my breechcloths and this eagle-feather headband." Jumping Jack offered the items to me.

"I give Sunchaser tobacco pouch to hold his Wasichu money. No place for his wallet," Full Moon said to Jumping Jack. While I tried on the Native American attire, Jumping Jack brought out a container of face paints and made two horizontal streaks across each of my cheeks, one blue and one yellow.

"Sunchaser look very good. He should dress like Indian all the time," said Jumping Jack as my friends stepped back with folded arms to examine me. Then Jumping Jack and Full Moon put on animal skin headgear that I had never seen them wear before.

"Are those fur hats?" I asked.

"These powwow dress hats. Mine otter skin," said Full Moon as he adjusted the turban-like headdress.

"What's yours made from?" I asked Jumping Jack. His hat reminded me of a punk rocker's hairstyle.

"This porcupine skin. Now we all ready for parade, " Jumping Jack said as he painted streaks across Full Moon's face.

"Tawny girl will like Full Moon's powwow dress," Full Moon said as he looked at himself in my mirror. "We go find Tawny girl now."

It was only seven o'clock, but a huge crowd of inebriated people dressed in outrageous costumes already lined both sides of Duval Street. "These people are higher than a kite!" I said as we weaved our way toward Sloppy Joe's. From the sidewalk outside, we saw Tawny and Briana dancing on top of a long wooden table inside the bar.

"Look! There they are…boy, those cowgirls look hot tonight!" I pointed into the pub, screaming to be heard over the noise. A crowd of guys had surrounded the table where the pair of Texan vixens, dressed up like Dallas Cowboy Cheerleaders, was driving them crazy by gyrating to the song "Susie Q" by Credence Clearwater Revival. Briana fired her cap pistol into the air and then, with pursed lips, sensuously blew the smoke from the tip of the barrel of her pistol. The crowd of horny men erupted with cheers, and one guy began grabbing at Briana's legs. A burly man wearing black-rimmed glasses and sporting a thick black beard was standing next to me. He said to no one in particular, "That's the scene I've been searching for! The *Playboy* Bunnies from the U.S.O. arriving at the frontlines—this is the scene for my movie, *Apocalypse? Wow!*"

"That tabletop dancing *would* make for a good scene in some apocalyptic Hollywood movie," I agreed. Then the guy looked at me dressed up as an Indian and said, "Better yet, one cowgirl and one Indian girl—that will be perfect for my U.S.O. *Playboy Bunny* dancers!"

"What movie are you talking about, sir?"

"I'm a Hollywood director. My new movie is about the Vietnam War. I'm still working on the screenplay, and in a scene where the U.S.O. brings in *Playboy* bunnies by helicopter to perform for the troops; I couldn't decide how the girls would dress and what they would perform. But now, *that* is perfect!" he said and pointed at the girls, who were now bent over and shaking their butts at the crowd. "Here, take my card." The guy handed me a business card and I looked at it. ***Francis Ford Cappella, Hollywood Director.*** When I looked up, the guy was gone. I could see the back of his head as he wormed his way through the crowd and into Sloppy Joe's.

"We better get those girls out of there before they drive these horny bastards crazy!" I said and then began jumping up and down, waving my arms to get the girls' attention.

"Full Moon go get Tawny girl now," Full Moon said.

"How are we gonna get them past that crowd, dude?" Tawny finally saw us outside; she tapped Briana on the shoulder and then said something to her. Both girls turned their backs to the crowd and stood at the edge of the table.

What are they doing?" I wondered as a guy grabbed Briana's calf again. Suddenly both girls fell backward into the crowd, and the guys up front caught them and started passing them overhead toward the front of the pub.

"What they do?" Jumping Jack asked.

"They are crowd surfing." When the girls got near the front entrance, the crowd began to pass them back inside.

"Get them now!" I yelled as all three of us grabbed the girls and carried them over our heads away from the bar. The crowd inside began booing us as we escaped with our cowgirls.

"Those boys are madder than a skillet full of rattlesnakes!" Tawny said as the booing grew louder.

Briana said, "Well, tie me to a pig and roll me in mud, Tawny! I ain't been groped that hard since my sixteenth birthday—the night I met my West Virginny cousins for the first time at a family reunion."

A few of the angry guys from Sloppy Joe's were following us. "Let's duck into Captain Tony's!" I yelled. The place was packed, but just as we arrived, a couple began to leave a small table near the rear of the joint. Like a contestant playing musical chairs, Tawny sat down just ahead of a guy dressed like an extraterrestrial spaceman.

"I'll get us a round of beers." I said and went to the bar. As I waited for my order, I glanced over to the entrance, and my heart faltered. Obstructing the entrance was the enormous body of Otis, the giant. The good news was that Otis had two black eyes and a disabled right arm, which dangled at his side in a cloth sling. The bad news was that he looked meaner than hell, and he had two other boulder-sized guys with him. Otis seemed to be scanning the crowd, looking for someone. *Oh shit!* I turned my back, took the feathered headband off, and bent down toward the bar just as Otis's menacing glance was coming around my way.

As I leaned over, my face only inches from the bar, I peeked out from under my right armpit. *Whew! He didn't see me.* Otis, followed by his two buddies, walked toward the far wall and stopped beside a table that was occupied by three girls who had dressed up like 1920s-era flappers. As I nervously watched the brutes talking to the girls, the beers arrived, and I paid the bartender before scurrying back to our table, still keeping a low profile by bending over at the waist.

"Did you see who just came in?" I asked as I passed out the beer. "It's Otis, and this time he has two gigantic friends with him." I pointed toward the far wall. Everyone looked at the broad backs of the three hulks.

"No problem. If they not nice we disco them again…three against three…very good," Full Moon said. But just as he finished that observation, four more behemoths wearing jackets with big varsity letters sewn on the front and the name OKLAHOMA BISONS emblazoned across their backs joined Otis.

"They must be linemen for a football team, dudes! We gotta get out of here pronto!" I said.

"But those boys are right next to the exit. We'll never get past them," said Briana.

"What we need is a diversion, dudes," I said as I stared at Jumping Jack's spiked porcupine fur hat.

"What that is—what diversion?" asked Jumping Jack.

"Hurry—just give me your fur hat," I said and snatched it from his head and put it on the table.

"Hey!" Tawny protested when I ripped two ruby-red rhinestones off her skin-tight hot pants. Then I reached under the tabletop searching for a couple of wads of fresh chewing gum.

"Oh gross!" the girls said in unison as I held two gooey wads of chewing gum in my hand.

"Eddie, what the hell are you doing?" Tawny asked as I glued the rhinestones onto the porcupine hat, one on each side near the front.

"These are eyes. Now give me that lasso." I said and took Briana's toy rope lariat and tied the bitter end of the thin rope to the hat.

"I'm making a giant rat!" I said.

"A what?" the girls said, again in unison.

"Chug down those beers and follow my lead, dudes. When I give you a signal, walk toward the exit." I said and then I went over to stand behind the crowd gathered at the end of the bar. After signaling my friends with a thumb-up sign, I tossed the porcupine hat onto the floor at the end of the bar.

"What the hell is that?" I screamed and pointed at the furry ball of spikes as I used the rope to drag it slowly along the floor through the dark shadows. The "rat" stopped directly beneath a scarecrow's barstool.

"Ahhh! A rat!" the scarecrow yelled, lifting his feet from the floor and then climbing up onto the bar as a shower of straw from his pant leg fell on the rat. More patrons began climbing up onto the bar; others ran for the exit. The bartender was creeping cautiously around the end of the bar holding a Louisville Slugger. He paused wide-eyed when he saw the giant "rat" crawling along the floor. People rushed past me, and I began running with them, still holding the thin rope. Now the giant rat was chasing us, its ruby-red eyes glinting from the dark shadows under the bar.

"Rat! Rat! Rabid rat! It's coming for us!" I screamed in faux horror but stopped beneath the hanging tree that grows in the middle of Captain Tony's Bar. My friends were swept up in the stampede and ran past me toward the exit as I paused next to the tree trunk and then threw the rat up into its branches. The hat went up and over a branch, and its weight began pulling the lariat rope upward, so I let go. The porcupine hat began to slowly descend from the tree.

"My god! Now a giant tarantula is coming out of that tree!" I screamed. People were no longer looking at the floor, worried about the rabid rat. Now they were bent low, covering their heads as they ran for the door. When the loop of the lariat snagged a branch, the "hairy tarantula" stopped its descent and began swinging through the air above the heads of the panicking crowd; strands of straw wedged between porcupine quills hung off the hat resembling skinny spider legs.

"Ahhhhgggg!" Superwoman screamed and fell over a chair, sending her sprawling across the floor. She got up and used her red cape to cover her head as she ran for the door.

Otis was across the room, standing with his friends trying to figure out what the commotion was all about, when he spotted me and pointed. I couldn't hear what he was screaming, but I could see the angry scowl on his face.

"Spiders! Spiders! They're all over the place!" a woman near tears was wailing. For the first time Otis saw the porcupine hat, and his expression went through a series of changes. Anger morphed into surprise, and then the look of fear flashed across his face as he looked up at the ceiling and covered his head with his one good arm. The bartender came up next to me and, like a kid attacking a piñata, began swinging the baseball bat at the tarantula, nearly taking my head off with his follow-through. I moved away to avoid his spastic attack on the spider, and the crowd enveloped me. The crush of the stampede took me through the exit and spit me out onto the sidewalk like a slippery watermelon seed. I regained my feet and ran to my friends, who were standing halfway down the block.

"Don't just stand there, dudes, run! Otis saw me!" Just before turning a corner, I stopped to see what was happening. Two blocks behind us, I saw Otis and his buddies emerge from the bar, knocking people to the ground as they pushed people to get away from the spiders. The brutes stopped and huddled in the middle of the street. Otis began giving out orders and using hand signals to direct his team. Three guys took off running south and Otis and the other three began jogging our way.

"They're looking for us, dudes. Hang a right!" I said as we turned the corner and ran over to Duval Street. The parade had started, and the crowd swallowed us up.

"Let's walk along with these floats," I said as we joined the procession.

"Get up here!" a guy wearing a yellow hardhat said and offered his hand. One by one, he helped us up onto the flatbed parade float. The theme of the float honored current 1970s-era rock music. "We can always use more Indians and a couple of cowgirls," the guy said. I recognized our old friends from Miami, the Village Dudes, dancing to the song "Macho Man."

"Look, those fellows are the Village Dudes. We do the 'Dance of Honor' song for them now. They like that," Jumping Jack said to Full Moon. He and Full Moon began making the movements of the ancient ritual dance in time to "Macho Man." They raised their arms spread wide to the sky in honor of the heavens and then pointed to the ground with arms at their sides to honor the earth before bending sideways and forming a round, rising sun. Finally they placed their palms together above their heads to honor the great teepee in The Meadow of Tranquility.

"Hey, look! Those guys dressed like Indians want to do the 'YMCA' dance!" a guy dressed like a fireman said and then changed the song to 'YMCA.' Instantly, everyone joined Jumping Jack and Full Moon in the ritualistic movements of the Dance of Honor. People lining both sides of the street began doing the YMCA movements.

"Look! All the Wasichu people know the Dance of Honor!" My friends were amazed that everyone was joining the traditional Native American dance that honors the stars, the earth, the moon, and the great teepee in the sky.

"Time to wrap up this party, dudes. Otis and his boys are coming!" The float was moving slowly, and Otis was walking toward us, searching the crowd and looking for us. We jumped off the float and cut down a side street, heading for Key West Bight and the safety of *Orion*.

After we boarded the boat, Tawny asked me in a pleading tone of voice that was more appropriate for an eight-year-old girl, "Captain Eddie, can we please stay on your boat one last time?" I was about to say no but saw how Full Moon was looking longingly into her fluttering blue eyes.

"Okay, but we have to sail at five in the morning, girls—five o'clock sharp."

The next morning it was four forty-five when the sleepy cowgirls walked down the dock and away from our boat.

"Full Moon find Tawny girl when he come back to Florida," Full Moon yelled. Tawny turned and waved to him one last time.

"Don't worry, dude. I got her Texas home phone number for you," I said to Full Moon as his round face took on the look of a lovesick puppy.

Chapter 17

HAITI

Off the port quarter, the eastern horizon began to lighten, and then a sky burst of brilliant orange and red light greeted me as the sun rose out of the deep purple water of the Atlantic Ocean. It was Friday morning, November 1st, and we had been underway for nearly three hours. Behind us, Key West was now just a dark, distant speck of land sinking below the horizon of the Gulf of Mexico.

At the helm, I examined my nautical chart and set our south-easterly course. In the days ahead we would be skirting the northern coast of Cuba and sailing well offshore to avoid a run-in with Cuban gunboats. The low-lying land of the Bahamian Islands to the east was too distant to be visible, but it was comforting to know that in the event of a problem those islands could provide us a safe harbor.

Our hope was to complete the 651 nautical mile voyage to Haiti in three days by sailing non-stop and working in six-hour shifts. It was 7:11am, and my shift was nearly over when Full Moon came topside to relieve me.

"Full Moon, if you take the helm early, I'll cook up some eggs and grits."

"That idea good, Sunchaser," Full Moon said as he sleepily gazed at the land off our starboard beam and stretched his arms high above his head. "What land is that?" he asked and pointed to the mountains in the distance.

"That's Cuba, dude. When you tack to the south, don't take us in too close to shore. We don't want to enter Cuban waters and get arrested for being American spies," I said before going below to cook.

Jumping Jack came out of his cabin when he heard me knocking pans around in the galley. "Yum. Sunchaser cook now?"

"Yeah. Hey, do you know where the salt is?" I asked as I searched a cupboard.

"Me not know."

"Well, I'll be damned. We got grits but forgot to buy salt." When the scrambled eggs and grits were done, I took a bowl up to Full Moon, and then Jumping Jack and I sat down in the galley to eat.

"This food not good. Eggs taste dull. Needs to be brighter," Jumping Jack said with a frown.

"Yeah, it's bland—needs salt, dude." My friends always used an excessive amount of salt, probably a taste acquired from a diet that included lots of dry-salted fish and meats.

Full Moon agreed. "What wrong with food?" he called down from the helm.

"Sorry, Full Moon. We have no salt!"

Jumping Jack squeezed some lemon juice onto his eggs and said, "Later Jumping Jack make us some salt from ocean water." He was referring to the process of evaporating ocean water to obtain sea salt.

"Okay, dude, but that will take a couple of sunny days," I said.

"Maybe we can cook ocean water to get the salt," he said.

"I tried boiling down ocean water once, but the heat ruined the sea salt. We will have to do without salt for a couple of days."

After breakfast I took out my charts again to plot a necessary change of course, a jog to the southeast that would take us down to Haiti after we cleared the eastern tip of Cuba. A large island close to our course and just northeast of the tip of Cuba drew my attention.

"Hey, Jumping Jack. I know where we can get some salt, and it's not much out of the way," I said as I pointed to the island.

Jumping Jack looked at the chart and asked, "What place is that?"

"It's Great Inagua, the southernmost island in the Bahamian chain."

"Do they have bitter root water?"

"Sure, but better yet, they have plenty of salt! The Morton Sea Salt processing plant is on that island!"

"Good, we get salt and bitter root water. Yum yum!"

"Maybe we should lay over there for one night to rest up before we tangle with those Vandalic Bats in Haiti."

04:30, MONDAY, NOVEMBER 4TH

I had come topside to relieve Full Moon and found him at the helm pointing to something in the distance. "Look out there, Sunchaser. A light blinks off and on!"

I looked out into the darkness but saw nothing. "Where?"

"Wait. It come back soon."

Suddenly a light flashed for the duration of three seconds. "That must be the lighthouse on Great Inagua Island," I said as the old kerosene-powered light went dark again before coming back around to beckon us to shore. "We will be there by sunrise," I said.

"I go tell Jumping Jack. He want bitter root water!" Full Moon said excitedly.

"No—let him sleep. You should get a couple hours yourself before we dock, dude."

Two hours later, with the morning sky lightening, I roused my buddies, and we prepared to enter Matthew Town Harbor. After docking the boat, we went to investigate the sleepy little harbor town that was just starting to come to life.

"This village very quiet. Not like Key West. Are you sure village has bitter root water?" asked Jumping Jack as we walked along a deserted street toward the Morton House Lodge.

"Sure, but it's a bit early for drinking," I said.

"You know what Mr. Buffett, the Wasichu singer, say in Key West: 'It's five o'clock somewhere,'" Jumping Jack said and then smacked me hard on my shoulder and yelped, "Whatchacallit!"

"Damn, I hate that!" As I rubbed the sting out of my left shoulder, I spotted the inn. "Hey, there's the lodge." We quickened our pace and walked onto the porch of the Morton House just as an elderly man sporting a pencil-thin mustache was coming out of the building. He was dressed in a safari outfit, complete with a pith helmet.

"Morning, mates," he said with a heavy British accent.

"Good morning, sir. Do you work here?" I asked.

"No, my good man. I'm afraid the proprietor of this establishment does not rise until after ten am. A sleepy fellow, he is. If the old chap doesn't get an afternoon nap, he is completely knackered by tea time."

"Well, sir, do you know if there are any vacancies here?"

"Not likely, mate. This place is packed with birders like me."

"Birders?"

"Bird watchers, my good man. People come here from all over the globe. The flamingos are the main attraction, but the vast variety of species makes this place a birder's paradise." Several people came out onto the porch; they all wore similar safari outfits and all had binoculars hanging from their necks.

"Is there other lodging to be had in this town?" I asked the Brit.

"This is an island of fewer than a thousand people, mate, and everyone seems to work at the Morton Sea Salt factory, across town. You might find a local at the factory who has a room for let."

"Thank you, sir. We need to go there to buy salt anyway."

The Brit had been eyeing my companions. "Jolly good costumes your mates are sporting, but Halloween has long passed." He nodded toward the Indians and then lit a tobacco pipe.

"That's their normal attire. That's how my friends always dress, sir."

"Huh—very strange birds, indeed," he said with an arched eyebrow and blew a puff of sweet, cherry-scented smoke into the air. "Do you and those odd fellows wish to join our expedition this morning?"

"Expedition?"

"Yes, to the rookery—a sight that should not be missed."

"No thanks, sir. We are looking for a shower, a hot meal, and some relaxation time."

"Very well. Maybe we will see you later this evening at the lodge. My name is Professor Derbyshire," he said as a rusty old minivan rattled to a stop in front of the lodge.

"I'm Eddie Ocean."

"Jolly good show, Eddie. We will see you later then. Ta-ta!" he said as he followed his entourage to the minivan.

"Ta-ta!" I said.

We spent the morning exploring the island and snorkel diving off a rocky, Pleistocene limestone beach. The pristine, vodka-clear water held an abundance of sea life. Fish and crustaceans darted in and about the magnificent coral heads and sea fans. By noon we were all starving again.

"Let's see if they are serving lunch at the lodge," I said as we collected our belongings and then walked back to the town center.

The Morton House dining room was open for business, and a tall woman with cocoa-colored skin, who was wearing a bright yellow sarong, directed us to a table.

"Are you boys guests here?" she asked.

"No, ma'am—no vacancies here. But we *are* looking for a room for one night. Our sailboat is giving us cabin fever," I said.

"My niece rents a small beach cottage. Want to see it?"

"Sure—right after lunch." We all ate a hearty lunch of conch ceviche and fish, then ordered a round of Kalik Beer. Just as we finished, a young woman came into the dining room and approached us. "Are you da boys needin' da room?" she asked.

"Yes, ma'am."

"Come wit me, den. I show you."

"I'm Eddie Ocean, miss. What's your name?"

"Carina," she said and walked away. We followed her down the road, and then we veered off toward the west and went to a beach house that had a small limestone cottage beside it. "This be $10 American a night, and I make de breakfast fer five more," she said.

"Sold!" I said as we looked over the two-room cottage and then stowed our diving gear. We returned to the *Orion* to fetch our toiletry bags. On board the boat, I opened the engine compartment and engaged a hidden kill switch to disable the fuel line to the engine, a trick to make it harder for anyone to "borrow" the boat during the night.

Back at the cottage, Carina was sitting on the porch of the main house, weaving something out of palm fronds.

"Carina, we're going to get dinner. Want to come?" I called out to her. Without looking up, she just shook her head no.

After dinner at the Morton House, we saw Professor Derbyshire sitting in the parlor smoking his pipe and reading a book. "Look guys, it's the old professor. You fellows go on ahead to the beach house. I want to talk to the gent."

I walked into the parlor. "Hello, Professor. How was the birding?"

He looked up from his book. "Oh, good evening, Eddie. The birding here is excellent—most excellent indeed—so many species concentrated in such a small habitat. Were you lads able to secure lodging?"

"Yes, sir—a small beach cottage. We will be sailing out early in the morning."

"Oh, what a pity. Sorry to hear that you are leaving. What is your destination?"

"The mountains of Haiti, sir. We are on a quest to capture a giant Vandalic cave bat."

"Vandalic bat? So sorry to inform you mate, but those bats do not exist. They are about as real as that Romanian chap—Count

Dracula, who transforms from human being into vampire bat. Vandalic bats are mythical creatures—inventions of practitioners of Haitian vodou. The folklore of Haitian vodouists, I'm afraid."

"Vodouists?"

"Yes. A vodouist is a person that practices vodou."

"Do you mean voodoo?"

"No. That is a common mistake of the layperson. Haitian vodou is not the same as, say, Cuban Santeria or even Louisiana voodoo. Vodouists believe in a distant and unknowable Creator they call 'Bondye.' According to vodouists, Bondye does not directly intercede in human affairs. Therefore vodouists must direct their worship toward spirits subservient to Bondye. These spirits are called loa. Each loa is responsible for a particular aspect of life. Vodouists cultivate personal relationships with the loa through the presentation of offerings and the creation of personal altars. They participate in elaborate ceremonies involving music, dance, and spirit possession. I'm sure you have seen re-enactments of those practices in the movies."

"Yes, I have, and that's all very interesting, Professor—but how do you know that the giant Vandalic bats do not exist?"

"My department at the university received a grant to research Haitian vodou and specifically to investigate the existence of the giant Vandalic bats said to be indigenous to Haiti's Tiburon Peninsula. We searched extensively throughout the Chaine de la Sella Mountain Range—all the way from the Massif de la Sella region at the border of the Dominican Republic to the Massif de la Hotte region in the southwest of Haiti. I'm afraid the giant bats of Haiti are poppycock—merely the folklore of the locals. Sorry, mate."

"Sir, we have traveled hundreds of miles. Are you certain of this?"

"Yes. But so that all is not lost, maybe you would like me to give you and your mates a seminar on the wonderful birds that inhabit this island."

"Thanks for the offer, sir, but we are bound by our oath to have a look for ourselves—to search for those bats."

"Well, you are in for a treat. The cloud forest mountains of the Tiburon Peninsula are quite spectacular."

I stood up, disappointed by the news that our journey was in vain. "Thanks for the info, professor, but now I need to pick up some salt and then get some shuteye, sir."

"Happy sailing, mate."

I went to the Morton Salt Factory and found the evening supervisor. "Hello, sir. I would like to purchase salt."

"How much you need, mon?"

"Just one, please."

"Just one order, mon? Dat hardly worth de shipping cost."

"Oh, I'm not shipping. I want to take it with me now. I sail in the morning."

"Where de ship? I don't see no ship." The man stood at the window, looking out into the commercial harbor.

"My sailboat is over at the private docks, sir."

"Sailboat? What you talkin' 'bout, mon? You want de salt put in de sailboat?"

"No. I want to take back one box of salt."

"A box? Don't jam me up! I be talking bout one ton of de salt. One order—one ton! We sell de salt by de ton, mon!"

"A ton? I don't need a ton, sir. The store in town was not open. Where can I get a box of salt?"

With a frown the man walked over to a kitchen area and took a Quaker Oatmeal box from a shelf. He emptied the remaining oats into a bowl and then offered me the empty container. "Fill dis up wit de salt and den go away!"

"Thank you, sir." As I was leaving the office, I heard the guy mumbling something about how my head was stuck up an improbable orifice. Outside I was amazed to find two huge piles of white, crystallized salt rising about five stories high. After scooping up a box full, I waved goodbye to the guy and left. *Two mountains of salt! No wonder that guy thinks I'm nuts for coming here for one box.*

Back at the cottage I found my buddies sitting on the beach with a stranger. They were sharing a smoke. When I approached them, I recognized the sweet smell of cannabis.

"Hey, dudes, who is your friend?" I asked.

The stranger stood to greet me. He was shirtless, had long dread-locks, and wore dingy white cotton pants cut off just below his knees and tied with a cord at his waist.

"My name is Juma." He offered me the reefer.

"No, thanks. Are you a Rastafarian?" I asked.

"No. I'm Obeah shaman."

"What's an Obeah shaman?"

"The conjurer of great magic spells and miracles," he said, tilting his head back to blow a puff of smoke into the air.

Full Moon reached up for the joint and said, "Sunchaser, this fellow great witch doctor just like Weeping Willow. We smoke his paper peace-pipe together—for good luck."

"Well, that's nice that you made a new friend, dudes, but we must get some sleep. We sail early."

"Yeah, mon, dey tell me during dis here reasoning dat you go to Haiti to kill de giant hell bats."

"That's right, but I'm afraid that I have just discovered from a very learned man that those bats do not exist. The bats are merely part of the Haitian vodou folklore."

"Dis not so, mon! I have seen dees bats. I study with vodou man in Haiti last year. He shared many secrets. I learn many tings from Daca. We also see de giant bats in de mountains. Dey come out of hole in de ground at night. Dey fly up from hell into de sky. Dey look for blood."

"Do you know exactly where this hell-hole is located, Juma?"

"Of course, mon. It be in de mountains south of Jeremie Town."

This guy must have been hallucinating—high as a kite—the night he thought he saw the bats, dude, but I guess it's worth taking a chance on him. "Juma, are you interested in working as our guide?"

"What you pay, mon?"

"We're low on money, but I'll pay you what we have left, minus what we need for our trip home—maybe $10 a day."

"Okay, mon. I needs to go to dos mountains to gather plants and de herbs for my potions and poisons. I come back tomorrow, mon. Den we go to Haiti."

"Great! Just be here before seven."

"Dat too early, mon!"

"We won't wait, dude. It's up to you."

Juma snuffed out the reefer and put the roach into his pocket. "Okay den. Juma be no leg short, mon."

"Let's get some sleep, dudes," I said as I led my spaced-out friends back to the cottage.

"Why Sunchaser not smoke paper peace-pipe with nice witch doctor man?" Full Moon asked.

"Someone has to keep a level head, dude. We are far from home and danger awaits us," I said, recalling Weeping Willow's warning that one of us would not be returning home to the Whatchacallit village. That night I had a dream about Katarina. In the dream she had regained her sight, and we could both fly. We soared effortlessly on the wind like two Florida swallow-tailed kites, riding the wind currents ever higher into the sky.

The next morning my crew and I waited impatiently on the boat. Juma had not arrived. I checked my watch, "Ten past seven. Where is that damn Rasta-man?"

Jumping Jack corrected me. "Juma say he is Obeah shaman, not Rasta-man. He not come. We leave now."

"Give him a few more minutes, dude. Maybe he blew out a flip-flop hustling over here to the dock." *You can't leave Juma behind, dude. You'll never find that bat cave without him.* At eight o'clock Juma came strolling up to the dock carrying a small sack. He was walking in slow motion with glazed eyes.

"Welcome, Sleeping Beauty. Glad you could join us!" I said with a sarcastic scowl.

"What da wybe is? I come early morning like I promise, mon. I come before you leave, so dat een nothin' den!" Juma said as he boarded the boat, still moving in slow motion.

"Jumping Jack, stow Juma's stuff below and let's cast off."

Juma seemed to know his way around a sailboat, and although he was a bit slow, he was actually helpful. Once we were out on the open ocean, I beckoned Juma over to the helm and took out my navigation charts. "Juma, show me the port that's nearest to the bat cave. My current course is set for Port au Prince."

"No Port au Prince, mon. We go here." He pointed to an area on the western tip of the Tiburon Peninsula. "We go to dah Jeremie Town." I calculated the new heading and adjusted our course farther to the west.

We covered the remaining 165 nautical miles in just over one day and arrived in Jeremie Town, Haiti at 3:00 am on Wednesday November 6th, 1974. We rested on the boat, waiting for daybreak.

Just before sunrise, a fisherman arrived and, for a small fee, he agreed to have his family watch over our sailboat in our absence. Once again I engaged the secret kill switch on the *Orion*, and then we all boarded the longboat and untied the painter line. Juma directed us up a long, narrow, winding creek that led us to a rural fishing and farming commune called Beaudrounin. The villagers knew Juma, and they greeted him warmly. He spoke to them in Creole and then turned to me and said, "Let's go, mon." He began following an elderly man.

"Where we going?" I asked.

"I ask to see my friend Daca. He da vodou shaman I tell you about. He conjures de bats from hell."

"Conjures them? You said the bats are real!"

"Oh, dey real all right! Dey just needs a bit o' conjuring. You see dem soon, mon!"

We followed the old man along a narrow path into the dense forest. The trail began to ascend up the foothills of a great mountain.

Halfway up, the trail leveled out and we began walking horizontally below the peak until we came to the mouth of a cave. On both sides of the entrance, effigies of humans carved from hardwood warned us away with menacing stares from wild eyes. Above the entrance, the carved faces of three beautiful goddesses smiled down at us.

"Those very nice totems," said Jumping Jack as he walked over to closely examine the fierce wooden figure standing to the left of the cave's entrance. An angry voice echoed out from the depths of the cavern, and our elderly guide with fear in his eyes scurried back down the trail.

Juma answered in Creole and then said with a smile, "Dat be Daca." A moment later, a very old man with wrinkled, gray-colored skin emerged from the entrance to the cave. He had many beaded necklaces hanging down over his bare chest, and he carried a long black walking stick. The knob was carved to resemble a bat's head. His vision seemed to be impaired by cataracts.

Juma spoke to him again in Creole; the only words that I recognized in his sentence were "Daca" and "shaman." The witch doctor's angry expression softened as he recognized Juma, but he did not smile or make any friendly gestures toward him. With a grunt, the witch doctor motioned with his staff for us to enter the cave. Inside, torchlights of burning oil dimly lit the cavern. As my eyes adjusted to the dark, I saw a room that reminded me very much of Weeping Willow's lodge back at the Indian village. We all sat cross-legged on a large mat woven from palm fronds, and Juma, the Obeah shaman, had a long conversation with Daca, the vodou shaman. At one point Daca gasped and angrily shook his head *no!*

"What's wrong?' I asked.

"Wybe, mon! Daca don't want to help us!"

"Why?"

"He say you tree conchy-joes ain't no shamans. He say you con-chy-joes will bitch-up and de giant bats take yo asses down de hell hole!"

"Here, Juma, show him these containers." I took out the container with the talisman hieroglyphic that Weeping Willow had given to me and motioned for my friends to present theirs to the old man as well. Daca looked at the items that we placed in front of him with a puzzled expression. Then he opened one, sniffed it, and paused as a look of recognition spread across his face. For the first time the old man smiled, a wide toothless smile, and grunted approvingly before speaking in Creole.

"Daca says dat a powerful shaman guided you to Daca's cave. Daca says dat wit dees powerful potions you might have de magic to summon dee giant hell bats and survive. Now Daca say he will help us!"

"Excellent, dude!"

"Daca say we be good in de morning. We make fire and camp outside tonight."

That night as we sat around the campfire, Daca joined us and, through Juma, he introduced us to the effigies that protected his cave from evil spirits. He stood in front of the figure to the left of the cave, which Jumping Jack had admired, and explained that this was Ogun, a wild man who roams the Haitian forests. Ogun was once a king but returned his crown and went to live in the woods. The fierce fellow on the right was Agwe, the god of the sea, who can be called upon to calm the ocean waves. Above the entrance, the faces of three goddesses are represented: Oya, the goddess of wind and fire; Yemaya, the goddess of the sea; and Obatala, the goddess of the heavens. The three nymphs gazed down seductively as Daca went back into the cave momentarily and then emerged with four long, black, intricately carved walking sticks similar to his own staff.

"Baton jeu-jeu," he said as he passed them out.

"Dees be vodou sticks," Juma said.

"It's a beautiful staff, but what is it made of? Surely not wood or stone—it seems to be made from ivory or bone," I said. The staffs were carved from a heavy, dense material. The top of the knob was large, and mine resembled a dragon's head. The shaft was tapered and narrowed until it was about the diameter of a dime at the end. *This knob could be used as a club or, turned this way; the point of the staff could be used as a spear!*

Juma examined his staff as he spoke with Daca and then said; "Daca say dees sticks carved from giant spider legs! Dat be ginned-up, mon! Dat not righteous!" Juma dropped his stick and stepped back from it.

"Dude, that's probably a vodou myth. Look at the size of these sticks—they can't be spider legs! Anyway, they can't harm us now, brother," I said as I swung mine like a club. Reluctantly, Juma picked up his walking stick and sniffed it. Jumping Jack was admiring the eagle head carving on the knob of his beautiful staff. Daca came over to him, turned his face to the sky, and chanted an incantation as he rubbed a string of crystal beads over the staff. One by one, he repeated that ritual for each of us and then, without another word, retired to his cave for the night.

Chapter 18

MASSIF DE LA HOTTE

The anticipation of our expedition in search of the giant Vandalic cave bats kept me restless throughout the night. *In Weeping Willow's vision, she said that one of us would not be returning home to our village. Which one of us?* I looked up from my bedroll and saw Jumping Jack and Full Moon standing silently side-by-side. They were gazing down at our dying campfire. It was 5:00 am. *They must be wondering the same thing.*

I got up and, without speaking a word, joined them. The warmth generated by the pit of glowing red embers was comforting and took the chill out of the early morning mountain air. I listened to the gentle popping and crackling sounds and found myself once again wondering who among us would be the one that would not return from our expedition into the Massif de la Hotte Cloud Forest.

Juma lay curled up in the fetal position, sleeping soundly on the far side of the fire pit, when suddenly a booming voice echoed out from the cave behind us. We turned toward the cave.

"Whatchacallit!" my friends gasped in unison.

"Holy crap!" was my response as I nearly backed up into the pit of red-hot embers. Daca was standing at the entrance to the cave with his arms raised toward the sky, holding a machete in one hand

and the body of a bloody, decapitated chicken in the other. On his head was a headdress with two long, corkscrew-shaped horns, one horn protruded out from each of his temples. Black horizontal lines were painted below his eyes and extended down each side of his wrinkled, gray face, ending at the tip of his chin. The vodou shaman began chanting loudly in Creole with a singsong cadence to his voice.

"What de wybe is?" Juma said and rolled to his other side then covered his ears. "Too damn early, mon!" Daca stopped chanting and pointed the machete at Juma. Then he called out a command that grabbed Juma's attention. Juma reluctantly sat up and began rubbing his eyes and whining, "Dis early? Dis not righteous, mon!"

"What's happening, Juma?" I asked him.

"Daca want ta put de spell on us."

"The spell? That don't sound good, dude! What kind of spell?"

"Daca performin' de ritual for de protection." Reluctantly Juma picked up his walking stick and slowly came over to join us. Then Daca stood before me and began chanting an incantation as he dripped chicken blood over my hands and my walking staff. Suddenly he threw the machete into the ground, where it stuck into the earth less than an inch from my bare feet. With wild eyes, the ancient vodouist bent toward me and placed the palm of his open hand near my face. I could see a pile of white dust on his palm.

"Aethyr! Cymble! Fait accompli!" Daca chanted and then blew the white powder up my nose and into my eyes. The dust smelled fragrant, like a bouquet of flowers, but blinded me for a moment. Then the powder seemed to dissolve in my eyes, and I felt refreshed. Daca went down the line, repeating the ritual for each of my friends. To everyone's relief, the ritual ended when Daca threw the chicken carcass onto the embers. The dripping chicken blood sizzled, and then the feathers burst into flames. Daca watched the bird flare up like a torch and then pointed at the containers given to us by Weeping Willow. He spoke Creole.

"Daca say for you to drink de potions now." We all drank our potions that Weeping Willow had given us, and then shared the fourth one that had the wolves depicted on the container. Suddenly, without a word, Daca abruptly turned and went back inside his cave, not to be seen again.

"Is that it? Are we free to go?" I asked Juma.

"Yeah, mon. Daca done de jumbey hurt. He won' be back. Now we go ta de mango tree and eat."

Juma led us away from the cave to a small, cultivated orchard. After eating a breakfast consisting of delicious mangos and bananas, we began hiking higher into the mountains. By noon we were 7,000 feet above the sea and standing just below the highest peak. Through an opening in the dense foliage of the cloud forest, we could see the vast, blue sea stretching out to the horizon far below. Surrounded by lush ferns, we walked through wispy patches of cool mist that hovered just above the ground.

"This is the cloud forest that Professor Derbyshire described to me. It *is* a beautiful place!" I exclaimed as I marveled at the variety of lush tropical plants and the abundance of birds flitting to and fro, squawking in protest as we walked past, disrupting their isolated habitat. Suddenly I felt something grab my walking stick and pull it to my left.

"What the hell is this?" I said when I realized that no vine or any other obstruction had caused the stick to pull left. Then I noticed that the walking sticks of the others were all pointing to the left as well. The long black staffs vibrated in our hands as they pointed toward a hidden crevasse. We had nearly walked right past the chasm, which was concealed by a dense cover of ferns and vines.

"Daca's jumbey sticks come alive!" With a gasp, Juma pulled his staff back but then dropped it. It fell to the ground and then rotated like the needle on a compass so that the narrow end once again pointed toward the crevasse. Juma stood with his hands raised up to his shoulders, staring wide-eyed at the walking stick and said, "What de spider sticks do, mon?"

"Sticks point the way!" Jumping Jack said.

"De sticks be true, mon! I remember now! Dat where de bat cave be. Dey fly out of dere in de night. Dat be de place, all right!"

"Let's take a look," I said and went to the mouth of the long, wide crevasse and peered down.

"It's an opening into a large cave below. It's pitch black down there. The crack goes straight down," I said.

"Yeah, mon, straight down to hell. But der be nahtin' ta see now. We wait till de darkness come. Den de bats fly out."

Confused, I set my backpack on the ground and removed the map that Weeping Willow had given to me. "Juma, Weeping Willow, the Whatchacallit witch woman, gave me this map. This cannot be the cave that is shown on her map. This is the wrong location."

"Dis de cave, mon. Dis where I saw de bats before."

I turned the map 90 degrees. "But look, the cave on the map is somewhere to our south. Maybe there is another entrance to this bat cave…a more accessible entrance."

"Let me see dat map, mon." Juma knelt beside me. "Dat cave over on de udder side of de mountain."

"You're right, dude! We can circle around and be on the other side before dark. Let's go." I said and slung my backpack over my shoulder.

It was after five o'clock when we saw the mouth of the large cave that was depicted on our map. We were at a slightly lower altitude and on the opposite side of the mountain from the crevasse that Juma claimed was where the giant Vandalic bats exited at night. As we approached the cave, the walking sticks once again began vibrating and pointing toward the entrance.

"The sticks are coming to life again! This must be another entrance to the same cave!" I said.

We entered the mouth of the cave and peered into the darkness.

"I've got a flashlight, but the batteries are very low," I said as I took it from my backpack.

"We make torches and save flashlight for later," Jumping Jack said as he and Full Moon walked out of the mouth of the cave and into the nearby foliage. After a while they returned with two tree limbs. Each had a wad of dry moss bound by vines to the end of the branches. The moss was covered with a tacky, dark tree sap.

"Sunchaser, give me the fire sticks," Jumping Jack said. I took a box of wooden matchsticks from my backpack, and the Indian lit up a torch.

"We go now. Torches not last long time," Jumping Jack said and began walking into the cave. We all followed. The air inside the cave was cool and damp, with a musty odor. As we went deeper into the grotto, the wide cavern began to narrow into tunnels, which had probably been formed by flowing water. Twice we came to bifurcations in the subterranean passages but did not have to guess which way to go. The vibrating walking sticks pointed the way forward. At one point the tunnel became so low-ceilinged that we had to "duck walk" forward.

"Dis place be ginned up. I can't breathe, mon!" Juma said as he became overtaken by claustrophobia and refused to continue.

"Dude, you'll be left alone in the dark. You won't find your way out of here," I said and prodded him forward with my staff. We squeezed our way through the tunnel, and suddenly the narrow passage opened up into a huge cavern. We stood under the dome of rock, admiring the many flat-topped stalagmites rising up from the floor. Above us, pointy, icicle-shaped stalactites hung down from the high ceiling. The light of Jumping Jack's torch was casting dancing shadows throughout the cavern, giving the place an eerie air. The musty smell had now turned to a pungent, acrid odor.

"This place look pretty but smell like animal crap," Full Moon said. High above, in the center of the cave's ceiling, a long but narrow beam of dim sunlight filtered down though the cloud forest above.

"That is the crevasse that we found—the place that Juma said the bats exit. That means that the Vandalic bats must be in here somewhere," I said, just as the torch began to flicker and go dim.

"Hey, hey, hey," Jumping Jack said as he hurriedly touched the dying flame to Full Moon's torch. It caught fire just before Jumping Jack's went out. The new torch was brighter, and now we could see the rock ceiling. Hundreds of dark, shadowy bodies were hanging upside down from the rocks above us. "Hoka hey!" Startled by the sight, Full Moon shouted and thrust his torch higher.

"Oh my gosh! Professor Derbyshire was wrong! The giant bats *do* exist!" I gasped as I squatted down low to the ground. Everyone besides Full Moon followed my lead, and we covered our heads with our arms in fear that one of the monsters might swoop down at us. I tried to raise my walking stick in a defensive position by pointing it toward the ceiling, but the staff kept pulling my arm toward the cave wall on our left.

"De stick pulling me dat way. It telling me to get de hell outta here, mon," Juma said as he stood up and began walking in a crouch toward the left side of the cave.

"I gotta get a look at those bats!" I said and opened my backpack, took out the flashlight, and directed the beam at the bats above. "They're huge—bigger than us!" Hundreds of beady, silver eyes reflected the beam of light. Glowing like stars above us, they began to move about. The hanging bodies, which were larger than those of human beings, were becoming agitated and walking upside-down across the rock ceiling.

"They're trying to get out of the light beam," I said. Suddenly, from the left, a deafeningly loud hissing sound reverberated throughout the chamber. I directed my light in that direction and illuminated Juma. His eyes were wide with fear as he crouched low to the ground. His staff was pointing upward and vibrating violently. At the periphery of my light beam, and just above Juma, a movement caught my attention, so I elevated the beam.

"*Aggghhhh!*" All at once, everyone except Juma screamed in terror. The hairy face of an eight-eyed monster was hovering just above Juma and gazing down at him. The creature seemed to be levitating and floating in midair. Juma's wide eyes stared into my light beam apparently unaware of the monster hanging less than two feet above his head. With a quick twitch, the hideous face jerked toward me. Two rows of eyes reflected my light. Now I could clearly see two rows of four eyes glistening from atop a large, round, brown, and hairy head. Just below the rows of eight eyes and forward of its ugly mouth, two long fangs dripping venom protruded from a hairy set of chelicerae. Now I could see that the creature was dangling from a thick thread of silk that was attached to the ceiling.

"It's a giant spider!" I screamed. The enormous spider returned its attention to Juma and reared its body back, exposing the two long, curved fangs. For the first time, Juma looked up just as the spider raised its two front legs, preparing to strike.

"*Aggghhhh!*" Juma's screams were drowned out when the monster rubbed its rear legs together, once again a loud, deafening hissing sound reverberated throughout the cavern. The spider's stridulating warning-call terrified us but seemed to excite the giant Vandalic bats above. They began chirping and squeaking loudly like a pack of rabid rats.

The horrible sounds only added to our terror. We were all frozen with fear and mesmerized by the horror show as the spider struck down upon Juma with lightning speed. We saw its fangs pierce Juma's back, one fang through each of his scapulas. He let out a muted grunt, and then the spider brought its front legs down hard upon Juma's limp body, and the hideous mouth snatched Juma by his head. Jumping Jack regained his composure and stepped forward, holding his staff. Assuming the position of a javelin thrower, he took aim. But just before he could release his makeshift spear, the spider, with Juma's body in its clutches, began racing up its silk thread.

"Hoka hey!" Jumping Jack and Full Moon both threw their staffs, narrowly missing the fleeing spider as it disappeared with Juma into a dark recess above us. Full Moon and Jumping Jack dropped to one knee and began chanting a prayer for Juma. When they had finished, they stood up and retrieved their staffs. Since the spider had left, the mysterious sticks were no longer vibrating.

"Look, the sun has set." I pointed to the crevasse above that had become dark.

"Now bats might go away…they fly out into night sky. How we get up there to get one?" asked Jumping Jack. But just as he finished his question, bats began dropping off the ceiling and flying in a circle around the huge cavern. The whoosh of giant wings stirred the air as some began exiting through the crevasse.

"We gotta get one now! They are afraid of our lights. Snuff the torch!" I yelled and turned off my flashlight. Now it was pitch black. The loud thumping sound of the bat wings grew closer and surrounded us. We stood close together, holding the heavy staffs.

Whump! Whump! Whump! "Hoka hey! Spread apart so that we can swing the sticks!" Jumping Jack yelled as a bat passed close to our heads. Most of the bats had exited the cave, but now, without the fire and flashlight beam to protect us; the stragglers began to mount an attack.

"I can't see them!" I yelled out just before hearing a dull but loud thud. The sound was like someone striking a hollow log.

"I got one!" Full Moon said. I began swinging my heavy club around blindly over my head and then felt it connect with another bat. *Thump!* "Me too!" After several minutes my arms were becoming weary, and I squatted down and retrieved the flashlight. When I turned the light to the ceiling, we could see that all but two of the bats had gone out from the cave. The two remaining bats swooped down at us but then were repelled by the light beam and flew out through the crevasse.

"They are gone." I said and then directed the light to the ground. A giant Vandalic bat lay dead at Full Moon's feet. Besides the giant spider it was the ugliest creature I had ever seen. Its smooth, black, hairless body was over six feet long, and it had the snout of a dog, complete with rows of razor-sharp teeth. Protruding from the upper mandible were two long, hollow fangs designed for sucking blood.

"We must hurry. The batteries are dying," I said as I tapped the flashlight with my palm. The Indians used their walking sticks and my backpack to make a pony drag to haul the bat's carcass out of the cave, and we were just about to leave when a loud squeal came out from the darkness. I turned the light toward the sound and saw a giant bat crawling rapidly along the ground, coming at us with a snarling snout, its long fangs exposed. One wing was broken and dragging limply at its side.

"Hoka hey!" Jumping Jack ran forward to meet the beast and attacked the injured bat by clubbing it over the head with Daca's heavy spider-leg walking staff. With a final loud squeal, the bat collapsed to the ground, quivered, and died.

"Good! Let's go!" I said as I directed the dim light into the exit tunnel.

Chapter 19

RETURN TO KEY WEST

With the failing flashlight in hand, I led the way into the exit tunnel. Jumping Jack and Full Moon followed me, pulling the dead Vandalic bat strapped to the pony drag behind them. Suddenly the batteries of my flashlight died.

"Keep moving, dudes," I said as we stumbled forward, bouncing along the rock walls in the pitch-black darkness. *I hope we did not make a wrong turn. We could be going deeper into this labyrinth.*

Suddenly, to my great relief, I saw illumination up ahead. "Look! Light at the end of this tunnel!"

"Hey, hey, hey, hey!" the Indians chanted with joy. We exited the cave and stood gazing up at the night sky, sucking in the cool, fresh air of the cloud forest. "That was not fun, dudes!" I said and flopped down on the soft, green moss.

"We no should leave Juma with the giant devil spider," Jumping Jack said.

"We had no choice. The monster took him out of our reach. Besides, the spider's venom killed him instantly."

"That spider heap uglier than this demon bat," Full Moon said and then kicked the dead beast lying at his feet.

"Weeping Willow say she only need the wings." Jumping Jack said. With disgust, the Indians cut the huge wings off the monstrous bat and then heaved the body into the underbrush and covered its hideous carcass with foliage.

"Let's get the hell out of here!" I said as we all looked up at the sky, wondering where all the giant bats had gone in search of prey.

That night shortly after midnight, we boarded the *Orion*, and our voyage home began beneath a moonless sky.

As I steered the boat, and Jumping Jack helped set the sails, Full Moon looked back at the towering mountains. "Look!" he yelled and pointed to a black, craggy precipice silhouetted against the starry night sky. Dozens of the giant Vandalic bats were flying in a circular pattern above the summit of the cloud forest mountain. Suddenly several bats peeled off from their flying formation and started descending fast and moving in our direction.

"The demons come for us!" Jumping Jack called out before grabbing the pony drag to untie the spider-leg walking sticks from the straps of my backpack. "Here!" He tossed one staff to Full Moon, and they both took up defensive positions in the stern. We watched the black silhouettes of the monsters draw closer. Flying fast with a spastic, jerky motion, they continued to descend. As I ducked below deck to retrieve my spear gun, again I remembered Weeping Willow's warning, *One of you will not be returning!*

"This is it, dudes," I said and placed the pistol grip of the gun to my chest and then pulled down the three elastic bands to engage the spear. We could hear rat-like squeals as the excited, bloodthirsty beasts began dive-bombing the boat and using echolocation to nimbly avoid the boat's rigging.

A huge bat swooped down to attack Full Moon from behind. "Hoka hey!" Jumping Jack screamed, leaping forward to bash the dive-bomber with his heavy staff. After a loud thud and a high pitched squeal, the monster dipped down to skim the surface of the water before rising back up several feet in an attempt to fly off, but with a broken wing it went spiraling back down and crashed with a splash into the ocean, where it floundered around at the surface.

From the stern, Full Moon swung his staff hard and made contact, sending another bat flopping and convulsing across the deck of *Orion*, where it came to rest lying belly-up near the bow. With its fangs bared and its huge wings flapping frantically, the bat began to right itself until both Indians ran forward and rained down blows with the heavy staffs. The pummeling sent the devil beast back to hell. With the Indians' attention directed at the dead creature, another Vandalic bat swooped down and grabbed Jumping Jack from behind. The huge bat embedded its long, sharp talons into Jumping Jack's shoulders and, with several powerful thrusts of its massive wings, it lifted him off the deck and began to ascend with him, flying along our portside beam.

"No! Jumping Jack!" Full Moon screamed out in horror. A look of resignation crossed Jumping Jack's face as he passed by us, dangling limply beneath the huge beast. I had no time to take carful aim, but I fired my spear gun from the hip just as the bat passed the helm.

Skrrreeek! The monster let out a shrill, ear-piecing shriek and released Jumping Jack, who dropped feet-first into the ocean behind the boat. My spear gun was jerked from my hands as the impaled bat tried to fly away. "Hoka hey!" Full Moon said and then dove overboard and began swimming to rescue Jumping Jack. I tossed a life ring toward them and then turned the boat into the wind to stop our forward progress. My spear had gone straight through one of the bat's wings, and it was flapping violently 15 feet above my head as it tried to escape, but the cord connecting the spear to my gun was fouled in the standing rigging.

Now the tethered beast was flying in short circles above me like a remote-controlled monster. Unable to escape, the huge beast suddenly went from flight mode to fight mode and tucked its wings as it dove down at me. I barely had time to release the ship's wheel and raise my arms to fend off the bat, which knocked me to the deck and landed on top of me. An incredibly long tongue flicked out from the beast's mouth and tasted the skin covering my carotid artery on the right side of my neck. Then I felt a searing hot pain in my abdomen as the creature sank the long, sharp talons on its hind legs into my belly and thrust its head down toward me, going for my throat with two needle-sharp vampire fangs.

I grabbed a handful of the loose, hairless black skin on both sides of the bat's neck to fend off its grotesque head. The snarling, dog-like snout filled with razor-sharp teeth and vampire fangs was only a foot away from my neck when my arms began to fatigue and shake under the weight of the beast. The fangs slowly inched closer toward my neck.

It's me! I'm the one who will not be returning! Resignation to my inevitable demise began to overcome me, and I closed my eyes so that I would not have to watch the hideous creature suck my blood. *Carlos, my friend, I will soon join you in the Meadow of Tranquility!* Suddenly the image of Katarina sitting alone, blind and helpless on the terrace the night that I visited her in Key Biscayne filled my mind. *Kat needs me! I must survive!*

"Hoka hey!" I screamed as a rush of adrenaline surged through my body. Startled by my outburst, the bat pulled its ugly head backward, relieving the downward pressure for an instant. But then it thrust its jaws toward me again. This time instead of holding it off, I pulled the bat down, yanking it hard toward me but directing its head off to my left as I rolled to my side. With a thud, the bat's head slammed into the teak deck, stunning the creature momentarily, which allowed me to push it away and roll onto my stomach.

I felt the flesh of my abdomen being ripped open by the talons as I separated myself from the bat. The spear that had gone clean through the webbing of the bat's wing was dangling in front of my face, suspended by the cord attached to the spear gun that was fouled up in the standing rigging. I grabbed the spear.

"Hoka hey! See you in hell!" I yelled and plunged the spear into the Vandalic bat's throat.

"*Skrrreeek!*" Giant bat wings pummeled me as they flapped frenetically; the beast's lifeblood poured out, pooling thick, sticky, and black on the deck around me. With a last powerful flap of its left wing, the bony thumb protruding from mid-wing bashed me on my right temple, and everything went black. As I began to regain consciousness, I thought I was asleep. I was dreaming of swimming on the reef off of Inagua Island. Water dripping on my face revived me and I awoke to familiar voices.

"Jumping Jack, is Sunchaser dead?"

I opened my eyes and saw Jumping Jack and Full Moon standing over me. The saltwater dripping from their long hair stung my eyes, and my abdomen felt like it was on fire.

"It's my stomach, dudes. That thing tore me up. Are the monsters gone?"

"You kill last bat, Sunchaser," Jumping Jack said as they pulled the spear out of the bat's throat and tossed its body overboard.

"We get away from here now, then I clean and bandage both of you!" Full Moon said as he nervously watched dozens of Vandalic bats continue to circle the Massif de la Hotte Mountain peaks in the distance.

FRIDAY, NOVEMBER 8TH, 1974

After three days of sailing nonstop, we entered Key West Bight. It was 7:00 pm. Most of the sunset worshippers had abandoned Mallory Square to investigate the local watering holes.

"Jumping Jack need cheeseburger and bitter root water," Jumping Jack said as he tied a spring line to the dock cleat.

"I hear you, bro!" I said and cut the engine. Jumping Jack's puncture wounds on the back of his shoulders were healing nicely, but a deep gash on his left pinky finger looked infected, and the slashes across my abdomen were still tender and oozing a clear liquid.

"Let's pick up some bandages and ointment at Rite-Aid and then hit Sloppy Joes," I said.

We made a brief stop at Rite-Aid for the first aid supplies.

"Jumping Jack, you need to keep that finger dry." I was about to tell him to buy a finger cot to protect the wound on his pinky from the saltwater, but then thought I might have a little fun at my friend's expense.

"How I sail and keep finger dry?" he asked.

"You need to put a finger cot over it, dude. Ask the girl at the counter for a rubber, but tell her it must only be this big and show her your pinky finger so she will know what size to give you," I said.

"Okay, Sunchaser." Jumping Jack took his place in a long checkout line. I positioned myself near the register pretending to look at the candy display as Jumping Jack stepped up to the counter.

"May I help you, sir?" the young, attractive girl working the register asked.

"Jumping Jack need a rubber," he said in his usual loud voice. The girl blushed, and everyone in the checkout line turned his or her attention to Jumping Jack.

The red-faced young woman turned her back to locate to the condoms and then asked over her shoulder, "What brand do you want?"

"No matter to me. Just give me this size rubber." Jumping Jack held out his pinky as the girl turned to see. Several people in line burst into laughter as Jumping Jack looked at them with a dumbfounded expression.

"What funny?" he asked the laughing, middle-aged man in line directly behind him.

The young girl giggled and began examining the boxes of condoms behind the counter. "Sir, I'm no expert but they don't seem to come in sizes. I think that one size fits all." Now everyone was laughing including me as Jumping Jack and Full Moon stood looking at each other with expressions of bewilderment. Finally I stepped forward to rescue my poor friend.

"Miss, I think he is trying to buy a finger cot for that wound on his pinky finger."

"Oh! Thank goodness. I felt so bad for him. Look on aisle five," she said as I pulled Jumping Jack out of the line.

Perplexed, Jumping Jack asked me, "Why the people laugh at me?"

"Just a little innocent misunderstanding, I guess." The Indians looked at me with blank faces, and again I could not help but burst into laughter.

"The Wasichu people very crazy people," Jumping Jack said to Full Moon.

"I think Sunchaser play Wasichu joke on Jumping Jack," said Full Moon as the pair eyed me suspiciously.

Still chuckling after paying for the finger cots I said, "Come on, dudes. Let's get some grub."

Outside, Full Moon changed our dressings, and then we went to eat dinner at Sloppy Joe's as a rock band covering the Tumbling Stones played songs.

"That is Nick Dagger music. Maybe they play Jumping Jack's song tonight," Jumping Jack said as he toasted the group with his beer mug. During a break I requested that the band play "Jumping Jack Flash," and after the band played the song, to Jumping Jack's great enjoyment, we finished the pitcher of Miller Lite and went down the street to Captain Tony's Bar. I stopped just outside the door and looked up at the giant goliath grouper head mounted on the wall above the door.

"Let's see who can flip a nickel into that fish's mouth. You have to flip it with your thumb like this." I demonstrated by flipping the coin head-high and then catching it. "Here you go first," I said and handed the nickel to Full Moon.

"Oh, that was close!" I said as I caught the nickel after it had bounced off the fish's upper lip and fallen back to earth. Then I flipped it toward the gaping mouth. Mine hit the lower lip but didn't go into the fish's mouth.

"Your turn, Chief," I said to Jumping Jack. His flip went right down the grouper's gullet.

"That too easy!" Jumping Jack said with a smirk and puffed out his chest.

"You win, Chief! That means you have to buy us a round of beer!"

"That good trick, Sunchaser! Now Jumping Jack pay for bitterroot water, ha- ha!" said Full Moon. Then he turned to face Jumping Jack and smacked him hard on the shoulder. "Whatchacallit!" Full Moon yelled, and then we all went inside for a beer.

"Hey, Indian dude, Mr. Moon!" a bartender called out to Full Moon. "Last week some chick left a letter for you. She said to give it to you if you ever came back to the bar." The guy took an envelope from beside the cash register and gave it to Full Moon.

"Huh, a letter for me?" Full Moon said as he opened it.

"What is that?" I asked.

"This letter from Tawny girl. Cowgirl leave letter for me," Full Moon said as he struggled to read the note. In addition to the letter I saw him holding a ticket.

"Is that a ticket?"

"Full Moon not know. What is a ticket?"

"Let's see." I looked at the ticket and then read the letter for him. "This is a plane ticket to Dallas, Texas. Tawny wants you to visit her at her father's ranch."

"Ranch?" Full Moon said.

"Wow! Get a load of this! Tawny's last name is Pickings! She is the daughter of the oil tycoon Bone Pickings. Hey, dude, that means Tawny is a filthy rich cowgirl!"

"What is rich? Is rich bad? Full Moon no care. Full Moon no care if Tawny girl is filthy. Full Moon will marry Tawny girl."

"You have a ticket to ride in those jets that you Indians call silver birds. Are you really gonna fly to Texas, dude?"

"Yes. Full Moon fly in silver bird to find Tawny girl."

"Awesome, dude! We'll get you on a bus up to Marathon airport first thing in the morning."

SATURDAY, NOVEMBER 9TH, 1974

After saying our farewells to Full Moon and putting him on a north-bound bus to the Marathon Airport, Jumping Jack and I set sail on the final leg of our journey home to the Big Cypress Preserve and the Whatchacallit Village.

"Jumping Jack, Weeping Willow was right when she said that one of us would not be returning home. But I thought the old witch woman meant that one of us would be killed, dude!"

That evening we navigated the shallows leading to the banks of the Whatchacallit Village and anchored just off shore. We were both excited and eager to greet our loved ones.

"They must not have spotted our sail," I said when we realized that no one had come down to the shore to greet us.

"I get the bat wings and we go to village to find the people. Jumping Jack want to see Little Hooters."

Chapter 20

THE BATWING MASK

MONDAY, NOVEMBER 11TH, 1974

The warm glow of dying campfires greeted us as we entered the Whatchacallit Village. It was a ghost town; the people had turned in for the night.

"Hoka hey! Who goes there?" The command, which was spoken in the Whatchacallit tongue, came from a warrior named White Cloud. He was standing guard duty and stepped out from the shadows beside the main lodge wielding a long spear.

"It is Chief Jumping Jack and Sunchaser," Jumping Jack responded.

"Hey hey ho, hey! Welcome home, Chief Jumping Jack!"

"Hey ho! Jumping Jack go home now. White Cloud help Sunchaser take bat wings to Weeping Willow's lodge. Then Sunchaser sleep. I see Sunchaser in morning." White Cloud and I each carried a bat wing to Weeping Willow's lodge and placed them outside her door. Then White Cloud returned to his post, and I placed my bedroll under a tree to settle in for the night. I was exhausted and was almost asleep when I heard Weeping Willow's voice call to me.

"Sunchaser, come in." I went to the doorway, picked up the bat wings, and entered the lodge. Weeping Willow walked slowly over to me, gazing intently at the huge black wings. She stroked the smooth, webbed skin with her fingertips, then touched the long, sharp, bony fingers protruding from the end of the wing and gasped.

"The wings are the same as in my vision—they are beautiful wings!"

"I guess beauty *is* in the eye of the beholder. Those Vandalic bats are the ugliest creatures I have ever seen—well, maybe with the exception of the giant hairy cave spider."

"Cave spider?" She looked up from the wings with a quizzical look on her face.

"Yes, a spider the size of a pony! It killed our friend Juma."

"That was no spider. That was *him*, the devil. The devil can take many forms, and the entity that I could not identify in my vision was the devil! So you say he took the form of a spider?"

"Yeah, a huge one! It killed Juma," I said.

"The devil did not kill your friend Juma, the Obean shaman."

"How do you know about Juma?"

"Both shamans were revealed to me in my vision. Juma, the young one, and Daca, the old vodou shaman."

"Juma *was* killed. I witnessed it happen from a mere ten feet away."

"No! Juma's soul was taken. The devil now possesses Juma's soul. Now Juma's zombie body will walk the earth casting evil spells and doing evil black magic; he is a servant of the devil beast." Weeping Willow returned her attention to the wings. She was clearly fascinated by the huge, black, silky-smooth bat wings. "The Vandalic bats are magnificently efficient killing machines. You did well to survive your encounter with them, Sunchaser."

"I know. They nearly killed both Jumping Jack and me. One nearly gutted me like a fish—look." I opened my shirt to show her my wounds. The bandage was wet from the oozing, open slashes."

"I must treat that! Quick, Sunchaser, come here!" She guided me to a table. "Lie down. Even a scratch from the filthy talons of a Vandalic bat can lead to a fatal infection." Weeping Willow took three powders and mixed them together, and then added water to make a poultice. She applied the paste over my wounds and then bandaged my abdomen.

"Weeping Willow, you must warn Jumping Jack about infection. A bat tore up his shoulders and hand," I said as I sat upright.

"Little Hooters will know how to treat his wounds. He will be fine. Now I must get to work on the bat wings immediately before they spoil. Sunchaser, you can sleep in Horny Owl's room. He is studying medicine at Night Owl's lodge all night."

"Thanks, Weeping Willow. Goodnight."

The next morning I came out of Horny Owl's bedroom and found Weeping Willow admiring a new mask that she had made from the bat wings.

"Is that another mask for Katarina? Last time a mask was made for her I thought it was a bra." I chuckled.

"What is bra?"

"Never mind. Weeping Willow, do you expect Kat to put that dead bat skin on her face? That's gross, dude...I mean ma'am!"

"This is more than a mask. This mask will give Katarina the sight of a bat. She will see again, but in a very different way."

"What are those cups for?" I touched the mask where the skin had been sewn into the shape of a cup.

"The flat patches will cover her eyes and those cups are ear covers. The string ties in the back like this." Weeping Willow put the mask on so that I could see how it fit. The batwing mask was a monstrosity.

"That looks hideous! The ocelot mask is much nicer."

"This mask is not just for esthetics, it is functional—very beneficial." She took it off and glared at me. Her eyes never seemed to be looking in the same direction. Her left eye was directed at my face, but the other was looking down and to the right toward scraps of bat flesh littering the floor.

"Sorry, don't mean to be so negative, but that bat skin is not just ugly—it even stinks!"

"You leave the work of the witch woman to me, Sunchaser. The bat mask is not yet finished. It will have a pleasing aroma when it's done." Her yellow eye stared out from the folds of wrinkled, leathery flesh as she pointed a long crooked finger at me and smiled, a cynical smile that exposed her jagged, broken, yellow teeth. She seemed to be contemplating what she was about to say next. "Sunchaser, did you know that while you were away Running Deer asked to look upon Katarina!"

"What?"

"That's right, and Katarina accepted! The council of elders has approved their courtship!"

"I don't believe you! You're just angry that I was critical of that ugly mask, right?" She turned away and went to her worktable to finish the bat mask. "Where is Katarina?"

Without looking up she said, "I have told you too much. You should go now, Sunchaser."

I slammed the door and went to search for Katarina. I went to the farming village and the fishing village but no one knew where Katarina was. Four hours later, on the path leading back to the main lodge, I saw Running Deer coming toward me.

Running Deer waved to me and called out, "Sunchaser, I've been looking for you. I need to tell you something very important!"

You're a ratfink, Running Deer! Anger turned my face red as I jogged forward to meet him.

"Is it true? Did you ask permission from the elders to look upon Katarina?"

"That what I come to tell Sunchaser...I sorry. It just happened... we fall in love."

"Weeping Willow already told me, you back-stabbing bastard!" I took off my shirt and tossed it aside.

"I no want to fight you," Running Deer said and raised his hands with palms turned out in resignation.

"I'm gonna kick your sneaky ass either way!" I threw a left hook; Running Deer ducked and was forced to defend himself.

"Okay, Sunchaser!" he said and raised his fists. Running Deer was the best marksman and the fastest runner among all the warriors, but Jumping Jack and I were superior to all the others when it came to hand-to-hand combat. With a few classic disco moves I was on top of Running Deer with both of my hands around his neck, choking him. His face turned red and was changing to blue as he lost consciousness. In my rage, I did not realize that I was killing my friend. Suddenly a painful, high-pitched clicking sound pierced my left ear, causing me to release Running Deer and cover my ears with my hands.

"Ahhhggg!" I rolled to my side and looked to my left. Standing ten yards away, Katarina was bent forward at the waist with her arms extended out to her side like the wings of an airplane. She was wearing the bat skin mask and had a short, round reed in her mouth. The high-pitched sounds were coming from the reed. The sound stopped, and Katarina took the reed from her mouth.

"Get off of him, Eddie!" Katarina said as if she could see us.

I sat upright and said, "I went away and risked my life to help you, Kat, and you repay me by falling for my friend Running Deer?"

"It just happened, Eddie. I don't know how...don't know why. I spent every day with Running Deer. He taught me many things about nature and the forest."

"Oh, I bet *you* taught *him* a thing or two, babe!"

"No, it's not like that, Eddie. He has not touched me...well, one kiss was all." Running Deer began coughing and gasping for air. Katarina put the reed in her mouth, and the clicking sounds began again, only this time they were barely audible. She ran to Running Deer and helped him sit up. *How did she do that? She must have followed the sound of his coughing.*

"Running Deer, are you okay?" she said as she touched his face.

"He'll be fine, Kat! I'm the one who's hurting. You two can't be serious, Kat. You have nothing in common with him."

"I'm different now, Eddie, not the angry, vengeful girl you knew in Miami. My hatred of Rafael Cato and the Communist bastards who killed my grandfather and stole my family's land was consuming me. My lust for vengeance was robbing me of my soul. Then when I lost my eyes, I completely lost my will to live. I wanted to die until you brought me here; now, for the first time in my life, I feel happy to be alive. Running Deer taught me to appreciate the beauty that surrounds us…the beauty of life! Ironic isn't it? Only after losing my eyes and my eyesight was I able to see the wonders of the world that had always surrounded me. Do you know I have learned how to communicate with the wild animals?"

"Yeah, the sixth sense—big deal! I could have taught you that."

"When I was with Running Deer I was no longer helpless. He made me want to live again."

"Great, so he makes you want to live, and when you are with me you want to jump overboard and die. I get it, Kat, and it's all my fault for your uncle's death."

"No, nothing was your fault. You have always been kind and understanding…"

"Wow, I'm the kind and understanding loser again! Just my usual fate…the Ancients must be getting a kick out of this little drama."

"Believe me, I have struggled with my emotions. I still have feelings and desires for you, Eddie, but I realized that I never want to leave this place, this village. I have found my home here…for the first time in my life I have a place where I'm happy and where I belong. I know you, Eddie. You will never put down roots. You are Sunchaser Eddie Ocean. They say you have saltwater running through your veins, and you would never be happy without the ocean breeze riffling through your golden locks."

Running Deer interrupted her, "Katarina, what happened?" Running Deer sat upright with a dazed expression.

"I kicked your ass, you back-stabbing bastard."

"Oh yeah, me remember—Sunchaser discoed Running Deer's ass real good."

Katarina hugged Running Deer and then said, "Eddie, Running Deer did not want to fall in love with me. He tried to avoid me when we began having feelings for one another. He said that he could not look upon me because I was Sunchaser's woman, and then he went away from the village to live in the forest. But I pursued *him*. I almost died out there stumbling around in the wilderness; I was lost in the forest until the farmers beat on hollow logs to call Running Deer home. The farmers told Running Deer that I was missing, and he tracked me down and saved me. Not only was I dying of thirst when he found me, but Running Deer told me that a panther had been stalking me. That was the day when we kissed, and it was then that we both knew our destiny was to be together."

"Sorry, Sunchaser. That is not good destiny for you," Running Deer said as Katarina helped him stand.

"Just shut up, dude! I'll leave you two lovebirds alone. Ciao!" I said with anger and then left to return to my sailboat.

"Wait, Eddie—I haven't told you about Weeping Willow's miracle!" Katarina called out to me, but I ignored her and walked away. Katarina put the reed in her mouth and made the clicking sounds. Her head continued to turn in my direction as if she were watching me leave.

"What's that? Is that new mask?" I heard Running Deer ask her before I was out of earshot.

The next morning I was sitting on deck eating grits when I saw Running Deer and Katarina racing fast, side-by-side through the forest. She was wearing the bat skin mask and had the hollow reed in her mouth. I stood up, very concerned and called out to them, "Hey! She's gonna kill herself!" My fear was that Kat would run full-speed face-first into a tree. They heard my call and suddenly turned and came running toward me, laughing.

"Have you both gone batty? Excuse the pun," I said as they caught their breath at the shore near my boat.

"Sunchaser, Katarina can see now. She see better than Running Deer now!" Running Deer was very happy; he was downright giddy.

"Sure...she sees better than you without eyeballs."

"That's not a very kind thing to say," Kat said.

"Sorry, been pretty grumpy lately, dudette!"

Kat put the reed in her mouth made some clicking sounds and then took the reed out before saying, "Running Deer speaks the truth. You are not wearing a shirt Eddie."

"Good guess, Kat. So what am I doing now?" I began waving my arms.

She aimed the reed at me, took it away, and said, "Waving your arms."

"Huh?" I said and then stood on one leg.

"Now you look like a flamingo standing on one leg."

"What the hell?"

"See, I tell Sunchaser, now Katarina see better than we see," Running Deer said.

"That is incredible!" I said with a smile. Katarina smiled too. She looked beautiful. The black mask matched her shiny, jet-black hair perfectly. She looked very mysterious and sexy wearing the mystical eye covers. *Only Kat could make that grotesque piece of dead bat flesh look so beautiful.*

"It's the batwing mask Weeping Willow made for me. She put a magic spell on this mask and on me. When I make clicking sounds with this reed, the echoes come back to these bat ears, and in my mind I can see everything! I cannot see colors, but I can see everything—even an insect flying a hundred feet away! It's amazing!"

My chest felt hollow inside as I looked at my beautiful Katarina Romero, but I tried to smile. "I'm glad for you, Kat." She must have sensed my sorrow.

"Eddie, it's because of you that I have this magical mask. It's because of you that I have found my new home and my new people. This place is where I belong now. Because of you, my life has been saved. I will always love you, Sunchaser Eddie Ocean!"

"Huh, that's the same speech that Little Hooters gave me... seems like a long time ago. Everyone loves me, but no one can stand to be with me."

Running Deer disagreed. "Sunchaser, you leave Little Hooters; she not leave you. You sailed away. I remember when Sunchaser make Little Hooters very sad for very long time. Little Hooters not want Sunchaser to leave her."

"You're right about that, Running Deer. But fate seems to always find a way of sticking me with the shit end of the stick."

"Ha-ha! Shit on stick? That funny, Sunchaser," Running Deer said and pulled Kat by the arm.

"We see you later, Sunchaser. Now we practice running in forest!" They took off, sprinting. I was amazed that Kat could keep pace with Running Deer. I watched longingly as she raced away. Her long, muscular, yet elegant legs seemed to carry her without touching the ground. Silky raven hair streamed through the air behind her. The runners melted into the dense foliage, and they were gone. I threw my grits overboard and watched a school of greenies begin feasting on the bits of corn pone. *Feels like it's time to blow this joint, dude! Nothing left here for you anymore.*

Chapter 21

CAN'T HURRY LOVE

After watching Katarina and Running Deer disappear into the dense forest, I stood in stunned silence, staring at the majestic, ancient cypress trees towering more than 100 feet above the Florida lowlands. Long, gray ribbons of Spanish moss hanging down from the tree branches were bathed in the early morning sunlight, making them stand out in stark contrast to the dark green blades of the cypress leaves. Specks of white, yellow, black, blue, green, and brown flitted to and fro throughout the canopy of the forest, as birds of every color happily started their day of hunting and gathering. *I can't blame her for not wanting to leave this place.*

I went below deck and rinsed my bowl in the galley sink, and then sat down at the charting table. *Running Deer and Kat? I sure as hell didn't see that one coming! Yeah, maybe you should be the one jumping overboard—put yourself out of your misery, dude!*

The conversation in my head continued as I spread out a navigation chart of the Florida Keys on the table. *You gotta get away, dude. But where should I go?* I wondered. *You're broke. You need to make some money. Miami is packed with snowbirds and tourists. In Miami you could pick up some good paying charters. Work...stay busy, dude. Get the girl out of your head.*

The passing of time had healed my broken heart when I was coerced by the Ancients to abandon Little Hooters, and I knew the same remedy was in order to get over Katarina. I decided to sail for Miami the following morning. *Maybe Jumping Jack will have some Native American crafts for me to haul north to the trading post.*

I rowed the dinghy the short distance to shore and then went to find Jumping Jack to offer my delivery service. On the way to the central lodge I saw Running Deer and Kat walking on the trail ahead of me. They were walking hand in hand, gazing into one another's eyes, or in Running Deer's case at Kat's bat-skin mask. Their demeanor could only be defined as blissful. I veered off on to a side trail to avoid another awkward encounter with the pair of lovebirds. *This path leads to Weeping Willow. I'll go say farewell to her.*

"Hello, Weeping Willow!" I called out and knocked on her door.

"Enter, Sunchaser." Weeping Willow was sitting cross-legged on the floor, shaking her fist, preparing to scatter her animal bones on the mat in front of her. She seemed to be in a state of deep meditation, yet she was conversing with me. She tossed the bones and then opened her eyes to look at them.

"I see that you will be leaving us again, Sunchaser," she said and collected the bones.

"Yes, ma'am, in the morning. I have come to say goodbye and to thank you."

"Why thank me?"

"For helping Katarina. I still care very much for her."

"Sunchaser, you love Katarina. But as with Little Hooters, Katarina is destined not to be in your future. You will never be with Katarina—it is not your destiny."

"You can be so harsh, Weeping Willow—so blunt. Are you still angry with me for dissing that bat-skin mask?"

"No. Did you see Katarina wearing her mask?"

"Yes, and I admit that you were right. When your mask is on Katarina's face, that ugly stretch of bat skin looks exotic and mysterious…almost beautiful. But what's amazing is how it allows her to see."

"She cannot *see*—not as we see. She can detect objects by echolocation, the way that bats do in the dark. Her perception of the detail of her surroundings is far superior than any human's eyesight."

"So what's with the reed that she uses to make clicking sounds?"

"The clicking sound echoes off objects, and the echo returns to those ear shaped cups on the side of her head. But when she is not sounding with the reed, she is totally blind again."

"That sounds like sonar."

"Sonar? I don't know sonar."

"Well, Weeping Willow, like I said, I'm leaving for Miami. Do you have anything you want me to take to trade for you in Miami?"

"Yes, some potions. Take them to Little Haiti. The vodou women there will know what they are useful for." She presented me with a wooden box containing two-dozen vials.

"What do you want in return for these potions?"

"A headdress. A Haitian shamanism animal spirit headdress. I will present it as a wedding gift to Running Deer when he marries Katarina."

"It's for Katarina's wedding? Man, how can you Whatchacallit people be so empathetic one moment and then so unvarnished the next?"

"We Whatchacallit people speak truth, not dance around the truth like the Wasichu people."

"We Wasichu people call it 'being polite.' We call it 'being PC.'"

"PC no good. People talk in circles around one another. Phony people hide the truth...hide what they feel...hide what they truly believe."

"Another clash of cultures, then? Well, I will deliver your potions, ma'am. But now I need to go to see the chief."

"Sunchaser, before you leave, let me see your hand." She took my right palm in her hands and drew it close to her leathery old face. One eye was directed at my hand; the other was looking off to my left. She strained her eyes to see the lines in my skin. "Hmmm," she said as she traced a line on my palm with her fingernail.

"What is it?" I asked.

"You have long lifeline. How old are you now, Sunchaser?"

"Twenty-two."

"That means you are here on your lifeline." She stabbed a long, crooked fingernail into a spot on my palm. "This line is lifeline, and you are now here." Another line in my skin intersected the long life-line right near the spot that she had placed her fingernail. "This other line is your love line. It intersects your life line soon, at this very point in your life." She pressed her pointy fingernail into my palm.

"Hey!" I withdrew my hand. "Love line?"

"Yes, the lifeline and the love line intersect at the time in your life that you will meet your soul mate. That time is near."

"I know! That's what I've been saying. My soul mate is Katarina, and now I have lost her to Running Deer. Must I live my life alone? I grow impatient for a love to call my own. Sometimes I feel that I…I can't go on."

"Sunchaser, my mama said to me 'you can't hurry love'."

"But how long must I wait, Weeping Willow?"

"That I cannot tell, Sunchaser. In time you will know—you will know soon. If your age moves too far past this intersection on your lifeline, then you will have missed your soul mate. Sometimes that happens—many people are destined to be lonely. I am one of those people."

"If what you tell me is true, and Katarina might be my soul mate, shouldn't I fight for her?"

"No, now her fate is sealed. Her love for you was a threat to her goal in life, and impediment to her getting revenge against the Cuban government. When she was with you Katarina was in a dark place hiding the light of her spirit behind a protective façade—behind a cloak of rage, anger, and hate. That is why she could not show love for you."

"I knew that about her. I called it her hard exoskeleton. I knew she was hiding her tender heart from me—hiding it from the world. But now she says she has changed."

"You are wise for your age, Sunchaser."

"Thanks Weeping Willow, but what is most frustrating is that she was just coming out of that shell and opening up to me when the Russian kidnapped her and blinded her."

"Yes, but after that happened, Katarina went even deeper into her darkness and despair, she was spiraling toward death. The healing trance saved her life. While you were gone, Running Deer played a large role in Katarina's healing. He was with her constantly, helping her to feel alive again. Her spirit was like a butterfly emerging from a dark cocoon of captivity and into a wonderful world of beauty and light. It was as if Katarina was born again, and Running Deer was there to welcome her into the world. Like the hatchling goose emerging from its mother's egg, an immediate and permanent bond was formed between Katarina and Running Deer. You were not with her—once again you went sailing off into the sea."

"You sent me on that quest, witch! It's your fault! Because of you I wasn't here to help Katarina when she was most vulnerable! Damn you, you evil witch!" I became very angry.

"Hold your tongue, Sunchaser! I am just a medium—a messenger to convey the words of a higher power. The Ancients sent you on the quest to Haiti. The spirits from the Valley of Tranquility sealed your fate with Katarina by sending you away when she most needed you, not I!"

"Those bastards! They sure seem to have fun toying with my fate...with my very soul. What have I done to offend them? Why do they continue to torture me?"

"Control yourself, Sunchaser! *You* must not offend the *gods*. It is a great honor to be used as a tool of our ancestors and to be a servant of the Great Wanaka. Your service and suffering will be greatly rewarded, if not on this earth then in the afterlife."

"That's me all right—a tool...a real loser!"

"Sunchaser, you must not lose hope, or you will end up living in the darkness, living like Katarina did when you first met her, consumed by rage and anger."

"That malady of darkness must have been contagious, because I've already caught it!"

"You are being tested. Sunchaser. You must not give up seeking the light. You will only find happiness…only find what you are looking for when you catch the sun."

"Catch the sun? What nonsense, woman!"

"This is why the Ancients gave you the name Sunchaser. It is your destiny to roam the seas, following the sun. Your spirit must always avoid the darkness and look for that rising light."

"I get it, ma'am—another myth. Like the Phoenix—the great bird that flies close to the sun and goes up in flames, only to be reborn from its own ashes. I'm growing tired of all your myths, mysteries, and tall tales, old woman. I need to blow this town!"

Disheartened more than ever, I left to visit Jumping Jack. *Great, dude. Rub some salt in your wounds! Little Hooters will probably be home. Now you get to see your other lost love, and she gets to see you with your tail tucked between your legs again, a loser!*

My bad luck continued; Little Hooters *was* home. Awkwardly she invited me in and listened while I talked with Jumping Jack, who was in the kitchen. He was busy skinning a rabbit. He agreed to have people bring their crafts and goods down to my boat for transport to Miami at dawn's first light. Little Hooters seemed tense; she must have sensed my deep sorrow.

"All the people will miss you, Sunchaser," she said with a gentle smile. Her empathy and kindness toward me only made me feel more lonely and pathetic.

"Jumping Jack need to hang pelt outside to dry. Little Hooters say goodbye to Sunchaser now," the chief said, generously giving us a moment alone.

"You *will* find what you are looking for, Eddie—that I know. You *will* be happy some day!" she said and rose on her tiptoes to kiss my forehead. The sweet smell of honeysuckle surrounded us, and I resisted the urge to kiss her tender lips. *Get your sorry ass out of here before you make a fool of yourself.*

"Well, Little Hooters, I've got a lot of preparation to do. Take care," I said and left the central lodge. As I walked through the village, I was aware that the Whatchacallit people were not out and about as often nowadays. They were not as active as I remembered them having been in the past.

In front of the main lodge, I stopped to see a large group of children sitting cross-legged on the floor in front of a small black-and-white TV, watching cartoons. *Hey, they have electricity now!* I noticed that FPL, the electric utility, had run a power line to the central lodge.

At the next lodge, two boys were sitting on the porch playing with hand-held, battery-operated electronic games. They both appeared to be overweight, a condition that I had never seen among the Whatchacallit people. The sedentary Chief Thunderbutt and his wife were the only obese Whachacallit villagers I could ever recall. At another lodge I observed three pot-bellied men playing a card game and drinking bitterroot water. *The ancients brought me to these "Invisible People" to bring them out of the shadows and into the light. But now I'm wondering if I have not done the tribe a terrible disservice! They are losing their culture.*

At the boat, I took Weeping Willow's box of potions below deck and switched on my transistor radio. Some guy was talking about investment strategies to financially benefit from the current economic stagflation. I turned the dial, and an old song from the sixties filled the cabin.

"I need love, love
To ease my mind
I need to find, find someone to call mine
But Mama said:
You can't hurry love
No, you just have to wait

"How apropos, dude! You can't hurry love! The same crap that Weeping Willow was preaching!" I said aloud and continued to listen as Diana Ross's sweet voice empathized with me.

*These precious words keep me hangin' on.
I remember Mama said:
You can't hurry love, No, you just have to wait!"*

When the song ended, I shut off the radio. *No time to sit around feeling sorry for yourself. You've got a lot of work to do before daybreak.* The rest of my day was spent preparing for the voyage to Miami.

At dinnertime I went back to the village to see if I could mooch a hot meal from someone. As I entered the central village I was surprised to see a large tour bus parked near the central lodge, and a group of Wasichu people milling around a table of Indian arts and crafts. A warrior called Snapping Turtle was wearing a full-feathered headdress, and some of the other braves had war paint on their faces. The Indians were posing for pictures with the tourists.

"What's this all about?" I asked Snapping Turtle.

"This new Whatchacallit business deal. The elders no like business."

"What does Jumping Jack think about having all these tourists coming into the village?'

"He no like either. But he say paper money good for tribe. Money help tribe. So what you want here, Sunchaser?"

Before I could answer him, Jumping Jack came up behind me, grabbed my shoulder, and said, "Sunchaser, the people have no things for you to trade in Miami. The people say that now they sell all the things here in the village when the Wasichus come to visit on iron bus."

A fat guy wearing a tropical shirt and baggy shorts snatched the headdress off Snapping Turtle's head, put it on his own head, and started hopping around and chanting, "How, wow, wow, wow!" as he moved the palm of his hand over his mouth. I know it took great self-control for the Indians to refrain from killing the guy.

"That is rude and a great insult to the Native Americans, mister!" I said and took the headdress from him.

"Sorry, kid! Was just having a little fun. Hey, Doris, did you film that dance with the super-eight?" the guy said and walked to where his fat wife was filming us with a movie camera.

"Jumping Jack no like so many strangers come here."

"You're being commercialized—and your people are becoming lazy. You're losing your culture, dudes," I said to the Indians.

The following morning, before sunrise and without fanfare, I sailed down the creek and into the Gulf of Mexico. Two days later I arrived at the Miami Marina to renew my sailing charter boat business.

Chapter 22

TWO YEARS OF DARKNESS

In 1975, my life began spinning out of control. My downward spiral into the darkness and despair of which Weeping Willow had forewarned me came on gradually and was at first imperceptible. Numbed by my loss of Katarina, I robotically went about my duties as a charter boat captain, hauling sunburned tourists out to sea for sunset cruises and sometimes for an overnight jaunt down to the Florida Keys. I was wandering through life, meandering aimlessly through each successive day, shrouded in a fog of disinterest. My normally pleasant demeanor and outgoing personality had become flat and emotionless.

My good friend, humor, a device that I had commonly used to cope with the trials and tribulations of life, became a stranger to me, and I'm afraid I was not good company for my clients. This fact was reflected in the mediocre reviews that I began receiving from customers and the drop-off in my business. In my downtime, the memories of both Katarina and Little Hooters haunted me, and I continued to long for their companionship. *Get over those women, dude. They ain't comin' back! You're screwing up your business.* It was not until the end of 1975 that my thoughts of the two women became less frequent and their memories began to recede into the past.

DECEMBER 31ST, 1975

This is New Years Eve and, as usual, you are all alone dude! I sat on the deck of *Orion* drinking beer and looking across Biscayne Bay in anticipation of the Key Biscayne fireworks display when the recognition of the pitiful life that I was living smacked me right between the eyes. I slammed the palm of my right hand into my forehead. *What am I doing? I can't believe 1975 is gone—it's over! Where did the time go?* Nineteen seventy-five was a blur to me, and I felt like the entire year had been a total loss. *Well, at least by moping around and feeling sorry for yourself every day you saved some cash. But you've got to start living in the present...start living for yourself. Try having some fun, dude!* The fireworks display began and then three beers later ended with a spectacular grand finale. "Yippee! That was real fun!" I said sarcastically and then laid down on my back to gaze up at the crescent moon.

A few hours later a roar went up from the area where the marina's tiki hut bar was located, and I knew the year was now 1976. I raised my beer and said, "This year, my resolution is to have some fun. I pledge to treat myself better. Screw the rest of the world!" *You know what you need, dude—a set of wheels! A car to take you out on the town, boy!*

Three weeks later, I was driving off the lot of a dealership located in South Miami. "Oh, yeah!" I said as I stepped on the gas pedal and listened to the grumble of the in-line six-cylinder engine. I was behind the wheel of a new 1976 Triumph TR6. With the convertible top lowered, I turned south on Biscayne Boulevard and felt the wind ruffle my hair. I had not owned a car for quite a while; it had been three years since I sold my 1971 Ford Pinto and bought the *Watermelon* boat. I had dubbed my Pinto *The Blue Firebomb* due to the cars penchant for an exploding gas tank. The new TR-6 was quite an upgrade. *Where should I go? How 'bouts a joy ride down to the Islamorada tiki bar?* It was about three o'clock in the afternoon when I pulled into a parking space right in front of the tiki bar.

"Hey man, nice wheels!" a young guy holding a bottle of beer said to me as a bikini-clad girl came up behind him.

"What is that?" the girl asked.

"A TR-6," I said.

"Who makes it?" she asked.

"Triumph. It's British. Want to go for a spin?"

"Sure!"

"Get in," I said as I got back into the car.

"Hey, what about me?" the guy asked.

"It's just a two-seater, dude," I said but then realized he was talking to the girl, not to me.

"Don't worry. We'll be right back, Joe," she said and waved to the guy, who stood frowning as he watched us speed away.

"Is that your boyfriend?" I asked her.

"Kinda, but nothing serious," she said as she tilted her head back to let her long brown hair catch the wind. "This car is fun!" She put her bare feet up against the wooden dashboard and glove compartment door.

"Hey, babe, your feet!" I said.

"Oh, sorry." She put her feet back on the floor, and I frowned when I noticed two footprints of limestone dust on the wood veneer.

"Okay, babe, the joy ride is over," I said as I made a U-turn on the Overseas Highway.

"Hey, I thought we might get to know one another. What's your name?" she asked with a look of disappointment.

"I'm taking you back. Your boyfriend is probably worried about you. You shouldn't jump into cars with strangers...especially when you're dressed like that, babe. I could be a serial killer."

"Oh c'mon! Let's go to Library Beach. It's nice and private back there."

"I'll take a rain check," I said and took another glance at her dirty footprints on my new car. After I dropped her off, I headed back toward Miami. *The old Eddie Ocean would not have gotten so pissed off at that girl, dude. Those footprints will wipe right off...and you didn't even get a cold brewski. What the hell!*

On the route back, I took the Card Sound cutoff road and stopped for a beer at Alabama Jack's. In the parking lot, a pair of chicks asked me questions about my new car as I wiped the dusty footprints off my dashboard. It was then that I realized that my new set of wheels was a chick magnet.

On the drive back to the marina I passed *The Carriage Trade* hair salon located on US 1 near Coconut Grove. The name of the joint rang a bell. *Hey, that's John Dumass's hair salon.* My old friend John from skid row had offered me a free haircut after his rich girl friend bought him his hair salon. I pulled over and went inside.

"Hi. Is this John Dumass's establishment?" I asked the receptionist.

"Yeah, but we're booked solid for the day," she said as she chewed on a big wad of gum, blew a bubble, and then looked back down at the magazine she was reading.

"Hey! Eddie Ocean! How ya doin'?" John said as he came walking out from the back room.

"Hi, John. I was just passing by and saw your sign."

"Well, now I'll give you that free haircut I promised."

"John, you've got that VIP from *The Forge* waiting for you," the receptionist said.

"Okay. Let Marla take care of Eddie," John said.

"She's booked too, John."

"Well cancel hers or make them wait until we take care of Eddie. Eddie's a VIP, too," John said and motioned for me to follow him to the back. "Sit here," he said and pointed to a chair by a sink. A girl washed my hair and then took me to a cubicle in the main room.

"Marla, John said to cut this guy's hair," the shampoo girl said.

"Sit down, hotshot. Boy, you have nice hair, but it is a mess! How do you want it cut?" asked Marla.

"I don't know. Haven't really thought about that."

"So, do you want me to decide?"

"Sure. It will always grow back, right?"

"Thanks for the vote of confidence, hotshot," she said with a short, derisive laugh, and yanked my hair hard to get me to sit back in the chair.

"Hey!" I whined. When she was done with the haircut, everyone was staring at me.

"Wow, you really clean up nice!" Marla said.

"Is that the same guy—the hippie who walked in here off the street?" another stylist asked Marla.

"Yeah, Lourdes. He's a friend of John's. Hey, John, come see your handsome friend," Marla called to John, who came out of his cubicle to see me.

"Hey, man, you look great! We close as soon as I finish up this cut. Let's go get a drink after that. Marla, want to join us?" John asked.

"Sure," Marla said with eyes wide as she admired her handiwork. She spun my chair to face the mirror, and I looked at myself for the first time.

I thought the short, layered haircut made me look prissy, even girlish. "Well, I guess it will grow back," I said disappointedly.

"What, you don't like it?" Marla grabbed my ear and twisted it.

"Shit! That hurts!" I said and knocked her hand away.

Lourdes spoke with a Cuban accent, "He looks like that hot young actor who played a role in *The Harrad Experiment!* I think the guy's name is Don Johnson."

"Now he's the spitting image of Don Johnson, and he doesn't even like the hairstyle," Marla said as she pinched my arm hard and twisted it.

"Hey! What's with you, girl?" I asked and rubbed away the pain.

That evening we went out for drinks, and I asked Marla to go out with me the following weekend. In short order we became a couple, and I dated Marla for the rest of 1976. She was a very moody chick, often rather cold, with a hardened heart. She was fashionable and a very good dancer, with a wild side that was appealing to me, but when life gave us lemons she did not make lemonade; she spit on them. Marla was the perfect girl for me at the time: She taught me how to be tough and heartless.

"You're a good-looking guy, but you need some fashion advice, Ocean," Marla told me one Saturday afternoon. We went to the Omni Mall, and Marla helped me choose clothing that was better suited for our nightclubbing lifestyle and my cute little sports car. A few days later, Marla surprised me with a gold necklace that had a big, gaudy, solid gold letter *E* pendant hanging from it. A week later she gave me a gold Rolex watch. Eventually I would discover that the expensive watch was stolen property.

We took turns being cruel to one another and hurting each other, but we always made up. Through these exercises in sadomasochism, Marla helped me harden my heart and become numb to the cruelties of the world—just what I thought I needed. She moved in to live with me on my boat and sometimes worked as the cook when I ran a multi-day charter. Everything was fine until she began suggesting that we get married.

"Marla, as friends we can't even get along for more than a week at a time. Can you imagine us as a married couple? That would be a disaster!" I said. But she was persistent, and somehow—I don't remember how it happened—we became engaged.

"We can tie the knot in the springtime. That will be nice," she said. But in November 1976, just before my 24th birthday, she disappeared for four days. When she returned, I discovered that she had flown down to Argentina with a South American guy we knew from the disco scene to learn to tango. I didn't realize it then, but I now believe that Marla was bi-polar. In December she once again disappeared.

The chick is insane, dude. You've got to break it off. Take a trip to the Bahamas and get your head straight. I hauled Marla's belongings over to the dock-master's office.

"What's this stuff?" he asked me.

"Rick, I'm kicking Marla out and going to the Bahamas until the shit storm blows over. Will you please keep her stuff until she comes to pick it up."

"Sure."

"I need to celebrate!" I felt a great weight being lifted off of my chest as I walked to the marina tiki bar.

"Hi, Fanny," I said.

"Oh it's you, Eddie Ocean!" Fanny said and turned her back on me. "You want the loaded Bloody Mary."

"No thanks, babes. Now that I've got some cash, I don't need to have that trailer trash drink for breakfast. Give me a Maker's Mark on ice."

"We named that loaded Bloody Mary the 'Eddie Ocean,' in your honor, and now you don't even drink them."

"That drink seems low-rent to me now, babe."

"Well, ta-te-ta, look at you, mister big shot! Isn't it a bit early for whiskey?"

"I'm celebrating. Today I moved Marla out and I'm about to blow this town."

"That's too bad, Eddie. You and that nasty little broad made the perfect couple. You two deserve one another," Fanny said with a frown.

"Why the hostility, babe? We used to be friends."

"Yeah, and you *used to be* Eddie Ocean. I don't know who you are anymore. Hey I gotta take care of my customers," Fanny said and walked away.

I slammed back the drink, took out my wallet, and tossed a 10 onto the bar. "Keep the change *Faaannnnyy Liiiicker!*" I said in a loud, mean voice, probably a taunt that Fanny had not heard since sixth grade. The new Eddie Ocean had become cynical, bitter, and sarcastic, a man to be avoided whenever possible.

After spending a week in Nassau, I returned to Miami and went to see the dock-master.

"Hi, Rick! Did Marla come back?"

"Oh, yeah. You missed all the fun."

"Did she take her stuff?"

"Oh, yeah. She was spittin' bullets when she found out you were gone! I thought I was gonna hafta call the cops."

"What did she do?"

"She was kicking the counter and throwing shit all over my office. Then she went outside and used a nail file to cut a hole in your convertible top."

"Shit!" I said and went out to see my car; Rick followed me.

"You got off easy, it could have been worse. She was insane, man!" Rick said as we examined the slash. Rick had put duct tape over the tear.

"Thanks for covering up the hole Rick." I said.

"Yeah. We had some rain the other day. If I were you, I would stay clear of that madwoman."

"Where did she go?"

"I believe she is staying with a co-worker from the beauty salon."

"Great. Let them deal with that crazy woman." I decided to drive over to South Beach to scope out the beach for some new blood.

"Give me a Heineken," I said to the middle-aged guy tending bar at a thatched roof tiki bar. I sipped the beer and watched a young woman attempting to windsurf. A group of people standing at the shore also watched her intently as she repeatedly fell off the board.

"She's on the wrong side of the sail. She's standing on the lee-ward side. The chick doesn't understand the physics of windsurfing. Someone should have given her a lesson when she rented the sail-board," I said.

"This has been going on for over an hour. Those people on the beach were laughing at her in the beginning, but now they must be impressed by her determination," said the bartender as someone shouted out words of encouragement from the beach.

"Why didn't they show her how it's done?" I looked over at the old fart that was in charge of the windsurfing rentals. He was laughing hysterically.

"She wasn't the one who rented the board. Her friend there rented the sailboard." The bartender nodded at a girl sitting at the far end of the bar, closer to the beach. "She's the one that got the lesson but she gave up after about ten minutes, and then that one out there decided to give it a try. That one out there does not give up so easy!"

"Oh man! She just went down hard near the rock jetty!" I said and stood up to see if she was hurt. She got back on the board, and I could see a red welt on her thigh. Suddenly the wind filled the sail, and the girl leaned back in the correct direction and took off flying across the light chop.

"Yahooo!" Everyone standing on the shore began cheering, and the girl's friend jumped off her barstool and went running toward the water, screaming, "You go, girl!"

"She figured it out. She is really flying now!" I said as the girl turned and tacked back toward shore. The windsurfer made a few more maneuvers and then brought the board to shore. The group of onlookers congratulated her, gave her a water bottle, and patted her back. Her friend dragged the sailboard back to the rental concession, and then the pair of young women returned to the bar. The windsurfer girl had thick auburn hair, blue eyes, and a sprinkling of freckles across her cheeks. *She's real cute, a wholesome "girl next-door" beauty.* The bartender was talking to the girls as I stood to go over to introduce myself.

"Here's one on the house! You are one very determined young lady," the bartender said and put a beer bottle in front of the windsurfer.

"Thank you, sir. Ouch!" The girl couldn't hold the bottle; the palms of both of her hands were bloody, rubbed raw by the boom of the sailboard.

"Wow! Look at those hands! You are one tough cookie too! Let me get you something for those hands," the bartender said as he bent down to fetch a first aid kit from under the bar. *Man, she must be another psycho chick, like Marla. Not what you need right now, dude!* I put money on the bar and left.

1977

Christmas and New Year's passed, and I fended off the loneliness brought on by the holidays with a string of short, superficial relationships and one-night stands. Most of the women I had been meeting would eventually bore me. The few I found interesting quickly found out what a self-centered, cold-hearted bastard I had become.

Fanny Licker would hardly talk with me anymore. My business was failing, and for the first time I decided I needed to advertise my charter boat services, so I went to see Rosalina Rossi, my friend who worked at the Miami *Post* newspaper. The grumpy security guard who had given me such a hard time in the past was still working at the front door of the *Post* building. I approached him, preparing myself for the barrage of insults and comments about my long hair that were sure to follow.

"Hello, sir. I need to see Rosalina Rossi."

"You got an appointment kid?"

"No, but I think she will be glad to see me, sir." The guard was skeptical, but then I noticed that he was looking at my gold Rolex watch and the gaudy bling hanging around my neck.

"You look okay, kid. Here's a temporary pass. Go to the third floor."

"Thank you, sir." *Huh—how about that! The guy didn't even recognize me. That old bastard hates my guts!* I went to Rosalina's office and knocked on the door.

"Come in."

"Hi Rosalina."

"Eddie, is that you? You look so different."

"Good or bad?" I asked.

"Weird!" The voice came from behind me. Ima Hooker had followed me into the office.

"Eddie, you look good I guess…but just so different," Rosalina said.

"Out of character *I* would say," Ima the sketch artist added.

"Well, I've matured, I'm no longer a stupid jerk. No longer a naïve sucker. No longer the loser—the bleeding heart do-gooder who gives away his money left and right."

"Eddie those were acts of kindness…generosity, not stupidity," Rosalina said.

"Oh really? Well what did all those kindnesses get *me*? One broken heart after another, that's what!"

Ima said, "You have helped many people…made many friends. You literally saved my life. That was a priceless gift, Eddie."

"Yeah, well, the last woman whose life I *literally saved* stabbed me in the back! I'm done giving. Now I plan on doing a little taking, babe."

"Is this a joke? You don't even sound like Eddie Ocean," Ima said.

"The joking is over, I'm all business now, babe. I just came here to place an advertisement for my charter services in your newspaper."

"Ok, we'll help you with that, Eddie," Rosalina said.

Rosalina helped me draw up an ad, and then I left to return to my boat. It had begun to rain, and water was dripping through the slashed convertible top directly onto my head. *I feel like going out and picking a fight tonight. I gotta blow off some steam, man!*

Up ahead I saw a family standing at the bus stop. A man and a woman had three children lined up in front of them. All the children were wearing bright yellow dresses, and their parents were holding umbrellas over them, trying to keep them dry. *So if I gotta have this water pouring in on me why should you people stay dry?* I accelerated and swerved off onto the shoulder into a big puddle of standing water right in front of the family. *Whoooosh!* My car sent a huge spray of dirty water high into the air and saturated the family. I cut the wheel to get back onto the road as I looked in my mirror to see the children standing in shock with brown stains covering their pretty, yellow dresses.

"Ha! Bulls eye!" I yelled just as my front tires hit a rut at the side of the roadway. The TR-6 began to spin out into oncoming traffic. I steered into the spin and narrowly missed being T-boned by a city bus but then my car went off the road on the other side of the street, crossed a lawn and crashed head-on into a palm tree. My chest impacted the steering wheel, knocking the breath out of me, and I was gasping for air as I crawled out onto the wet grass. Three men huddled over me as I rolled to my back and felt the gentle rain on my face.

"It's my chest," I gasped, barely able to speak, but I realized that the guys were not there to help me; they were picking me clean. They removed my Rolex watch and gold chains. Then one guy violently jerked me onto my side and took the wallet from my back pocket. The sudden motion sent a searing, hot flash of pain through my chest, and I passed out.

"Where am I?" I asked when I regained consciousness.

"Jackson emergency. We just did an X-ray. You've got a fractured sternum. We are admitting you to the fifth floor...need to check your heart."

"My friend Patty Whacker works on five," I said.

"Great. We'll tell your family that they can see you when you get up to the fifth floor."

"My family?"

"Yeah, real cute little girls. Little sisters?"

"Huh?" An orderly whisked me away and took me to my room on five, where a nurse came in to help me move over to the bed.

"Is Patty Whacker working today?" I asked the nurse.

"She is, but when she saw you brought onto her floor, she asked me to switch sections with her."

"Why?"

"Don't know. You tell me. I guess she doesn't want to see you… doesn't want to take care of you."

"Well we had a little disagreement a few months ago. I ran into her in the Grove."

"Yeah, she said you were drunk…had a fancy little car and were dressed up like a New York pimp. Says you treated her like a whore."

"Everyone is so touchy nowadays. I was just flirting, told her how sexy she looked…thought she would be flattered."

"Patty swears you used to be a real nice guy."

"Still am, babe—just not such a stupid sap."

"Don't call me 'babe,' mister."

"All right, chill out!"

"A family waiting outside wants to see you. Only God knows why. Do you want to see them?"

"No."

"Good, then I'll send them right in." My jaw dropped open when three little girls in stained yellow dresses followed by their parents entered my room. I was speechless.

"Hello, mister. We came to thank you and say a prayer for you," the tallest of the girls said.

"Thank me?"

"Yes, for swerving and crashing into that tree so that you wouldn't run us over. Our daddy explained what happened…told us how you are a hero."

"But I didn't…"

The man interrupted me, "It's all right, son. The girls were devastated when their Sunday school dresses were ruined—their only pretty dresses. But I explained to them that it was an accident and that you got hurt trying to avoid running over us." He gave me an intense stare with a furrowed brow. The woman stood at his side staring at the floor. She couldn't even look at me.

The tallest girl spoke. "Yes, so we want to pray for you to get better and to sing you a hymn of thanks." She took one step forward and then opened a small white Bible that had also been stained by the dirty rainwater, and read from the book. "Isaiah 41:10. *So do not fear, for I am with you: do not be dismayed, for I am your God. I will strengthen you and help you; I will uphold you with my righteous right hand.* Amen."

"Amen," said the others. I was becoming choked up with emotion, which caused the pain in my broken chest to intensify. My eyes, too, welled up with tears as the other two little girls stepped forward in their ruined Sunday School dresses to join the tall one, and they began to sing with the voices of angels.

When upon life's billows you are tempest tossed,
When you are discouraged, thinking all is lost,
Count your many blessings, name them one by one,
And it will surprise you what the Lord hath done.

Now I was gasping for air, unable to breathe, and in pain. Fighting back the tears, I blurted out, "Please forgive me!"

"Okay, girls. We should leave this young man alone now so that he may rest and heal himself," the father said.

The tallest girl said, "Thanks again, mister. We'll pray for you to get better." "You're our hero mister." A child said as they shuffled out of my room.

Then I heard a voice come from the area of my doorway. It was Patty Whacker's voice. "What was that all about?" she asked me.

"What kind of man have I become, Patty? I don't even know myself anymore. Even you hate me."

"You *have* changed. That is true, Eddie. But you can always change back. You can restore your soul. You must have suffered greatly to become such a bitter man."

"I've been selfish and greedy. Many people have suffered much greater hardships than me. I deserve everything that's happened to me and more, believe me. I'm not a good person."

"Recognizing your failings is the first step to changing…to healing. I have a Bible verse for you, too, Eddie."

"If it's for me, the verse should concern being sent straight to Hell!"

"The verse is short and sweet. It's Psalm 147:3. It goes something like this. '*He* heals the brokenhearted and binds up their wounds. Take care of yourself Eddie."

Patty never came back to visit me, and two days later I was discharged. Those days in the hospital gave me plenty of time to reflect on my life and how I had gone astray. I made a pledge to get my life back on track and to stop playing the role of a hard-assed son of a bitch. Since my TR-6 was a total loss, I took the bus back to my boat. After two months, my sternum had healed to the point that I was ready to go back to work. Insurance money from my car had tided me over, but now I was flat broke again and needed to get to work.

The spiritual healing was a long process and another year passed before the old Eddie Ocean was back. I had rediscovered myself.

Then in the summer of 1978, my life took a turn. There was a note left for me in the marina office.

"This guy saw your ad in the paper and called the office," Rick said and handed me the scrap of paper that contained the phone number of someone wanting to charter the *Orion* for a weeklong cruise. *Great! A week charter! I need the business!*

Chapter 23

MARGARET ANN

"**R**ick, do you mind if I use your phone?" I asked the dock-master. "A business call? Sure, no problem."

"When I dialed the phone number, a very flamboyant fellow answered my call. He identified himself as Angelo and explained that his partner wanted to surprise a co-worker named Maggie with a *birthday cruise* to the Keys. Angelo carried on and on about how wonderful the birthday girl was, describing her as nothing short of an angel haven fallen to earth.

"I get it sir. Maggie is very special to you and your friend, so you want the best for her. She sounds like a real saint."

"Yes, she touches everyone she meets." Angelo said.

We shall see. How could anyone live up to that introduction? I wondered.

"So Captain Eddie Ocean, are you the right captain for this job?" Angelo asked.

"Sure, I'll make it the trip of a lifetime. I know the Keys like the palm of my hand," I said, desperate for his business.

"We want to sail before dawn so that we can watch the first sunrise out at sea," Angelo said.

"No problem, sir. What day is Maggie's birthday?" I asked.

"July 20th, but we want to leave on Saturday morning July 18th."

"Perfect! We will be in the Keys to celebrate this angels birthday."

05:00, SATURDAY, JULY 18TH, 1978

I was sitting on deck in the dark, sipping a hot cup of strong coffee, when my clients came stumbling out onto the docks.

"Good morning! Come aboard!" I greeted them. They appeared to have been drinking, and Angelo was not a happy camper.

"Roberto, this is an ungodly time to still be up in the morning!" Angelo whined.

"Oh, shut up, snowflake!" Roberto said as Angelo, the drama queen, put on an Academy Award performance as he struggled to walk up the gangway.

"I must be sleepwalking…this must all be a nightmare! I never open my studio before ten!" Angelo said as Roberto pushed on his ass to get him aboard.

"Welcome to the *Orion*. Where is the guest of honor?" I asked the pair.

"She had to use the little girls' room. She'll be here soon."

"Looks like you fellows were doing some partying," I commented.

"We took Maggie out dancing all night. There she is!" Roberto said, just as a young woman came walking out of the shadows and approached the boat carrying three bags.

"You guys forgot your luggage," she called out to us. I went down to the dock to help her with the bags.

"Well at least *you* look bright eyed and bushy tailed," I said as I looked into her smiling eyes and helped her come aboard. "I'm Eddie Ocean…the captain."

"Good morning, Captain Eddie, I'm Margaret Ann, but everyone calls me Maggie."

"Where are the damn beds? I need to lie down!" Angelo whined.

"Go below and pick a bunk, but not the one with the knapsack on it. That one is mine," I said.

"If you don't mind I'm gonna get a bit of shuteye as well," Roberto said.

"Go for it sir."

"Enough with the sir kid, just call me Roberto."

"Roberto is a surgeon...Dr. Roberto...," Maggie said but was interrupted by the doctor.

"Just call me Roberto."

"Ok Roberto, have a nice nap. Maggie, you can rest as well. I don't need any help casting off and I can wake you in time for the sunrise if you want."

"No, thanks Captain Eddie. I'm fine. But I *would* like some of that coffee."

"Sure, in the galley. Would you mind getting me a refill while you're down below?" I started the engine and was casting off the dock lines as Maggie came back with coffee.

"How can you see in this darkness?" she asked as she sat next to me in the cockpit.

"I know this port like the palm of my hand."

She handed me my coffee mug and asked, "Have we met before?"

"You know, I was thinking the same thing." I examined her face in the dark. "Hey, you're that girl from South Beach!" I said.

"No, I live on Brickell." She scrutinized me for a moment and then said, "Hey, you got a haircut. You don't remember me, do you?"

"Guess not."

"A couple of years ago we met on Southwest 8th St., remember? I translated the Spanish inscription on the Cuban Memorial Wall for you, and then we had a cup of coffee together."

"Oh yeah! Small world!"

"You were kind of a jerk, remember that? You said that your name was Sunchaser and that you lived under a bridge like a troll, so I started calling you Joker."

"I *do* remember. But I wasn't joking. Back then I was homeless, and my nickname *is* Sunchaser. It's a name given to me by some Indians."

"Really!"

"Yeah, really." I looked at her closely. "You *are* that girl from South Beach—the windsurfer!"

"Oh no! You saw that embarrassing display of futility?' she said and blushed.

"You were very impressive! I've never seen such determination."

"Some people say I'm tenacious."

"Your friend Angelo didn't mention that you are tenacious. He described you as a mix of Mother Theresa, Florence Nightingale and Gandhi—claims you're some kinda saint in his opinion!"

"Oh, Angelo's just a sweetheart. He says nice things about everyone." Maggie said and then stood up. "Hey, look, the sky is getting light. I want to see the sunrise." She walked to the bow of the boat and stood looking out at the eastern horizon. Her silhouette outlined against the early morning sky jogged my memory. *She looks just like the mystery woman in my vision—a glimpse into my future that the Ancients had provided for me to ease my mind at a time when I was destitute and had little hope for my future. In that vision I was sailing my own boat, accompanied by the unidentifiable silhouette of a young woman standing at the bow. I always thought that the mystery woman would turn out to be Katarina.* Maggie turned around and came back to the cockpit.

"It's to early to see the sunrise, but the ocean is so beautiful," she said as she sat just behind me where I manned the ships wheel. The soft light of the daybreak on the horizon illuminated Maggie's face, and for the first time I could see her clearly. Suddenly a bright auburn-colored glow enveloped her head and shoulders. I leaned back to better see the hue.

"I see a glow. Maggie, an aura surrounds you. It's around you right now. It's the color of your hair!"

"An aura? The sun is on my face…probably just a reflection off my hair."

"It's an aura. I've seen this before."

"Don't be silly," she said and blushed.

"I swear; there is a dark ginger-colored hue radiating out from your body. Sometimes Little Hooters had a similar glow around her. Weeping Willow said the light came from her inner spirit...her kindness."

"Who is Little Hooters? Is that a real name? Are you going to start playing the Joker again?"

"Little Hooters is a Native American woman. When I was with the Whatchacallit Indians I developed extra senses...perceptions... and seeing auras was one of those extrasensory abilities." In amazement I moved closer and touched the air above her head. She looked up at me smiling, her light-blue eyes sparkling bright in the low sunlight.

"Now what are you doing?" she said in a tone of voice that more accurately conveyed the question "Come on, dude...really? Is this your best come-on?"

"Sorry, but it's been years since I've seen an aura like that around anyone. Weeping Willow said it emanated from the persons inner spirit. She said the glow around Little Hooters was generated by her inner kindness."

"You already fed me that line, and people say *I'm* persistent! Do these bizarre pick-up lines actually work on girls?"

"I'm not trying to *hit on you*. This moment was a long time coming, Maggie. So it *is* true what they say."

"What *do they* say, Eddie?"

"That love don't come easy—you just have to wait."

"Love? Captain Eddie, I don't even know you. Now you are starting to freak me out!" She stood up and returned to the bow of the boat, but she couldn't hide the smile spreading across her face as she left me. She turned back toward me, still smiling, and laughed, "Wow, you have the lamest pick-up lines I've heard in ages Joker."

The sun broke over the surface of the sea but was still low on the horizon. Maggie began performing graceful movements that at first seemed to be a Tai chi exercise routine but then I recognized her movements as ballet dancing. Her slow, graceful pirouette was beautiful to watch against the backdrop of the colorful, sunburst. *Dude, that chick not only has the elegant, athletic gracefulness of Katarina, she has the inner beauty of Little Hooters to boot!* Suddenly Maggie rose high on her tiptoes, arched her spine to lean backward, and with her arms outstretched formed a circle above her head. My mouth dropped open when I saw the distant sun perfectly framed by Maggie's graceful arms. *She has caught the rising sun!* She held that position for a moment and the extraordinary image of her cradling the sun in her outstretched arms etched itself permanently into my mind. *Amazing!*

The voice of Weeping Willow filled my head, causing me to stand up: "Sunchaser, you will only find what you are looking for… you will only find happiness when you finally capture that sun." *Weeping Willow, is that how you catch the sun? Is that all there is to it, just reach up and grab it?*

With outstretched arms I began to form a circle in front of my face, mimicking Maggie's *sun catching* technique. She pivoted on the ball of her foot and turned toward me. Still standing on one leg, Maggie lowered her arms and paused momentarily with her hands on her hips and her right leg bent at the knee.

"What are you doing?' Surprised by my odd posturing she ended her ballet demonstration. Now Maggie stood facing me with her legs spread wide and her hands on her hips.

"I said what are you doing Eddie Ocean? Are you mocking me?" she asked feigning anger with a furrowed brow. But apparently she could not suppress the wry smile that crept slowly across her face.

"No Maggie, I would never mock you—I'm just trying to catch that rising sun!"

"Catch what?" She took a quick glance over her shoulder to look at the sunrise, wondering what the hell I was babbling about.

This ain't working dude. The circle formed by your arms is too large. By cupping my hands in the fashion of a wide receiver catching a football I formed a smaller circle in front of my face.

"Margaret Ann, I got it!" I said and adjusted my hands to perfectly frame the distant sun.

"Eddie, you're not on drugs are you?" Maggie pretended to be concerned for my well-being but asked me the question with an amused smile.

"Finally! I did it! I caught that rising sun babe!" I was sure that by now the poor girl thought that I was completely insane. "You must think I'm crazy, but someday I'll explain everything to you. Someday all of this nonsense will make perfect sense to you."

"You making perfect sense? I doubt that will ever happen Eddie Ocean!" Now she was laughing out loud as I pulled my hands down and then made a motion as if I were releasing a dove into the sky. "Wahoo! You are free to go now!" I said with my arms spread wide and raised toward the sky.

"Free?"

"Yeah, the chase is over babe. I feel free as a bird."

With a look of amused resignation, Maggie slowly shook her head and walked toward me. "*You* are one strange bird mister."

"You'll get used to it." I put my arm around her waist and together we watched the sun rise higher into the early morning sky.

"Margaret Ann, *you* are the one." I said and exhaled deeply. For the first time since leaving Katarina at the Whatchacallit Village the hollow feeling in my heart was gone, the emptiness had been replaced by a warm sensation permeating my chest.

"I'm the one?"

"Yeah, the one who showed me how to catch and hold that elusive sunshine. I feel it inside me now." I said and nodded at the horizon.

We heard coughing sounds and then voices coming from below deck. I turned my head from the glorious sunrise to look at Maggie's gentle, smiling face, which was now clearly illuminated by the soft morning light.

When our eyes met she squinted as if she were trying to see deeper into my psyche, deeper into my soul.

With my arm around her shoulders I said, "Your eyes are like limpid pools...as deep and as blue as the sea."

Maggie's eyes widened and she turned her head away from me. She was trying to suppress a laugh. Suddenly there was a loud burst of sound from her; a choking snort that quickly turned into uncontrollable laughter. Her body began quaking under my arm.

"What's so funny?"

After regaining her composure she tried to answer me but when she looked up at my face she went into another hysterical, convulsive fit. Not until she was out of breath was she finally able to speak, "Whew! Oh brother Captain Eddie Ocean, I have a feeling that this is going to be quite an interesting journey!"

THE END

Margaret Ann

1980

2011

Other Novels by E. O. Test

Crocodile Island

Crocodile Island is a romantic, adventurous and humorous sojourn through south Florida and the Caribbean during the raucous 1970's.

In the great tradition of Forrest Gump, Eddie Ocean is an ordinary young man whose extraordinary zest for life makes waves for everyone around him.

This book will keep you intermittently laughing and cheering and you'll be nothing but sorry when it's over; you will be left longing to receive your copy of the sequel, *Street Life in Paradise*.

Street Life in Paradise

Street Life in Paradise begins with Eddie Ocean and a dog named Hobo destitute and homeless, living on the streets of Miami in the year 1974.

Eddie tries to reunite Hobo with his young master and along the way inadvertently sets inner-city fashion trends, finds romance, deals with a horrible boss, comes into conflict with Nicky the Knife, and serendipitously helps his friends find a pathway out of skid row. Join Eddie and a zany cast of characters for hijinks on both land and sea.

Gasoline Rainbow

Gasoline Rainbow is an action packed thriller due to be published in late 2017.

www.ingramcontent.com/pod-product-compliance
Lightning Source LLC
Chambersburg PA
CBHW050036180626
46810CB00002B/737